Author Certification

I hereby certify that I authored all the words in this book, with only minor editorial changes. The ideas and content are entirely my own. I employ no ghostwriters, nor do I have a writer's stable or company that employs writers to write content. I wrote every word of the following book.

John R. Takacs

SEALED TRUTHS

John R. Takacs

Red Engine Press
Pittsburgh, Pennsylvania

Paperback ISBN 978-1-943267453
E-book ISBN: 978-1-943267460
Library of Congress Control Number: 2017954244
Cover Design by Sandi Linhart
Editing by Betsy Beard

Printed in the United States.
Red Engine Press

Shohn Louis Turner-Takacs
Husband, Father, Novelist, Screenwriter, Son
May the Everlasting Light always guide your path.
May 24, 1974 – January 24, 2017

Chapter 1

Day 8
Three Days Lost

He knew evil, knew it well. Most of the time evil was insidious. Like rust, it corrupted slowly. It was at its greatest power when it was slow and sneaky, wrapped in the ordinary of everyday. Not often was it overt like the howls of an approaching pack of wolves. If it were, the viciousness would alarm, and he would have time to run or fight…although fleeing was never his strong suit.

The glare of light, constant and fierce, together with complex alarms and whirring noises had become a part of his confused world. Was it evil, once again on the attack, going for his throat this time? He gagged, tasting stale plastic and smelling his own puke. He tried to whip his right arm up to protect himself but it wouldn't move, snugly fastened down at his side. He instinctively knew this was no nightmare. This was real.

A voice penetrated the fog. "Stop fighting it."

He tried to shout, "No," as he struggled once again to command his restrained arms. He wouldn't go down without a fight and lifted his entire body up, determined to win this battle.

"Please. Stop fighting it." The female voice was soft and sweet.

He stopped thrashing about, wanting to hear the voice again. Could it be the voice of love, the voice of an angel? He felt the ominous blackness overtake him again and fell back into the depths of the great void.

"Jesse…sweetheart, open your eyes."

He felt a hand gently passing through his hair and slowly opened his eyes. They wouldn't focus; all was fuzzy. He knew the voice… but she was dead. She died many years ago in a car crash. Jesse closed his eyes, and his last thought before drifting off was that he also must be dead.

* * *

"He's coming to, again."

Who is? He was dead. But if he was dead, how could he hear voices murmuring? And what was that insane bleating sound? Jesse turned his head to the left. His vision cleared and he saw a face. For a time not measured in minutes but in heartbeats, he studied her.

The sunlight passing through the window filtered through her shining hair. It was shoulder length, both brownish and reddish in an impossible glowing mix. Her eyes were the color of the ocean and sky combined, contrasting sharply with her tanned skin. Innocent and knowing at the same time, they were the most stunning feature of her face. Like a movie star's, her teeth were incredibly white.

"Where am I?" he asked, trying to command the words to march out of his raw throat.

Leena leaned forward, and he could smell a mix of delightful aromas surrounding her like an invisible cloud. "I couldn't hear you, sweetheart. Say it again."

Why couldn't she hear him?

"Where am I?" Jesse whispered.

"Here, take a sip of water." She put a straw up to his lips.

"Am I dead?" he asked in a slightly louder whisper.

"No, of course not. You're in the hospital."

"In Khe Son?"

"Khe Son?" She turned toward the back of the room and said, "He thinks he's still in Vietnam."

Jesse strained to sit up and see who she was talking to, but the effort was too much. Instead, he closed his eyes and disappeared into the land of soft and fuzzy once again.

When he came fully awake a few hours later, her pleasant scent had completely dissipated. He looked around the room and studied each of the machines surrounding him. Slowly he looked away and fixed his eyes on the ceiling, trying to concentrate.

He was alone now, and the room stank like—it gradually came to him—the cleaner the Army used to clean the shit houses. He shuddered as a horrible feeling came over him. Something was totally out of balance. He understood he was in a hospital, but where? He closed his eyes and looked deep within, trying to dredge up his last memory. What had happened to him?

The last thing he remembered was seeing the long narrow field with the tall elephant grass surrounding him as he left the safety of the tree line. The jungle had been thinning out for the last half klick, not nearly as dense as the triple-canopy jungle they had been in for the previous couple of weeks.

He stopped walking, hearing a sound that didn't fit, slightly off to his right. He put his hand up to signal a halt to Humphreys, the new guy who was his slack man, soldiering fifty yards behind. The remainder of the platoon, back another fifty yards, stopped. The soldiers respected him, and when he stopped suddenly, all of them became tense. They crouched down, eyes everywhere, everyone alert. None of his platoon mates wanted to walk point. He didn't like being bait, either. But he was good at it.

If I were the enemy, he thought, I would pick this spot for an ambush. He turned and signaled back. The LT started moving forward and suddenly ran to his left, diving for the ground. The screeching sound of incoming ordnance was loud in his ears, but before he hit the ground he laid a long burst into the thick jungle with his M16. As he tried to become as small as the dirt he tasted, he heard the distinct sound of AK-47s and Soviet SKS rifles. He slipped out of his ninety-pound rucksack, slammed in a fresh magazine, and began low-crawling back toward his slack man. He knew from past experience that once the mortars stopped the enemy would begin the assault. As far out front as he was, he would be alone on an island of death.

He closed to within ten yards of Humphreys, a blonde kid from Wyoming, when a shell struck and the fucking new guy disappeared in a ball of fire and mush. The enemy mortars had his range and were thumping all around. It was just a matter of time before—

He got up and started to run when he felt a giant hand lift him up and fling him into the air. He landed on his head, just like when he carried the football in high school.

He lay on his back, quiet fuzziness surrounding him, the taste of blood in his mouth. He looked up through his tears at the once-clear blue sky. Darkness beckoned and he closed his eyes.

Jesse forced his eyes open and noticed a tube coming from the IV pole. He followed it down to where it was taped, just above one of his hands. He stopped and looked closely.

Alarmed, he forced himself to lift his hand. Turning it back and forth slowly, he studied it for many long moments. This was not the hand of a young man.

He was still too medicated to panic, but from the recesses of his brain a single thought came staggering into the daylight. *Whose body is this?*

He felt a twinge of pain in his side and reached down to lift the faded blue hospital gown. The wound was neatly stitched, surrounded by bruised and blackened skin. He didn't remember being shot… or did he? In another dream?

Jesse turned his head toward a large window and gazed at a reflection he didn't recognize. It was dark outside and he was alone, with no one to ask if this was all a bad dream. Or was he insane?

Chapter 2

Day 9
Suspended Memory

Jesse could feel the bright summer sunlight flooding into the room on his bare arms. He smelled her sweet perfume before he felt something touch his face. He squinted as he opened his eyes and could make out the face of that pretty woman again. She leaned in to kiss him on the cheek.

"Oh my sweet man, are you going to stay with me this time?" she asked. "You look much better today than yesterday."

He had to ask. "You know me?"

The woman knitted her brows. "Of course I do! I'm Leena. Don't you remember me?"

"I don't even remember me," he said, seeing the look on her face. "You act like you're my wife or something."

She smiled. "If you're asking me to marry you, that's the slyest proposal I've ever heard."

"I'm sorry. I, uh…I'm kind of confused…do I love you?" he blurted out.

She looked down. He seemed so innocent and somehow pure, even if his eyes remained blank. It occurred to her he really didn't know.

"You've never said it in so many words." Her voice cracked. "At times you act like you do. And we've become very close." She reached up and touched his face. "What's the last thing you remember? You know about the Take-Us car, don't you?"

"I remember being on patrol and being wounded, I guess." He lifted his gown and showed her his left side.

"No, sweetie, you were shot in your own home and then again in San Francisco. You were wearing a bulletproof vest in San Francisco, so the bullets didn't penetrate the second time."

He was quiet for a moment. "I keep having strange dreams, but I've never been to San Francisco."

"How old are you?"

He thought for a few seconds and then whispered, "Twenty. Twenty-one in April."

"No, Jesse, you're in your fifties. When you were shot in San Francisco, you fell and bashed your head on the sidewalk. Maybe it caused some kind of brain injury." She pointed at his head. "Or maybe it's the drugs they have you on."

"So these really are my hands." He gushed out a breath of relief.

"I'm going to get your doctor," she said, walking toward the door.

"Wait a moment." He tried to sit up straighter in the bed. "My mind seems clouded, but can you tell me a couple of things?" She paused at the door and he continued. "What was your name again? And, well, do you love me?"

"Leena. My name is Leena Delaney." She moved quickly back to the bed and put her arms around his shoulders. "You are a sly one, aren't you?" She nuzzled close. "I could stay like this for a long time, but time is something we're running out of. I need to go and find your doctor. Now."

He noticed she only answered one of his questions.

It was midafternoon before Dr. Chang, the staff neurosurgeon, arrived on his rounds. He put his right hand under Jesse's head, feeling the staples they put in to close the gash Jesse received when his head struck the sidewalk.

"It's been what? Four or five days now? We can remove the staples in another couple of days." Dr. Chang stepped back and studied the bags of medicine on the IV pole and then checked the rate of the drip. "Still on Versed. The latest scan indicates the brain swelling has decreased and you're out of the danger zone."

The doctor flashed a small penlight into Jesse's eyes. "Well, Mr. Christenson. I've been told you're having trouble remembering things."

"I can't say," Jesse replied.

"Of course not." Dr. Chang laughed. "It's normal not to be able to recall things after you first awaken, until you sort of re-boot" He pointed to Leena. "Do you know her name?"

"She told me it was Leena."

"How long ago did she tell you that?"

Jesse glanced up at the clock. "This morning, about eight o'clock."

"Good, good. There are only a few different types of amnesia. The drug you're still on, Versed, can contribute to your condition, but the dosage has been scaled back, so it's probably just a small factor. The more common form of amnesia is anterograde. It occurs after a traumatic injury and typically doesn't allow you to create new memories. If you had it, you probably wouldn't have remembered Leena's name from this morning. The other type is retrograde amnesia, and it involves loss of memories that were stored before the event occurred."

The doctor walked over to the window and peered out, lost in thought. "External physical trauma is probably what has caused yours. However, we can't rule out psychogenic amnesia, which can be caused by deep mental trauma brought on by the psychological commonalities of the two events of being shot. It's interesting that your memories seem to start at the same point as your first major injury—"

"Doctor, what's the cure?" Leena interrupted, her fingernails impatiently clicking against the table.

"Yes, well there are things we can try, like hypnosis or sodium amobarbital, but more often than not it just takes time to heal."

"How much time?" Leena asked.

"Could be days, weeks, even years—and in extremely rare cases, never."

"So I might never get my memory back?" Jesse swallowed hard.

"That's very rare. Usually your memory will progress from the point you are remembering right now—which I understand is over thirty years ago—and move forward. Many times it will be subtle. For instance, it's not often you think about the first time you warmed something up in a microwave, but the memory is stored in there somewhere."

"What's a microwave?" Jesse asked, a puzzled look in his eyes.

"This is going to be fun," Leena said. There was no smile on her face.

Dr. Chang began again. "Sometimes, once the memories start to return, they begin to cascade, somewhat like an avalanche. It starts with a pebble, and pretty soon the entire side of the mountain comes roaring down. Many times it's like a wave washing a memory in. When the wave goes out some of the memories go with it, returning again on another wave until they finally find some sort of permanence."

Dr. Chang and Leena looked at each other and she asked, "Is there a way to help him regain some of his memories?"

"Perhaps. Many times pictures or letters or even relatives and friends telling him things could trigger memories."

"We have a small problem with that. His house burned to the ground last week, and everything in it was destroyed. Actually, we have a much larger problem, but I'll save that for when he feels a little better."

"Wow, I owned a house?" Jesse asked.

Ignoring him, Dr. Chang asked, "Does this have anything to do with that car thing?"

Leena turned and walked over to the window where the doctor was standing and said in a low voice, "Yes, the Take-Us car is missing. Let me correct that. It was stolen.

"I owned a car, too?"

The doctor and Leena turned to stare at Jesse.

"There is one more thing," said Dr. Chang. "I'm not sure if this could be a benefit or a detriment, considering the physical trauma he's endured…"

Leena and Jesse waited quietly for Dr. Chang to finish.

"Extreme stress, either physical or mental, can provoke and instantly bring back certain memories. Of course it can also go the other way."

Chapter 3

Day 10
Truism Unadorned

The following morning Leena came into Jesse's room with a plan she was anxious to share.

"Good morning, sweetheart," she said, giving him a small kiss, her lips lingering over his mouth. "No more medicine mouth. And you've shaved and smell good." She also thought his blue eyes looked clearer than the day before.

Jesse was sitting in the bed, his knees almost to his chest. He had his bed cranked up and was watching television. He changed the subject, embarrassed.

"You should see how many TV stations you can get in here," he said.

"I hope we can get your memory working again, because you will not believe all the changes in the last thirty years. It will take me that long to explain them all to you. In fact, let's begin right here, right now."

"What's that?" he asked as she plopped a laptop computer on the hospital tray table in front of him.

"It's a portable computer, and I've downloaded some interesting stuff for you to see."

"It looks like a portable TV, only smaller."

"Sort of, with a DVD—kind of like a VCR—included." She saw his eyebrows pull together. "Let me guess. There was no such thing as a VCR back then."

When he didn't respond, Leena continued. "Okay, that's not important right now. Just watch and see if anything looks familiar."

She tapped the keyboard and soon had a video clip playing. Jesse recognized the face on the screen as the same one he shaved that morning. He was in a car, and Leena was asking him questions. Then they drove off.

Leena pushed a button, and the image froze on the screen.

"Sure," he said. "That's you and me. You work for a TV station?"

"I work for a network. We provide most of the content for individual stations, but it's good you can recognize us. How about the car? Does it look familiar?"

Something tugged at his mind. "Yeah. My dad has a Buick Wildcat."

"You never told me that." Leena saw a blank look flash across his eyes and said, "That's okay. Just watch the rest of the videos, and we'll talk after they're over. Okay?"

She restarted the computer.

When the videos finished, Jesse asked, "Did I really invent a car that doesn't use any gasoline?"

"You invented the drive system. The Take-Us was converted from a 1966 Buick Wildcat that belonged to my mother."

"Is that how we met?"

"Yes. How did you know that?" She bent forward, her face very close to his.

Her wonderful smell filled his senses. "I don't know. I sort of just felt it. You're very beautiful, you know. Like one of those centerfolds in a *Playboy* magazine."

"So even at twenty you were a silver-tongued devil. Oh my God, you're blushing." Leena stepped backwards, laughing. "This is just too precious."

He couldn't help himself as his eyes rolled over her, checking her out. "This might sound weird, but you're like…a real woman. And I'm more comfortable with, well, high school cheerleaders."

Leena crossed her arms over her chest and glared. "So I'm just a Playboy Bunny who is your mom's age?" Jesse started to speak, but

Leena cut him off. "You'd better remember you're in your fifties. If you start checking out high school cheerleaders now, the cops are going to haul your ass off to jail. Besides, you told me before that I was the perfect princess for you. Oh, and since you've forgotten everything, let me remind you that I'm a black belt in karate. And you're deathly afraid of me." She turned around and smiled at the closed door.

Jesse spoke softly. "My mom died three years ago, and you don't remind me of her at all. She was—"

"What year was that?" Leena spun around, once again interrupting.

"Nineteen seventy-five…how can I know that? That hasn't happened, yet." Jesse's face showed utter confusion. He put his head in his hands, dragging the IV tube. "If that's in the future, then you said I'm already there. But I'm not. I'm here in the hospital—"

"Jesse, stop!" She moved forward and took his hands in both of hers. "Maybe this is how it works, flashes of memories just showing up out of the blue."

He sat there, outwardly quiet. But on the inside, thought after thought collided in a huge, confusing kaleidoscope of impulses and feelings. Once again he wondered if this was how it felt to go insane. Breathing slowly, he forced his eyes to rest on the small screen in front of him. Leena had called it a computer. Why did she show it to him—the car thing?

He squeezed her hand. "I'm afraid I might be going crazy. The car, though…it's important, right?"

"I know you can't remember the car right now, but it became your reason for living after your wife died. Please forgive the pun, but it was the driving force of your life. Your attorney is currently in Japan, selling your concept to auto makers there—"

"Why not to American auto makers?" he interrupted.

She eyed him closely. "Okay, history lesson time. Since you're stuck in the seventies, I'll begin there."

Taking a deep breath, Leena started. "Since the seventies, American automobile companies are seen as second tier. Cars from Japan are cheaper, get better gas mileage, and are higher in quality. The Middle Eastern countries—and other oil producers, like Venezuela—have joined together into a monopoly called OPEC, and they control the price of oil for the entire world. The American oil companies have sold us out and screwed us the same as OPEC. In fact, whenever any viable alternative energy starts up, they drop the price of oil to put the new technology out of business. So the price at the pump is like a yo-yo, up and down, up and down. It's been as high as five dollars a gallon."

"Five dollars? It was just twenty-eight cents when I left for Vietnam. Why doesn't the government do something?"

"The federal government initially thought that if the price was higher we would conserve more gas, as if people were taking gasoline into their backyards to burn for the fun of it. But the whole thing morphed into political corruption that's totally out of control. Not all, but most United States Senators and Representatives—and even presidential candidates—are on the bribe list. No one calls it a bribe anymore. People now call it campaign donations, mostly from PACs—political action committees."

"Why don't the newspapers and television do anything about it?" he asked, letting go of her hand and sitting up straighter.

"It's become so expensive to run for office that politicians need tons of money for advertisements. Guess who gets the lion's share of the money they raise. That's right, the news media. No, wait, there's more," she said, holding up her hand to stop him before he could interrupt. "No one in the government will create a solution to our energy dependence, because they would lose those precious re-election dollars. Your invention that you call the Take-Us car is the catalyst to clean up this whole mess."

"And it's been stolen?"

"It's worse than that. But I didn't want to say anything until you were better."

He looked at her butt as she turned and walked over to her purse, her every movement conveying sensuality and grace. She pulled out a newspaper. It was folded open, and she had circled a story.

"They started today." She handed him the paper and he began reading the article titled TAKE-US CAR A FRAUD?

After he finished reading, he handed back the paper. "Is this true?"

"Of course not. You drove the car from California to New York City. And then we both drove it back to California." She saw the puzzled look on his face. "We never stopped to get any gas, and at one point we went over two hundred miles per hour. The original Wildcats had four hundred horsepower, but really…what kind of car do you know that could do that?"

"So what's the problem? We'll just tell them what we did."

Leena slapped the newspaper against her leg. "We already did that with the video we filmed. The problem is…" She held up one finger. "The car is gone. It was our proof." Two fingers up. "All the plans and specifications were in your computer, which completely melted in the fire at your home." Three fingers up. "You left a secure website with all the data, which only you can access with some kind of secret encrypted password." She saw he was closely watching her when her fourth finger went up. "All of the Take-Us car knowledge is locked up in your brain. Same problem as number three: you can't remember."

"Can't someone figure out how to open the, uh, web thing?"

She put her thumb up and then turned it downward. "Possibly. But it's considered private property, and no one can legally touch it…at least while you're still alive."

Day Eleven

Day One of the Grand Pursuit

Chapter 4

Survival, Nothing Else

It was after midnight when Supervising Special Agent Mike Nowiki of the FBI unobtrusively entered the hospital room. The short man, built like a pit-bull and with a matching temperament, quietly plopped down in the chair opposite the bed. He looked at the screen, scrutinizing the man's vital signs. Heart rate, blood pressure, oxygen saturation: all seemed normal from his perspective. Leena, covered with a blanket, was curled up in the other chair sound asleep. He was amazed at how her hair looked perfect even while sleeping.

It was just nine days ago this whole thing began with an anonymous phone call from the Christenson man, a.k.a. cop killer, who was now sleeping peacefully in the hospital bed. Christenson had unwittingly created an inordinate amount of chaos. Or maybe he consciously knew he was destined to create chaos. After all, he was some kind of a genius wasn't he? Nowiki didn't know the answer to his own question. All he knew was that these two had placed him in a real bind.

The big question was whether the car was for real. It was polarizing, like religious fervor. Inside the government, people seemed to be evenly split on who wanted to believe what. Of course, he had seen the car, even if from a distance. He knew that a car did exist, so he could dismiss the goofy objection that there wasn't even a car. But he didn't have the slightest idea how it was powered. He wished for the hundredth time that he had looked under the fucking hood.

Like so many other investigations, as he began the wrap-up phase, it seemed as if ten doors opened for every one that closed.

At least he had some control with the search to find the missing car. On the other hand, many eyes would be focused on him when he turned in his preliminary report on the terrorist actions of last week. He knew he would be okay. The FBI was very good at not killing the bearers of bad news.

He had promised to give Homeland Security a week before he announced to the inner world of "eyes only" government types that many of their agencies were filled with…what? Spies? Hidden terror cells? Even though his report would be secret, he knew from experience that the whispers would begin immediately. The many diverse and different branches of the government were too politicized to keep anything quiet if it could be twisted to hurt one political party or the other.

Leena must have sensed Nowiki's presence as she cracked open an eye and sat up with a start.

"What are you doing here?" she asked.

He sighed and said, "It's still my job to see that both of you are kept safe."

"When can I get out of here?" She impatiently straightened the blanket that had started to slip off.

"We think you're both on the hit list, Miss Delaney. If you hadn't disarmed the phony policewoman, she would have shot you, too." He reached up and ran his fingers through his hair.

"As you just admitted, I did disarm the woman. I can take care of myself. And I don't need you or the government looking over my shoulder," she said, distrust evident in her voice.

Nowiki stared at her and wondered how naïve it would be for people to judge her solely by her appearance. She was a petite woman. But under that veneer there was solid armored steel. Here she was, sitting beside her mate, protecting him like…what? Was it a lioness or was it a black widow spider? He was too tired to decide.

He turned his attention to the man in the bed, who was now fully awake and eyeing him coolly. Nowiki had a fleeting thought and wondered if Christenson knew what he was getting into.

"Miss Delaney, you signed the agreement trusting the United

States government to keep you safe under protective custody, and that's all we're doing."

"Bullshit! You know that agreement was only for us to get to San Francisco." She saw Jesse's hand come out from under the sheet and reach for her hand.

"What's the problem, Leena?" Jesse asked in a slow and steady voice. "Who is this guy?"

"The problem is this FBI jerk won't let me leave the hospital or even call my office," Leena took a deep calming breath. "This is Agent Nowiki. He interviewed you at the church after the incident at your home," she said, squeezing Jesse's hand. "But I have a job to do and my boss doesn't even know if I'm alive or dead."

"He knows you're alive. In fact, you're on paid vacation." Nowiki raised his voice and held his hand up to stop another violent outburst. "Okay, you want no bullshit. Then here it is. It's because you're a news reporter in possession of top secret information that is probably the story of the year, or even decade…and we can't figure out what to do about you, because we know you won't keep your mouth shut. Okay?"

"Is this true?" Jesse asked.

Leena, now fully under control, glanced at Jesse and then looked Nowiki in the eyes. "The people I work for deserve to know the truth about what goes on."

"World Cable Network has already promised their cooperation until the investigation is complete," Nowiki replied.

"WCN may pay me, but I work for the people."

Nowiki looked up at the monitor once again, checking the man's vitals. His heart rate had increased slightly.

"Mr. Christenson, as one man to another, trust me when I say this. You still have time to jump ship." He looked over and once again concentrated on the fiercely intense woman's face. "Miss Delaney, did you not hear one word I said?"

"Just something about how well I protected myself against the fake policewoman." She smiled coolly.

Nowiki raised his voice in a carefully controlled tone. "Well, how about one more thing. That phony policewoman had a gang tattoo on the back of her hand. You know about the Mexican Mafia, don't you? Altogether, they number about one hundred thousand gang members, scattered across the United States and Central America. I think that's just a few more than the total of hidden Islamic terror cells, don't you?"

Jesse was the first to break the tense silence. "Why would a gang steal an electric car?"

"What makes you think they stole the car?" Nowiki asked.

"It seems logical. If they tried to kill me and get me out of the way, then only they would have unfettered access to the car with all its technology. Where did they steal the car from?"

"The impound lot at the San Francisco Police Department," Nowiki replied, realizing he hadn't thought of this angle. This guy only had half his brain working, so maybe he really was some kind of genius. "Everybody else thinks that the hit attempt was a contract killing and the theft was committed by terrorists still out there somewhere."

"Well, there you go. Probably an inside job," Leena said.

"Inside, you can count on that. It's the same way they stuck a shank into the phony policewoman, straight into her black heart." He saw the blank look on Leena's face. "You know, dead. They murdered her in jail right under our noses…and did away with our only lead."

"Oh, God. I thought the killing would end when the car got to San Francisco," Leena said in a subdued voice.

"Okay, look. There's no easy way." Nowiki took a deep breath and hurried on. "I have to ask you directly. Was the car real or was it a fraud like the papers have been saying?"

"At the church, did you see me take anything out of the front engine compartment?" Leena asked. "We used the engine compartment as a trunk since there was no gas engine."

"I've seen the video. What I'm asking, Miss Delaney, is this. Did you ever see what was in the original trunk? Could he have somehow installed a gas engine back there?"

"I know what you're trying to do, Nowiki." Leena hesitated. "How do you explain the fact that we never stopped for gas from New York to San Francisco?"

"Were you with the car twenty-four hours a day, every second of every day?"

Nowiki watched her closely as she ticked back through her mind and searched for details. If she was in on the scam, she would've already had the answers to these questions. It was obvious she wasn't lying.

"The first night, Jesse took some General Motors engineers for a ride without me being present," she said slowly. "During the second day I was so sound asleep he could have gotten gas and I probably would have slept right through it. The second night he could have snuck out, I suppose."

"Really." Nowiki glanced over at the bed and observed Christenson's face. Nothing there but a curious look. "And the third night?"

"Let's see, the third night we would have been in Wyoming and Utah. After I finished driving, Jesse drove. And once again, I was so sound asleep, I don't know if I would have heard a thing."

"Do you always sleep that soundly, or could you have been drugged?"

"The first night I drank a little too much, but after that I was exhausted from the stress of being chased. Anything is possible, I suppose, but I don't recall waking with a headache."

"What about day four?" Nowiki asked still watching closely for the first sign of a lie.

"From the time we left Salt Lake City to when we arrived in San Francisco, I never left the car. Except when we both walked down to my mom's house." Leena smiled. "There's no way any car, even with a big gas tank, could go that far. Especially at the speeds we were averaging." She saw Nowiki's mouth start to open and rushed on. "We were in a hurry and were going over a hundred miles an hour most of the time. In fact, when they started chasing us in the helicopter, we were going over two hundred for some time, even pulling away from them."

"So you never left him alone with the car at any time?"

"We only stopped a couple of times. Once for breakfast. And I wasn't gone from his side longer than a few minutes. The other time we stopped at a gas station in the middle of the desert…" Leena started speaking slower. "I went into the store and…he was parked by the gas pumps…but he was just washing the dead bugs from the windshield and then he went to the bathroom. He could have…"

Nowiki zeroed in. "Could have what?"

Leena looked over at Christenson's piercing blue eyes. He was searching her face, innocent as a lost puppy. "He could have drugged me and put gas into some kind of specially modified car. He's certainly smart enough." She looked back over at Nowiki and stared at his deeply lined poker face.

"I'm a reporter and have been for a long time. I'm not as easily conned as I was when I was younger." She spoke in a soft voice. "That man lying in that bed is the most decent, honest man I have ever met. Yeah, I could be slightly prejudiced because I've fallen for him somewhat…" Nowiki raised his eyebrows, as Leena continued. "But that's the whole point, don't you see? It's hard for anyone to crack into my heart, and only someone so…so *real* could ever manage it."

They both looked at Christenson who had a huge smile on his face.

Nowiki said, "Sustained speed of over two hundred miles an hour, huh? There's no way a car with a gas engine stuffed in the trunk could do that and not run out of gas. In addition, you would have been able to hear that thing all the way to San Francisco."

"That's right! I forgot how quiet the car was…and smooth. Hardly any vibration at all."

"That's what O'Hallohan said."

"Where is he? He drove the car; he knows," Leena said.

"He's been recalled to D.C. to begin an internal investigation. Everybody always trusts a war hero." Nowiki stopped talking and looked over as a male nurse knocked and entered the room.

"Hi, I'm Robert. Your nurse for tonight." He glanced over at

Leena and Nowiki. "You two shouldn't be here this late."

Nowiki noticed that Robert was dressed in light blue scrubs and resembled the Michelin Man, as wide as he was tall. His smile was youthful and pleasing, which made his blonde mustache turn up at the corners in a perpetual smile.

"How's your head feeling?" Robert asked, turning back to Christenson. He walked over and turned Jesse's head to examine it and then lifted his gown.

"Pretty good. They took the stitches and staples out earlier today," Jesse said.

"That's what I read on your chart. You could easily reopen these if you're not careful. You realize, of course, it takes months to heal from this type of concussion. How about everything else?"

"The day nurse popped the plug out of my di—" He glanced over at Leena. "Uh, took the catheter out, and I've been walking to the bathroom by myself."

"Yeah, you're definitely a fast healer. And you were in great shape before all this happened. I'm going to get you off the telemetry monitor, and you've also finished your IV regimen."

"No more drugs, then."

"That's what the doctor ordered," Robert replied as he disconnected the various leads and wires that connected Jesse to the monitor.

Leena stood up, leaned over the bed rail, and kissed Jesse quickly on the lips. "I'll see you in the morning, sweetheart."

Nowiki mumbled, "Later," and then said to Leena, "I'll escort you out. So…you drove the car. Did you feel it shift? Or what about a noise, like from a starter or…"

Christenson didn't hear her answer as they moved out of the room and into the hall. Their voices slowly faded along with their footfalls as they moved down the hallway. He didn't know what to make of her kiss, and a sudden sense of foreboding came over him.

"She's a beauty, that's for sure," Robert said as if he was reading Jesse's mind while pulling off the sticky patches the electrodes were connected to.

"Yeah, I suppose, but I really can't…"

"Remember her," Robert finished. He looked down at Jesse's face. "It's okay. You are going to have good days and unfortunately bad ones also…days of great insight followed by bad ones when you forget your own name. It'll all come back. The one thing I've learned from my years in the medical field is that more often than not, time heals all. Just have a little faith."

"Yeah, that seems to be a recurring theme. Thanks."

Jesse watched as the nurse disconnected the IV tubing from its port and began to gather it up. He placed it in a special receptacle labeled Contaminated Medical Waste. Then he gathered up the electrodes. As he was heading out the room, he said over his shoulder, "I'll be back in a few hours to DC the IV site."

"DC?"

"Disconnect. Remove the port from your arm." Robert stopped and turned the main lights down, leaving only the soft glow from the night light. "Didn't anyone tell you? You're being discharged and released tomorrow."

Discharged to go where? Released to do what, Jesse wondered. But no one was there to provide the answer.

Jesse thought back on everything he'd heard in the last hour. He couldn't decide if he was some kind of alternative-energy expert or what. Rubbing his forehead, he thought it was just too surreal, not being able to remember anything at all. It did seem like there was something tapping at the inside of his head, telling him to move over or at least get out of the way. Maybe it was just the crack in his skull healing.

It was hard to believe that Leena had—what was it she said?— fallen for him. He didn't have those kinds of feelings toward her at all. He wondered what he did feel. There was no doubt she was a gorgeous woman, and he could imagine her naked. She really did look like she could be one of those nude women he had recently seen in a *Playboy* magazine. But wait, that was thirty-plus years ago. Still, the last thought drifted across his mind before he fell asleep, she sure was stacked. He realized he had a hard-on.

***

A few hours later, Jesse felt a presence in his room and just knew it was Leena looking down at him. He awoke with a start and sat up. It wasn't Leena, but a male nurse standing over him and searching his right arm for the IV port. The man had a huge syringe in his hand.

"Who are you?" Jesse asked, coming out of his X-rated dream.

"Your nurse." The dark-haired man spoke with an accent.

"What happened to Robert?" Jesse was much more alert now.

"Who? Oh him…uh, he is on lunch break." The nurse was trying to insert the large needle into the IV port, but his hand was shaking and he kept missing.

"I thought I was done with shots and drugs. In fact, what are you giving me?" In the weak light Jesse looked closer at the nurse and saw that the man was wearing a set of scrubs at least two sizes too large for him. There appeared to be a dark stain near the neckline. Jesse pulled his arm away from the nurse and drew it toward his chest.

"It's…it's the drug the doctor ordered. Now just hold still." The nurse's voice sounded loud and shrill as he grabbed Jesse's arm and pulled it down to his side once again.

Jesse looked at the nurse's hand as he finally inserted the needle into the small orifice. In the dim light, Jesse could make out a tattoo between the nurse's thumb and forefinger in the web of his hand. With a jolt, Jesse realized he had seen one just like it. The memory surfaced: a policewoman's hand as she brought her gun into firing position, aiming at his chest.

"No!" Jesse shouted and knocked the syringe out of the nurse's hand. It skittered across the room and came to rest against the wall. At the same time, Jesse grabbed the IV port and ripped it from his arm. There was no time to wonder if the drug had reached his bloodstream.

The nurse stepped back and said, "You should not have done that, señor. The end would have been muchos more pleasant for you. The drugs were supposed to send a message, but it doesn't matter to me. Dead is dead." He reached under the scrubs and pulled out a large knife. Dried blood on the shank dulled the sheen of the razor sharp steel.

With adrenaline pounding in his veins, Jesse hopped out of the bed, putting it between the two of them. He reached down and grabbed the pillow.

"What are you going to do, hit me with the pillow?" the man asked in a heavy accent and snickered as he started to circle the bed. "I'll soon be a rich man, once you are dead."

A surge of energy cleared Jesse's head. His Army training came back and he somehow knew he was a good knife fighter. In an instant he saw an advantage: his size. The fake nurse was a smaller man. And the oversized scrubs would surely slow him down. Jesse glanced at the man's feet. A lunge stance.

When the man stabbed directly at Jesse's heart, he was ready. He caught the knife in the pillow and immediately closed with the phony nurse. He grabbed the man's knife arm with his left hand and put his right leg behind the killer's legs. Letting go of the pillow, Jesse swung his right arm behind the man's neck, twisted, and threw his weight into the man. The fake nurse lost his balance and collapsed to the floor, landing on his back with Jesse on top of him.

That should have been the end of it, with Jesse in total control. But instead Jesse gasped in pain as he felt the gunshot wound in his side rip open. Worse, the shock of hitting the floor made him feel like his head had been put inside a steel drum that someone was pounding with a sledge hammer.

Jesse went numb for a few seconds, which gave the assassin time to act. The man moved quickly and Jesse barely held onto the knife hand as they rolled across the room. Jesse was now on the bottom and the fake nurse sat astride his chest while Jesse bucked up and down, trying to dislodge him. The killer was trying to force the knife into Jesse's throat and was gaining slowly. Jesse thrashed his head around and saw the huge syringe next to his right arm.

Suddenly the killer grabbed Jesse's hair with his free hand and began battering his head against the floor. Blackness started to seep in. In desperation Jesse grasped the syringe. With the last of his strength, he buried the needle in the man's eye, at the same time pushing the plunger and emptying the contents of the syringe into the man's brain. The phony nurse, after a loud gasp, collapsed and lay still, as still as only death can be.

Gasping for breath, Jesse pushed the would-be assassin off and lay unmoving, stretched out on the cold floor. Time, how much time? In waves, thoughts drifted through. Got to go on. Am I still in danger? He felt brightness behind his closed eyes, and in his mind a small voice kept repeating, "Get up. Finish your mission. Get up."

He opened his eyes, trying to focus, and ever so slowly rolled to one side. He groaned as he raised himself to one knee and then to his feet, swaying slightly, his head whirling.

Jesse looked around in the pale light and couldn't remember where he was. He couldn't even remember who he was. With a jarring thought, he realized that the only thing he knew was that he was still in the ambush kill zone.

He trudged to the door and peeked out. Where were the others, the enemy? Glancing down, he saw blood dripping off his fingers from the former IV site on his right arm. He quickly categorized it as a small flesh wound, of no concern. It was then he noticed he was wearing only a thin hospital gown, smeared in blood.

He opened the wardrobe locker and found jeans, a t-shirt, and a pair of shoes. He stripped and put them on, not noticing the bulge in the jeans pocket. The clothes fit well—even the shoes—and he briefly wondered if they could be his own.

His head still woozy, Jesse walked over and took the knife from the dead man's hand. He looked closely at the would-be killer's face. The man must have seen the needle coming and blinked, causing the needle to pin his eye shut. Hispanic? He seemed familiar, and Jesse wondered if he had seen the man before.

Breathing heavily, he eased the door open. Jesse looked up and down the hallway. Knife hand leading the way, he walked out. His sneakers swooshed as he stayed to one side of the hall and crept to a door with an exit sign. He glanced back one last time before opening the door and heading down the stairs, each step setting off a zap of lightning behind his eyes.

The stairs opened onto a deserted lobby. If more attackers were waiting, they would strike as soon as he walked through these doors. Jesse summoned the last of his reserves and gripped the knife. Seeing everything and nothing, he moved across the lobby to the electric doors. They whined as he walked through, out into the darkness.

He did not hesitate or feel relief as he crossed the u-shaped drive to the parking lot, noticing a tinge of light on the horizon. Almost dawn. When he was at the end of the massive parking lot, he stopped abruptly and tried to guess the time. It occurred to him that he didn't even know what time of year it was…or where the hospital was located. The effort of thinking increased the pain in his head, making him dizzy. He tasted stale vomit.

"Oh, God, not now," he said aloud and swallowed quickly. The burning pain in his side returned as the white-hot rush of adrenaline burned off.

Jesse heard the sound of a diesel engine in the far corner of the parking lot. As he stumbled closer, he felt like he was walking through black oozing mud. In the weak light he made out a bus-like motor home. Small cargo doors were open underneath it, and the engine was idling.

He had finally reached the end of his endurance and collapsed to one knee as a giant flash of pain went off inside his head. He dropped the knife and gagged like he was going to throw up. He slowly quivered off his knee and stumbled to the open cargo door. Crawling to the center of the space, he lay on top of a stack of heavy packing blankets. He instinctively knew it was all over. As the freight train of darkness overtook him, Jesse surrendered and passed out.

He never heard the doors slam shut. Nor did he feel the motor home begin to move.

Chapter 5

History Repeats

Homeland Security Agent Patrick O'Hallohan wondered why they had assigned him the crummiest office in the entire building, hiding him in the basement. It wasn't as if people wouldn't figure out what he was up to. The bomb in San Fran blew away whatever cover his team might have had. To top it off, his head was pounding from too much booze last night. Again.

It was becoming clear to him it was going to be hard to have a relationship with *any* woman when he got drunk and started treating them all like hookers. Maybe his little sister's best friend was right, years ago, when she described him as "lust another idiot."

O'Hallohan wondered for the thousandth time if some men were just destined to be single. He looked back down at the report he was preparing. Seeing Christenson's name, he thought about Jesse's situation, single for most of his life. And just look at the woman he found. Leena was older than O'Hallohan, but what a babe. He wondered if she liked younger men. He rested his head on top of the desk. Maybe he should look for an older woman…

The buzz from the telephone startled him out of the fantasy. "O'Hallohan," he said into the receiver.

"This is Agent Nowiki, FBI."

O'Hallohan wondered briefly if that was how his name was spelled on his birth certificate. "How can I be of service, Agent Nowiki?"

"Is this a secure line?"

"Of course. What's happened? More dead terrorists?" O'Hallohan reached for his pad of yellow legal paper.

"I hope you're sitting down." Nowiki took a deep breath. "Christenson is missing." O'Hallohan sighed but didn't say anything as the FBI agent continued. "I was called by the hospital staff this morning when a tech from the lab discovered that the staff nurse was missing. When I got there, security had already arrived and found two dead bodies. One was positively identified as the nurse who worked there. I saw him just last night treating Christenson when I was leaving—"

"What time was that?" O'Hallohan interrupted, scribbling notes as fast as he could.

"About midnight. Anyway, the other body was dressed in the nurse's clothing and was found on the floor in Christenson's room with a syringe sticking out of his eye. We think he was injected with some kind of poison. We're doing a blood analysis and awaiting the results."

"Oh, man! That Christenson guy can be nasty when he wants. Where was the guard you had outside his door?"

"Gone, missing, vanished…we don't know," Nowiki said.

"You think he was part of it?"

"Honestly, I don't know. He's been in the Air Force for six years and has a good record. No, I know what you're thinking, but he's a white guy, not Middle Eastern or Hispanic. At least we don't think so. Okay, he could be aligned with whomever. We've expanded our investigation into his background."

O'Hallohan crossed the question off his list.

Nowiki continued. "You remember we chose the Air Force hospital because we thought it would be more secure than any other place."

"Sure, and since they were in the middle of a remodel, the upstairs wing wasn't fully staffed. No other patients, and it allowed for complete privacy."

"We didn't know it at the time, but the drawback is they also treat veterans in the first floor clinics…and so they allow more civilians 'inside the wire' than other military bases. I'm not saying it was a veteran, but they don't screen very closely."

"Okay, but what's happened to Christenson? Abducted? Or what?" O'Hallohan asked.

"His clothes are missing, so he could have just walked out. Or been kidnapped or tossed into a garbage dumpster. We found a large knife toward the back of the parking lot and believe it to be the weapon used to murder the nurse. It's being flown to the crime lab. The Air Force has locked down the base, and they're searching for Christenson as we speak."

O'Hallohan had a brief insight. "Hey, aren't there cameras at the hospital?"

"First thing I thought of. But a couple years ago they passed a law protecting medical privacy. It's now a HIPAA violation. They can't have security cameras in the hospital or the parking lot because it violates the patients' privacy."

"Jesus Christ!" O'Hallohan exploded. "We're going to politically-correct ourselves into the paper shredder of history."

"Ain't that the truth? Well, listen. I just wanted to give you a heads up. I'll have more for you later today."

"Good luck."

"Luck." Nowiki breathed out. "I keep thinking about this poor guy's luck. I want to like him, but everywhere he goes, dead bodies keep popping up. In fact, why don't you start looking for a big stack, and that's probably where we'll find him."

"I'll do that. Hey, wait a minute. What about Leena?"

"I haven't told her yet." Nowiki sounded suspiciously quiet. He sighed. "I'd rather go to the dentist and have all my teeth pulled."

After he hung up, O'Hallohan's thoughts jumped straight back to Leena. He felt a little ashamed of his earlier fantasies. With an effort, he put aside his feelings and tried to recall the order of events after the sidewalk shooting in San Francisco.

After Jesse was shot, agents put him in the ambulance. The paramedic was treating O'Hallohan's leg wound; he seemed a good sort. They drove a few blocks to the hospital. The helicopter came in and flew them to Travis Air Force Base. They unloaded Jesse into another ambulance to travel to the other hospital…Damn it, dozens of people could have seen him. That was a fact, but someone gave away the hospital's location—or rather Christenson's. Someone with access to that secret and the right ear to whisper into.

That was the reason O'Hallohan was writing his report in the basement. Someone inside the government was selling sealed truths. He already knew about the Mexican Mafia angle, but why them? Gangs were usually into drugs, guns, and prostitution, not oil or alternative energy. Who would know about this angle?

O'Hallohan's headache disappeared, the way it usually did once the shit hit the fan. With a sudden brainstorm, he logged onto his computer, found the right phone number, and called the most knowledgeable governmental department he could find: the Department of Energy.

Little did he know that although the door to hell had been cracked open, he was kicking it the rest of the way open. Wide Open.

Chapter 6

Missing Heart

She reread the letter she had finished minutes before, and with a little too much anger pounded "Kaikalina Delaney" at the end. Most people knew her as Leena, but this needed to be as formal as possible. With a clenched jaw, she hit print and closed her laptop. She watched as the borrowed printer connected wirelessly and began spitting out her well crafted words.

From her perspective, today was the last insult. How could they not let her out of her room? She was locked in like a common prisoner. They had even doubled the guard at her door, and she could see an agent dressed like a maintenance man loitering outside her window, as if no one would notice the earpiece receiver.

She stood up and paced around the sparse room, stopping in front of the mirror to study herself. She had been in the media since graduating college and had been around many beautiful women. Some aged well; others didn't. For the ones who aged well, there was no common trait except perhaps being physically fit and staying active. She still looked pretty good and could pass for someone in her early thirties. Not so much what I've done as genetics, though, she thought.

It was an undisputed truth in the media that beauty was a weapon. She never tried to use hers as a weapon but was realistic enough to understand that sometimes you do what you have to do. She ran her hand through her hair, thinking it was starting to look shaggy and would require a trip to the salon soon. She suddenly stopped when she recalled how much Jesse had loved to touch her. The old

Jesse always had a gentle touch. The new Jesse didn't even know her. She was so conflicted. Was he just another assignment? Or was he something more?

Leena had spent many days and nights in his hospital room. When he was so helpless, the dam she had so carefully crafted had cracked. She knew there wouldn't be another moment in her life when she wouldn't think of him. After he woke from his coma, she could see him fighting for some kind of recognition when she looked into his eyes.

But recognition was a long way from love. He just had to remember her at some point. And if he didn't, he would just have to fall in love with her all over again. She didn't think anything could change those feelings.

There was a soft tapping at the door. Before she opened it, she spritzed on some perfume, thinking there might be a chance to flirt her way out.

Agent Nowiki stood at the door with two other men dressed in dark gray suits. So much for flirting. Leena turned and stomped to the other side of the room, hastily picking up the paper she had finished writing.

"What do you need these guys for, Agent Nowiki? Are they carrying the handcuffs and ankle chains to haul me off to the gulag?"

Nowiki slowly walked into the room, but before he could say a word she started to unwind. "You cannot keep me locked up without some kind of charge or court appearance. I have rights. I demand that you release me or at least give this letter to your superiors. You can't do this to me."

"He's missing," Nowiki said.

"Who? What?" Leena felt a chill start up her back.

"Your boyfriend…Christenson." Nowiki closely watched her face.

"Missing how?" Leena couldn't help herself as tears sprang to her eyes, her hand flung across her mouth.

"We don't know, yet."

"Oh God, no," Leena said weakly, stumbling backwards like a drunken sailor. The paper she was holding slipped out of her hand and fluttered to the floor.

Nowiki gently led her to the couch. Tears streamed down her face, and Nowiki automatically reached into his pocket to give her his handkerchief. She was an excellent actress, he knew, but he had spent enough time around her to know she was not acting this time. He waited a few moments for her to gain her composure.

"A lab tech went into his room for a routine blood draw this morning and found Christenson missing and a dead guy on the floor," Nowiki said. "He called the sergeant in charge of the security detail. When the guard stationed outside the door didn't respond by radio, the sergeant went to personally check. It was around six this morning."

Agent Nowiki went on to summarize what they knew up to that point.

"I put his clothes in the closet. Are…are they missing?" Leena asked, faltering badly.

"Yes. And a hospital gown we presume was his, was found on the floor, with blood on it."

"Lots of blood?" She put her hand back to her mouth.

"Not so much. It was smeared around, but not soaked. The nurse you and I met last night was murdered with a knife. We have to assume the killer had it when he went for Christenson… uh, Jesse. If so, he might have been stabbed or cut during the fight."

"So he could still be on the base," Leena said, her voice coming out weak and tired but a sudden spark showing momentarily in her eyes.

"I know you haven't been off the base since you got here." He saw her eyebrow rise and continued quickly. "At the gate, they photograph all vehicles going in or out. Security examines the occupants coming in, but going out it's just a matter of slowing down and driving through. Since this morning, they're inspecting all outbound vehicles. But he could have been smuggled out hours before anyone knew he was missing."

"So you think there was more than one of them?" Leena asked. "Then why wouldn't the other person just kill him? Why abduct him?"

Nowiki looked into Leena's eyes. "We don't have a working hypothesis as yet. I've already told you more than I should have, but I figure I owed you that much. And I'm only going to tell you one more thing."

Leena stiffened and sat back.

"We have preliminarily identified the dead guy in Christenson's room. He's a Mexican national and has been in and out of prison a couple of times for real bad-boy crimes. He was easy to ID when we saw the Black Hand with *La eMe* tattooed on his chest. Mexican Mafia."

"So there was a contract out on Jesse."

"You figured that out, huh?" Nowiki said. Leena didn't respond, so Nowiki continued. "Yeah, word on the street is five million. The poison they were going to inject was pure cocaine—not street grade, but uncut right from the jungle. You never see it that pure unless it comes right from the top levels of the cartel. Incidentally, pure cocaine is one of the deadliest poisons on earth. And the contract is still in force." The skin bunching up around his eyes conveyed it all.

"What about me?"

"There's no word of a price on your head. I guess they figure you for an innocent bystander. Of course, as brutal as they are…"

Pushing her shoulders back, Leena stood up and walked over to the window. The silence was like dense fog. After a minute, she took a deep breath and turned slowly, facing Nowiki and the other two FBI agents.

"You got me. I don't think you're lying to me, except for the innocent bystander part." She lowered her eyes and with an unfocused gaze said, "All for a man. Okay, I promise I won't do the story—probably the story of the year, and an Emmy Award winner—until you give me permission or whatever."

On demand, Leena's eyes filled with tears. This time they left trails running down her face. "I can't help it, I care so much for him.

I'll do whatever you want."

Nowiki turned to the other agents and barked out an order. "Put her acceptance into your report. Don't forget the date and time. You can leave now."

After the agents left, he walked over, noticing her perfume. "I believe you. No, not what you just said. You're a very good actress. But you are now legally obligated, so you're free to go. But just because our source doesn't know if there's a contract out on you doesn't mean there isn't one. I can assign an agent to be with you if you'd like."

Leena straightened and looked directly into his eyes. "Agent Nowiki, you have been honorable, and I do want to thank you for that. But I'm not the fool you must think I am. I understand that you're going to have me tailed. You think I'll lead them to him. I know what it feels like to be used as bait."

"It's nice working with another pro. If they already have him, you're in no danger. If not…"

"I think I'll take a little time off and kick back for a while. If Jesse does somehow contact me, I'll let you know."

Nowiki handed Leena his business card. "Yeah, right. You're a pretty good mind reader, but don't forget… if you dig too deep—how did you write that up?" Seeing the look on her face, he continued. "Yes, we hacked your computer and read the news article you're preparing. I believe you wrote something about how many hidden cells and sleeper agents there are in how many different agencies."

"Hacked me? There was a day I used to think that was against the law."

"Court ordered and legal," Nowiki said solemnly. "I'm not your enemy, Ms. Delaney. And you better believe the real traitors know who you are."

Chapter 7

No Mother's Son

The hot summer sun beat down on Miguel. He bent over and scooped up a handful of dirt from between the rows of grapevines. When he straightened, he rubbed the dirt between his fingers and thumb.

"What do you think, Lino, need more water?" Miguel handed the dirt to his oldest friend, who was standing next to him.

"You never could read the dirt," Lino said, hardly a trace of his Mexican accent noticeable. "This is just the topsoil. You have to dig deeper to know about the moisture in it."

"You should have become a farmer like you father." Miguel turned away. "I might not know how to read the soil, but I can read men." He walked over and kicked the kneeling man in the ribs.

"I know a thief, a liar," he spat, "and a user when I see one." He reached down and grabbed a handful of greasy hair, pulling the man's head up. "Luis, what happened to you? I trusted you, and now look at you. The smell of your own shit and piss fills your nose."

The black-haired man grunted through the gray duct tape stretched across his mouth as tears flowed from his eyes, dripping onto the parched earth.

"You have a nice fat wife," Miguel continued, "and cute kids. But you had to start using our own cocaino and worse, lying and stealing from the rest of us." Miguel's eyes bugged out as he shouted. "And worst of all, I gave you a simple errand to do and you totally blew it. Si."

Miguel let go of the shaking man's hair, stepped backwards, and put out his hand. One of the five men standing nearby opened a ziplock bag and pulled out a black semi-automatic pistol.

Miguel spun around impatiently, reaching for the pistol. "I never kill one of our own for stupidity. It's too common a disease in our family. However, I cannot tolerate lying to me about something we could easily have taken care of at the time. That's a death sentence."

Miguel spun back around and in one quick motion blasted into the back of Luis's head. Blood sprayed up as the man fell forward into the dirt. Miguel handed the pistol to his compañero on the left. The man stepped forward and fired a single shot into the downed man's head. He then handed the gun to the third man who repeated the action until all of them had turned Luis's head into an unrecognizable bloody pulp. The last was Lino. Instead of stepping forward, he moved backward and in a blur of motion shot twice, taking off one of the dead man's ears with each shot.

"Why do you always have to show off, eh?" Miguel asked, a repulsive smile spreading across his face.

"He won't need to hear, where he's going," Lino said, removing the magazine. Seeing no ammunition remaining, he dropped the pistol and magazine into a five-gallon bucket of sulfuric acid. The other men bent down and picked up their spent casings, dropping them into the bucket and securing the lid.

One of the men walked over and started the waiting tractor. Lowering the attached backhoe bucket, he scraped up the dead man along with the dirt under him, removing any spent bullets, the last of the evidence. As the bucket curled upward, two of the men loaded bags of lime into it and then placed the bucket of acid on top.

"Deep, real deep, José," Miguel ordered. José nodded, backing the tractor away from the remaining men.

The men started back toward the farmhouse.

"So what was the big lie, Miguel?" Lino asked.

"I gave Luis an easy job. Get a tow truck and pull a car from the San Francisco pig's parking lot. Instead, he gets high and fucks these two cochinas for two days, and when he goes to get the car, it's gone. Tells me it was never there."

"That's all?" asked Pedro, the lieutenant from the south bay.

"He was also supposed to waste this gringo, and he blew it twice. Hey, that happens and I understand, but no motherfucker is ever gonna lie to me and live to tell about it." Miguel jerked a thumb back at the growling tractor. "Goes for all of you. As long as I'm El General, you can't just lie and tell me a story you think I want to hear."

They reached the porch of the old farmhouse and sat around a large metal table with an old beat-up cooler on top of it. Lino opened the lid and started handing Buds to everyone.

"Hey, Miguel, this gringo and this other shit. What's it all about?"

"I've been south for the last couple of weeks." Miguel's eyes darted around table.

"Mexico?" Lino asked.

"No…further. Venezuela. I met with the chief security officer and the minister of Petroleos de Venezuela." He took a swig of his beer and the men looked at him in stunned silence. "Let me back up. Did any of you see a report on this guy driving an old Buick across the United States? It doesn't use gas. Somehow it makes its own power going down the road."

"Was that on TV?" Pedro asked.

"Si, every night for a week."

"Didn't he blow up in the San Francisco bombing?"

"No. We tried to kill him on the sidewalk. We shot him, but he didn't die. I'm getting ahead of myself. The oil minister is worried that if this car is successful, his oil won't be worth spit. They called me down, and I made a deal to kill him and get the car to Venezuela." Miguel smiled wickedly. "In return, we get free shipping rights for all our blow and weed, brown heroin, meth…any fucking thing we want, to anywhere we choose."

"This is great news, Miguel, especially with Mexico ready to explode," Pedro said. The rest of the men nodded in agreement.

"True, there is too much competition in Mexico now. We will wait for it to settle down before we make our move there. Then we will be even more powerful than the Columbians." Miguel turned and spat.

Lino stood up, crushed the empty beer can in his hand, and reached for another. "Aren't we getting a little ahead of ourselves? Where's the car and this gringo right now?"

"Chico, don't we have carnales in all the towing shops in Frisco?" The swarthiest of the group nodded. "So it shouldn't be too hard to find the car. The car is this really clean '66 Buick Wildcat, got big wheels and tires. We were supposed to take it from the cops, but someone beat us to it. I got a DVD for each of you, showing the car and the guy. His name is Christenson…Jesse Christenson."

"Where can I find this gringo?" Lino asked.

"He got away, but only since this morning. So he's probably still in Cali. And we also know he's not in too good of shape, got a bullet hole in him and a cracked head. So he's probably hanging low."

"Not much to go on. Anything else?" Lino asked.

"Si, he's got an old lady we're watching."

"What do you want to do with him and the car?"

"We gotta have the car and if you can take the gringo, that's cool. If not, waste him. Listen to me. This is mucho importante. Get everybody—and I mean everybody—on this right now."

After the others left, Lino and Miguel walked to their parked cars.

"I take it you're getting all your info from the FBI stooge you have in your pocket," Lino said.

"How do you know he's FBI?" Miguel asked, narrowing his eyes.

"Too good of stuff, got to be someone high up."

"Even if we have history and go back a long way, you don't need to know, Lino," Miguel said.

"You're the general." They walked together in silence for a while. "We have known each other a long time. I think I'll stop by and see my papa on the way down to LA tomorrow."

"Ernesto…right? I still remember him and your pretty mama. Got to be ten, twelve years since I saw them last. I know your mama's been a long time gone." Miguel had a strange look in his eyes. "Ernesto still working for old Franklin?"

"Loyal as a lap dog. He'll never leave. He's been there almost his entire life." Lino wondered about the look in Miguel's eyes.

41

An ugly smile appeared beneath his crazy eyes and Miguel said, "You sure you're not going down to see Juella? You always had a thing for her, at least for those nice chichis of hers."

"Me? Oh man, I remember when you tried to squeeze them behind the gym and she knocked you on your ass." Lino shook his head. "Her, Ronnie, and me were always close…and you," Lino quickly added.

No longer smiling, Miguel said, "Skinny girl with big tits, ever since they popped out in seventh grade. She was always way taller than me. Even in the seventh grade she must have been at least six inches taller."

Catching his friend's mood, Lino said, "Maybe she needed those six inches you had back then."

"Yeah, maybe if I get the chance, I show her now."

"Heh, heh, I bet you would." Lino tapped the DVD against his leg as he opened the door and got in, tossing the DVD onto the passenger seat.

Miguel bent down, looking inside the car. The way he spoke left no doubt it was an order.

"Hey, Lino, go kill this fucking gringo."

Chapter 8

Re-Awakenings

Jesse came awake when the motor home stopped. He was drenched in sweat and had slept through the entire journey. At first it was an all-encompassing sleep; later it was more of a waking dream. There were so many thoughts colliding in his head he couldn't hold on to any. It felt like two totally separate and different people were living inside his brain.

In his dreams, he kept seeing the outline of a beautiful woman, but when he tried to see her face she would somehow turn into a…a tornado or something and zoom off in some kind of car. He fell back into a deep sleep.

The sound of voices brought him once again to the surface. They grew louder and then moved off. He heard the clank of a lock being undone, and daylight burst into the compartment where he was hidden. He closed his eyes against the brilliance.

Someone was taking bags and boxes from beside him, and he would soon be uncovered. He decided it was time to get out of the sweatbox, so he rolled over to get closer to the door. He let out an involuntary gasp when the bullet wound in his side came into contact with a bungee strap lying on the floor. From this position he could see the backside of the person unloading the boxes.

At the sound of his gasp, the woman spun around and let out a scream. "Don't you come near me," she yelled, backing away.

He moved to the door and sat on the edge of the opening. "I'm sorry. I'm not going to hurt you. I just—"

"Don't come any closer!" She turned and picked up a shovel that was leaning against a wall behind her, ready to defend herself.

Jesse's eyes adjusted to the bright light and he saw the woman for the first time. She was tall—maybe three or four inches shorter than his six foot two—thin and athletic, but she filled out her t-shirt nicely. Her jet black hair was pinned up, except for a few long wavy strands that had escaped. However, it was her face that drew his attention. She was fiercely gorgeous, with eyes as dark as coffee. Even if his eyes had not yet adjusted to the light, he could tell her eyes were cold and bright.

"I'm sorry. I mean you no harm. I—"

She pushed the button of the intercom mounted to the wall and yelled, "Dad!"

"I'm sorry. I didn't mean to startle you. I'm leaving." Jesse stood up and the world started to go upside down. His knees buckled and he fell to the ground. When he looked up, the woman was standing over him, still holding the shovel.

"What happened to you?" she asked. "You have blood all over you."

Noticing the change in her voice he said, "Someone tried to kill me."

"Serves you right for stealing rides. Whose blood is it? Yours?"

"I think so."

"Who tried to kill you?"

"I don't know." Jesse vaguely remembered the violent episode in the hospital room. "A guy at the hospital."

"I know who it was," said a voice behind the woman. "Juella, are you okay?"

"I'm fine, Dad. But it looks like you brought home a hitchhiker. And he scared the crap out of me." She turned and faced the old man, who was holding a shotgun, aimed from the hip and pointing at Jesse.

"Did you hit him with the shovel and knock him down?" the old man asked as a dog ran up and started to sniff Christenson, immediately wagging his tail.

"No! He tried to stand up and just sort of crashed," Juella said, looking down as the dog began licking Jesse's hand.

"Not much of a watchdog, anymore, is he?" The old man studied Jesse's face. "Lucky for you, Mr. Christenson—"

"You know this man?" Juella asked, her voice rising.

"That's your name, right?" the old man asked Jesse.

"Yeah." Jesse reached over and scratched behind the dog's ears.

"Juella, you remember the TV show last week about the fellow traveling from New York to San Francisco in a new type of car?" Looking at her face and not seeing an answer, the old man continued. "He got there just before that suicide bombing. Well, this is the fellow with the car. Bet that bombing was no coincidence, was it, Mr. Christenson?" The old man placed the butt of the shotgun on top of his scuffed boot. "I swear this is just like déjà vu."

When Jesse didn't answer, Juella said, "What do you mean *déjà vu*, Dad? Here, let me look at you." She put down the shovel, reached for Jesse's arm, and helped him up. He swayed slightly and promptly sat down on the edge of the motor home's storage compartment.

"I mean Clem," the old man said. "This here fellow reminds me of him. I haven't thought about Clem for a long time, until I saw Mr. Christenson on TV last week."

Juella got down on one knee and inspected Jesse's right arm. "This looks like an IV site ripped open. Where did all the other blood come from?" Juella asked, and then turned to the old man. "Clem who, Dad?"

"Clem was his last name, Dick or rather Richard. He was my neighbor back when I lived in Texas…before I got out of the Air Force."

"Hmm, I'm going to lift up your shirt," Juella told Jesse, a frown creasing her already serious face.

"Why do I remind you of him?" Jesse asked as Juella lifted his bloody shirt.

"Back in the seventies he invented a motor—"

"Mary, Mother of God, you've been shot!" Juella exclaimed.

"Yeah, that's what they told me."

"You don't remember being shot?" Juella asked.

"They said I sort of bonked my head…"

"Where? Let me see. Bend down."

Jesse leaned his head forward so she could see the shaved area and the wound on the back of his head. Juella's long slender fingers probed the gash, which had reopened. After a few seconds, she said, "We need to get you to a hospital. Right away."

"No, I can't go. I'll be okay. Just…I'll…where am I?"

"Don't be a moron," Juella said. "You're seriously hurt."

"I told you someone at the hospital tried to kill me. He was dressed as a nurse and there was a guard outside my door. I think they killed the guard, too."

"Well I'm a nurse. And I'm telling you, you need to go to the hospital."

The older man stepped forward and said, "Mr. Christenson, there's something about nurses you need to know. They're good at being bossy." The old man looked over at Juella. "I told you I know who tried to kill this man. Same ones that killed Clem. You see, Richard Clem invented a motor that could run without any gasoline. He drove from Dallas to El Paso and back without stopping for gas. I was there when he got home. I'm telling you, the government killed him."

"What government? You mean *our* government?" Juella shook her head, dislodging a few more of the long black curls amassed on top of her head. "Dad, why does it always have to be the government's fault?"

"I know we go round and round about this all the time. But after Clem died, the FBI came in. They confiscated all his papers and drawings and scared his family into hiding the real truth.

"How did he die?" Jesse asked.

"They said it was a heart attack. Don't look at me like that, Juella. He was only fifty years old and could out-work two of me…and I was in my twenties. I would see him lying on the driveway when they would drop him there after 'negotiating' with him." The old man shook his head. "They would beat the shit out of him and just dump him like a pile of garbage. And think about it. Why would the FBI come in to investigate a local man dying of a heart attack?"

"Why didn't he just sell them the idea? Must have been worth millions," Juella said, trying to calm her father.

"Oh, he wanted to sell it, all right. But he was a man of high moral fiber. He wanted a guarantee—"

"That they wouldn't just shelve it," Jesse finished.

"Yep." The old man stared into Jesse's eyes. "That what they tried to do with you?"

"I don't know. I can't remember anything about any negotiations." Jesse reached up and touched his forehead. "God, my head is just killing me. But please, no hospital."

"You might have blood collecting around your brain. It just might be killing you, you know. At the very least, you should have a brain scan." Juella glanced up, trying to read her father's weathered face. "Okay, what do I know? I only do this for a living. Geez, another stray. Well, I guess if we're going to keep him, we should get him into the house. At least it's cooler in there. Here, let me help you up."

She put an arm around Jesse, getting him to his feet. He wobbled slightly and would have fallen if Juella hadn't clutched him tightly. When he leaned up against her, he could smell her hair.

"Apricots," Jesse said aloud.

"Of course…Mr. Fruitman," Juella replied.

"I'm a tellin' you, this is just like déjà vu. I used to help Clem into his house after the beatings. Do you think you can walk, Mr. Christenson?" The older man looked around. "Where is that bum Ernesto when we need him?"

"He took a tractor and went out past the walnuts," Juella said. "I think we can manage without Ernesto. Come on, try and take a step, Fruitman."

"Please call me Jesse. And I don't know your name, sir," he said, looking at Juella's father.

"Franklin Roosevelt Garcia. My family always named their first-born after the president who was in office at the time. Everyone wants to know how come a Mexican is named Franklin. But I'm not Mexican. My family is fourth-generation Californian. Probably been in America longer than your family. And—"

"My dad is a bit touchy about his name, as you may have guessed," Juella said, raising her eyebrows. "Just call him Frank. How are you doing?"

"I'll be okay," Jesse replied.

"I've seen many strong men injured. You don't have to fake it with me, Mr. Fruitman…Jesse," Juella said.

"Okay. I feel like shit."

"I love honesty." Juella broke into a smile for the first time in what seemed like ages to her. They walked to the farmhouse, navigated the wraparound veranda, went inside, and climbed the steps to the bedroom on the second floor.

Frank yelled from the bottom of the stairs, "I'm needin' to sit down. Maybe take a little snooze." He started to turn away, but stopped and asked, "You think he's going to be okay, Juella?"

"I'll do a quick assessment and let you know, Dad. I'll be down in a little while."

Juella looked at Jesse's eyes. They were blue, slightly dull, and full of pain. "Your head hurts pretty bad, huh? Is the pain here in the back?" Juella inspected the injured site very closely. She could see the marks left by the staples that once held the edges of the wound together.

"No, well, it's really kind of all over."

"Here, let's get that shirt off." She peeled his shirt off, walked into the bathroom, and dropped it into a trash can. Then she pulled a washcloth off the towel bar and rinsed it in warm water. First she cleaned the blood out of his hair and then gently washed the blood from his arm and his torso. She retreated to the bathroom and returned with some Neosporin and band-aids.

"Looks like you were stitched up and you've torn open the wound, but it's stopped bleeding." She applied the Neosporin and put band-aids over the wounds. "This will keep you from getting blood all over the sheets. You have blood on your jeans. Were you also shot down there? Sit down on the bed and let me pull those off."

"I don't know—"

"Oh, for Christ's sake, I'm a nurse. Don't flatter yourself," she said with a heavy sigh.

"Nurse or not, I'm not hurt down there…at least I don't feel any pain."

Juella raised her hand and started ticking off her fingers. "You fell down and can't walk. You can't remember being shot. Your brain has probably swelled. You're most likely in or going into shock—"

"I don't have any underwear on," he interrupted, looking at her raised countdown hand. It seemed somehow familiar, and a memory tugged at his mind. "Have we met before?"

She put her hands on her hips and glared at him until a smile slowly spread across her lips. She began to laugh. "So…if we met before, it would be okay for me to see your huevos? No, I don't think we've met. I would never forget someone like you."

She went to the closet and pulled out a robe. "This belongs to my husband. I'll turn around while you put it on…Fruitman. And then we can get those jeans off."

Jesse stood at the edge of the bed, pulled off the filthy jeans, and put on the robe. "Okay. I'm done."

Juella inspected his legs, occasionally reaching down and feeling for a pulse here and there. "You were right. No bullet holes down here. You have really good muscle tone, must exercise a bunch."

He didn't answer and she reached over and started petting the old dog that had crept into the room. "Well, Barney, he can't even remember if he works out. What are we going to do with him?" Barney raised his ears. "Yeah you're right, looks like I'm stuck with him." Directing her gaze back to Jesse, she said, "Do you remember if you slept while you were in the motor home compartment?"

"I don't know if you would call it sleep. More like I passed out."

Juella left the room and returned shortly with a glass of water and a pill. "It's a narcotic painkiller from my dad's stash. Probably shouldn't take it with a head injury. You should know that you might have a TBI—that's a traumatic brain injury. In the military, it's most often caused from being too close to an IED blast, which is too damn common for soldiers serving in Iraq or Afghanistan. Those people, the enemy, are such chicken-shit fuckers…"

Her dark eyes teared up and she said, "Sorry, I don't even know why I should care. You made your own choices, so…here. You decide." She handed him the pill and water, spun around, and stomped out of the room.

Jesse wondered if he had done something wrong. His head continued to scream out in pain, somehow making him believe he'd missed a vital clue or something. In the past few days, he had taken a bullet, banged his head, and almost been murdered in his bed. Beyond the point of caring, he placed the pill in his mouth and swallowed, washing it down with the water.

He thought he heard her voice from the bottom of the stairs saying, "And you better not crump on me. This time."

Day Twelve

Day Two of the Grand Pursuit

Chapter 9

Manipulative Officiousness

Ah, the day *after* the day-after-being-blitzed was the best, O'Hallohan thought. He had arrived early, around five, and now it was only a little after seven in the morning. Once again he was buried in minutia and was surprised when he heard a tap on his closed door.

"Hang on," he yelled out as he closed the Secret: Eyes Only computer file he'd been reading. He crossed the room and unlocked the door.

"Excuse me for bothering you. Are you Agent Patrick O'Hallohan?"

"Yeah, that's me." O'Hallohan stepped back and looked down on the smallish man dressed in a gray suit at least a size too big for him. The man clutched a brown leather briefcase close to his chest. He wore dark-rimmed glasses and looked to be an escapee from the Grade School Teachers Hall of Fame.

"Agent O'Hallohan, I'm Agent Howard Entersane. I'm with the EIA."

"What's the EIA?"

"Energy Information Agency." The small man blinked and, not seeing any reaction, continued. "We're part of the DOE. You know, Department of Energy."

"Oh, yeah." O'Hallohan snapped his fingers. "I called you guys yesterday. Come in. You must have had a hard time finding my jail cell."

"Jail cell? Oh, you mean this room. No, I figured this must have the thickest walls," he said, looking around at the stark room.

"Thickest walls?" This time it was O'Hallohan who was perplexed.

"Well, you know…you Homeland Security guys are always dealing in secrets, I suppose."

"Secrets, yeah. Well, the reason I called was I needed to know if you have any information on gangs interested in energy."

"You mean gangs like Al Qaeda?"

"No. Domestic gangs or maybe Mexican."

Raising his eyebrows, Entersane said, "By *energy*, do you mean nuclear? The DOE is in charge of all nuclear material in the United States… actually, for that matter, most of the world."

"No. I meant oil, I guess."

"Could you be just a little more specific?" Agent Entersane sat with his hands folded on top of his briefcase, waiting like a second grade teacher for a student's first oral book report.

O'Hallohan sat back, frowning. He was no detective. He was a soldier and now an agent for Homeland Security, but not a secret agent. If he had his choice, he would rather be out shooting at someone. "Agent Entersane, do you have any kind of secret clearance?"

"Yes, of course I do. I read secret reports all the time. In fact they wouldn't have let me in this building without clearance."

O'Hallohan nodded. "Have you heard of a car called the Take-Us?"

"That's not secret. It was on TV last week." Agent Entersane sat forward. "Were you involved with that?"

"Yes. Look, there's no other way, so let me tell you. The inventor was shot by a gang member."

"You don't say!" Entersane took off his glasses and wiped the lenses with his pastel colored tie. "So you're wondering if there are any 'oil' gangs in the United States."

"I looked at the Department of Energy website because you guys keep track of all the oil and—if I were to venture a guess—oil companies." When Agent Entersane didn't react, O'Hallohan continued. "Do oil companies hire gangs? You ever heard of such?"

"I've heard of many things." Agent Entersane reached up and

replaced his glasses. "However, logic dictates that if you use a gang once, they would own you forever. Oil companies are much smarter than that."

"I never thought of that. Of course, no legitimate company would take the risk of getting ankle-chained to a gang." O'Hallohan massaged the back of his neck.

"Not necessarily true. Here in the United States it may be. However, when you talk about overseas, that's what the terrorist movement is mostly about."

"I thought it was about religion." O'Hallohan began softly tapping his pencil.

"Religion is often the excuse used for many things. I believe if you do your research, you will come to the conclusion that the whole thing boils down to a quest for power. It's about money, which creates power. And that stems from oil."

"So if a gang was interested in stopping this alternative energy car, there has to be some quid pro quo. Either a money or power benefit for them, right?" O'Hallohan flipped his pencil around and jotted a note on the legal pad in front of him.

"Gangs would take a bite out of any apple offered. If I were a betting man, I would bet their concern is mostly the drug trade, which also translates to money and, once again, power."

"What about cash for a hit?"

"When was the last time you heard of gangs going after someone that wasn't connected somehow to drugs? It just doesn't happen, Agent O'Hallohan."

"Are you saying that if we find a drug angle we'll be able to find the car—I mean the shooters?"

Agent Entersane glanced down at his briefcase and then consciously looked up into O'Hallohan face. "Agent O'Hallohan, the Department of Energy is responsible for all the nuclear weapons in the United States. Actually, we are the owners…not the military. We have the additional responsibility of watching over and developing all the energy resources in the country. We also have a large intelligence branch, as you can probably imagine. We know the car is missing. We also would like very much to have it. In fact, it's a top priority…a grave matter of national security."

"Almost everything that walks in the door here is a matter of national security," O'Hallohan stated flatly.

"Of course it is. It's just that we have jurisdiction over all energy resources, in the same way that you have everything to do with suicide bombers walking down the sidewalks trying to blow up buildings and the sort."

O'Hallohan felt like he was being played…and now put down. He thought briefly about reaching over and grabbing the condescending little twerp by the throat, something he was much better at than sitting behind a desk.

"Does that mean it's going to be a race to find the car?" O'Hallohan asked.

"Of course it's a race," Entersane said. Seeing O'Hallohan's stare, he continued. "I surmise that you're new here in D.C. Each department has its own priorities. The real race is not between our agencies. More like some dictator or national entity that doesn't have our country's interest at heart. Face it, Agent O'Hallohan. They most likely already have the car—at least that's our consensus. However, when it does surface, and eventually it will, we need to be clear here. The Take-Us auto will belong to the Department of Energy."

"Doesn't it belong to its rightful owner, Jesse Christenson?"

"Minor detail. We'll clean that up," Agent Entersane said as he handed O'Hallohan his card and stood up to leave. "Please remember: by law after 9/11 each department is to keep the others apprised of current investigations affecting each other. Don't forget to keep me in the loop. Good day."

As the man was leaving, O'Hallohan thought he somehow looked larger than when he first stood at the door. He glanced at the card and immediately Googled the Energy Information Agency.

After reading for a few minutes he came across these words: "The Administrator shall not be required to obtain the approval of any officer or employee of the United States in the collection of any information. It will be independent from review of any Executive Branch officials."

Damn, O'Hallohan thought, most people were worried about Homeland Security becoming a government within the government. This was an agency that had no oversight whatsoever. And the clever thing was that they were right out in the open. The more O'Hallohan thought about it, the more he wondered what they would do with the car if they found it. And what about Christenson?

"He never even brought up his name," O'Hallohan said aloud. "Do they already have him?"

Chapter 10

Flight Risk

Leena reflected on the events of the previous twenty hours following Nowiki's delivery of the devastating news of Jesse's disappearance. When the two cut-from-the-same-mold, faceless FBI agents escorted her to the San Francisco airport and straight to the boarding area, they seemed relieved to get rid of her. Maybe it was her imagination, but she also noticed they watched her walk down the ramp into the plane, and she knew they waited until the plane's door closed before they left.

While flying nonstop to LaGuardia she finished typing out the final details of the story. After arriving in New York, she waited for a taxi in the cold rain and asked to be taken directly to the World Cable Network headquarters.

Even though it was after seven in the evening, the never-ending work of a twenty-four-hour news station hummed on. Once she was inside the huge tower, the only stop she made was to the printer before she handed her boss the manuscript which detailed everything that had transpired in the past week and a half.

Leena looked out the window from the 24th floor, her foot tapping out a steady beat as Max Puglisi finished reading and slowly took off his reading glasses.

"It's a great story, but then you probably know that." He handed back the manuscript. "Only two problems."

"I know the feds won't allow us to release it yet." Leena fidgeted on the edge of her chair. "The other?"

"There's no physical proof the car works as you say."

She sighed heavily. "I believe I know where the proof is."

"Leena, what makes you think you can locate Jesse Christenson, when every cop in the country is looking for him? This *is* just a story, correct?"

"Of course. It's not Jesse. The proof is physical. You can reach out and touch it."

"What do you have?"

"You know I trust you to the hilt, but I'd rather not say until I know for sure. Agent Nowiki told me they already hacked my computer once."

"Jesus, Leena! Everybody in this building has a story they're coveting, holding tight to their chest." He drummed his fingers on top of the desk. "So be it. I don't need details, just a story."

"Story, alpha and omega," she said, methodical as ever. Catching his look, she said, "Beginning to end. By the way, am I still on vacation or was that bullshit, too?"

"Where are you heading? You want to keep digging, huh?" he asked with a jaded smile. "Better yet, we'll tell everybody you're on your honeymoon."

"Yeah, right."

"Watch your back, honey."

"Honey? Isn't that sexual harassment?" Her slow smile appeared.

"We were talking about your back. I don't think that's classified as a sexual part. Of course, by next week political correctness might include it as well," Max said, rising to his feet. "Call me and keep me informed on what's happening."

Leena went to her office, leaving her laptop computer, manuscript, and other items on the desk before leaving and locking the door. The only thing she took from her office was a pair of running shoes she kept under her desk and the cell phone she used only for Jesse Christenson.

Many well-wishers offered congratulations as she was leaving, but like a woman on a mission, she quickly departed.

Shortly thereafter she entered her apartment, which was tastefully decorated, and kicked off her shoes as usual. But this time dark dread struck her like a slap. Cautiously walking into the living room she could feel the violation as she warily looked for an intruder.

Before beginning the cross-country trip with Jesse, she had left three different traps: one in a kitchen cabinet, one in her desk, and the last in her bedroom closet. All three showed that someone had searched her place.

She sat down at her desk, and her skin began to crawl as she realized that whoever had done this could be watching her at that moment with a hidden camera. Her knees shook, but she forced herself not to look around.

That's when she saw the letter from Jesse. On top of the letter was a business card: Agent Howard Entersane, Energy Information Agency of the Department of Energy. She felt like a fool for setting all the traps when right in front of her they all but told her they had searched her apartment. Printed neatly on the back side of the card were the words CALL ME.

Jesse's letter had been neatly opened. Inside, there was a small note that simply said PUT THIS SOMEWHERE SAFE. There was nothing else inside the envelope. What did this Entersane creep get? Safe deposit key, flash drive, instructions to open the website? The bastard! Stealing what Jesse sent and then having the balls to leave the envelope and make sure she knew it. But he likely didn't have Jesse…or the other.

Screw him. She was safe as long as he believed she would lead him to Jesse. Rising slowly and putting her back to the room, still mindful of hidden cameras, she went to her closet and stuffed some well thought out items into her soft-sided travel bags.

* * *

Leena caught the red eye out of JFK and transferred planes in Vegas, taking a short hop to Reno. She felt trapped sitting in the window seat, looking down through the dark sky at the cloud cover thousands of feet below the slick aluminum shell. With a little luck she could be back to her childhood home in California by late morning. She placed her hand over her mouth and stifled a huge yawn.

It had started over six months ago but the last ten days were the most intense and draining of her entire life. And she was starting to feel it. Leena sat up straight in her seat, no time for sleep. She had to stay alert.

Casually she glanced around the plane, wondering which one of the people on board was shadowing her. Maybe more than one. Even if that sounded paranoid, she wouldn't underestimate them again. Not after what she'd been through.

A feeling of emptiness engulfed her, knowing she alone would have to do what needed to be done. And what about Jesse? He must be miserable not knowing who he was or what his life had been about.

She had to find him. And if that was not possible at least she would not let his…their…dream die. Oh crap, now she was taking ownership of the dream. She wondered how that had happened.

Always independent, she reluctantly admitted she would need some help to prove Jesse's idea. She didn't fully trust Nowiki, although she really didn't distrust him. It was just that they were always butting heads about the whole by-the-book thing. It limited her creativity and just wasn't her way. What she needed was a more spontaneous partner, someone like Agent O'Hallohan. He was definitely a man of action, someone you could trust, and maybe—

"Get a hold of yourself, girl," the rational part of her mind yelled, feeling a bit guilty that she was thinking of O'Hallohan when Jesse was missing. Why did she always get horny when she was tired and stressed? It wasn't her fault Jesse had opened the door of sexual passion that she had successfully locked years ago. Once again, she glanced around the airliner. What was it about danger that brought those feelings out? Still, she needed help. Maybe she could enlist O'Hallohan…enlist or entice. Her fingers subconsciously smoothed out her blouse.

As the cabin lights came on in preparation for their descent, Leena checked her cell phone. It was just after five in the morning, Pacific Standard Time. She took a deep breath just like she did before going on live TV. Then she stood up and slipped her arms into the blue pinstriped jacket that matched her short blue skirt and sat back down. She slid her feet back into her smart stiletto heeled shoes. The plane had barely stopped when she gathered her carry-on bags and moved to the door for deplaning. Only then did she casually turn and try to memorize as many faces as she could.

Once she arrived in the terminal, Leena exaggerated her walk by swinging her hips back and forth. Truly feeling like a whore, she moved as quickly as she could through the crowded airport and chose the last bathroom before the exit. She selected the furthest stall and locked the door, immediately kicking off her shoes. Her bright red-painted toenails gave her pause. Too late. Disgusted by her bare feet on the dirty floor, she shook her head and opened her bag.

She donned her oldest pair of flip flops, took out a pillow, and tied it with a sash around her waist. Then she pulled out the muumuu she'd worn for Halloween the previous year and pulled it over her head, completely covering her smart business suit. Next came the long red-haired wig. Finally, she applied rouge and bright red lipstick. She tugged out the folded backpack she had stuffed into one of her soft-sided travel bags, shoved everything into it, and slung it over her shoulders.

Disguise almost complete, Leena dug out a pair of too-big, lightly tinted glasses, stopping only briefly in front of the mirror to adjust the wig. The whole process was complete in less than a minute. She took a deep breath to slow her racing heart as she made her way out of the bathroom with a slow deliberate waddle.

Fighting the impulse to run, Leena concentrated on the slow but stressful pace as she shuffled to the taxi stand. She handed the driver a piece of paper with an address she had typed out and climbed awkwardly into the back seat. With her best-worst Russian accent, she said, "You take-a-me, please," and handed the cabbie a twenty.

"Lady, you don't pay until we get there."

"No, you keep." Leena sat back and ignored the driver.

After several miles, the cabdriver dropped Leena at a hotel in the heart of downtown. She made no move to collect her change, playing the part of a naïve foreigner to the hilt. She plodded into the hotel and proceeded directly to the restroom in the lobby. This time she morphed into a blonde, wearing six-inch heels, painted-on-tight jeans, and a low-cut top that showed almost all of her well endowed breasts. She hoped everyone would be looking at her tits and ass instead of her face, which was hidden with a different pair of sunglasses.

She reversed her travel bags and piled her backpack and clothes—pillow and all—back into them. She emerged from the hotel, walked a short block, and entered the discount auto-rental dealer where she had reserved a car from her throw-away cell phone and paid in advance with a corporate card. She was reluctant to show her driver's license but insistent that the contract be made out in the corporation's name, hopefully harder to trace.

After leaving the parking lot, Leena slipped a baseball cap over her wig, which was starting to itch like hell. She drove a few blocks until she sighted a dumpster behind a bar. Then she stopped and hurriedly took off the high heels, thinking only briefly about the eight hundred dollars they cost. She sighed and put on the running shoes from her office and removed a small plastic bag that contained a few personal items. Glancing around and seeing no one, she marched over to the dumpster and threw the luggage, along with all its contents, away. If they had placed a bug anywhere, she was sure it wasn't attached to her.

The exits flashed by on Interstate 80 as Leena drove to California, where she would exit and take the back way around Lake Tahoe. When she arrived at the lake she turned left and drove through Incline Village, doubling back to Carson City where she stopped at a clothing store to de-whore herself. Then she was off to the military surplus store where she and Jesse had shopped the previous week… before they'd nearly been killed.

Paying cash, she purchased a set of night vision goggles, the same as last time, along with other items that might come in handy. Now it was only a matter of hours before she would arrive at her mom's house. She wondered if they would still be watching it.

Bait. That's what her girlfriends used to call her twenty years ago when they went bar hopping. She had always been pretty, but never wanted to be known as just that type. Rather, she wished to be appreciated for her smarts. Of course, it was fun at times, drawing all those boys to their table. Her friends sure liked picking some of them off, like plucking cherries from a tree or maybe more like bananas from a tree. Leena realized years ago that she was the aggressive one and chose who she would have sex with. It was never an accident. Her face hardened into a frown as she glanced in the rearview mirror. Now she was bait of a different sort.

She turned what would normally be a two-hour drive into a four-hour adventure, doubling back two times. At the top of Kit Carson Pass she got out of the car, ducked behind a tree, and watched closely as cars drove by, looking for the driver who seemed to be more interested in a car than the expansive mountain views.

Finally satisfied that no one was following her, she continued her journey, all downhill now. She didn't want to do it but she couldn't think of any other way. Fluffing her blonde hair and gripping the steering wheel tighter than necessary, she turned off the main highway and started down the side street toward her mother's home.

Jesse's property, down the street from her mother's, came within sight as she drove down the hill and rounded the corner. The scene was one of complete devastation; his house had burned to the ground. Someone had installed a chain-link fence around the remains and attached yellow crime scene tape to it.

Trying not to be too obvious in staring at it, she found what she had hoped and prayed was still there. She almost squealed in delight as a feeling of elation spread though her. If they had overlooked it as an insignificant piece of property, she would have her chance.

Leena pulled her eyes reluctantly back to the road and continued to drive, deliberately passing her mother's house. All looked peaceful and calm. She was pleased her mom had taken her advice to go and stay with friends after all the havoc from last week's big shoot-out.

Leena took a few more turns and ended back at the highway. She drove to the parking lot of the only bar in town and parked in the far corner under the shade of the massive pines. Taking off the blonde wig and reclining her seat, she stifled a yawn. She figured she would have to wait for dark, but without consciously wanting to, she fell into a deep dreamless sleep.

The darkness was close around her when she woke. For a moment, she couldn't remember where she was. Then it all came rushing back. With a feeling of impending doom, she started the car and drove to her mother's house, turning abruptly into the drive. She turned the lights off and stopped in front of the detached garage.

Jumping out of the car, Leena unlocked and went in the side door. She pushed the button that opened the garage door and ran back to the rental car, driving it into the garage. She waited in the recess of the door, breathing as silently as possible, watching and waiting. It was a half hour before she left the garage and unlocked the back door of the house.

The door creaked as Leena walked into the dark empty house.

She used the tactical penlight she'd bought at the surplus store and went through the entire house, looking for intruders. All was neat and tidy. But when she returned to the kitchen, she saw it. A business card was propped against the vase of fake flowers on the kitchen table: Agent Howard Entersane, Energy Information Agency of the Department of Energy. She picked it up and flipped it over: CALL ME. It was dated with today's date and she realized the guy was still one step ahead of her.

Chapter 11

Resilient Guest

Bright morning sun streamed through the window, waking Jesse. Juella was sitting in the chair next to his bed, a book resting on her lap. Her dark eyes watched him intently.

"How do you feel? Head still ache?"

Jesse pulled his arms out from under the sheet and stretched. "You're not a dream, then." He stopped mid-stretch and said, "Unless this is just a part of the same dream."

Juella stood and pressed her fingers on the bullet hole in his side. "Ouch!"

"Does that feel like a dream, Fruitman? How's your head?"

"Damn! Yeah, it's okay. Wait a minute—you're not her! Where am I?" He took his eyes off her face and looked around the room.

"Listen to me a second. This is important. Tell me about your head wound: does it feel like there's pressure inside or just soreness around the gash in the back of your head?"

Jesse ran his fingers around the area. "It feels just like any cut or bump you get, a little tender. Why is that so important?"

"Any time you have a traumatic head injury, an aneurysm can develop. If it bursts, blood leaks into your cranium and you can die very quickly. We just have to keep an eye on you."

"You probably already told me, but are you a doctor or such?"

"Such. I'm a nurse." She sat back down on the edge of the chair. "You showed up yesterday, stowed away in the luggage compartment of Dad's motor home." When he didn't reply she said, "Your name is Jesse Christenson and you—"

"I know my own name…and the dream about the fight in the hospital was real, wasn't it? I'm sorry, what was your name again?"

"Juella. It's Spanish"

"Hway-ella. That's different. Wait, did I already say that? Sounds like déjà vous."

"Déjà vous. That's what Dad said yesterday. He's been up since early morning trying to figure out what's going on about you. There's no news of you being shot, hospitalized, escaping…nothing." She sat back and crossed her arms. "You're a big mystery to us."

Jesse looked out the window, saying nothing.

"Why don't you take a shower and come downstairs for breakfast. You like coffee?"

"I would kill for a cup," he answered. Then seeing the look on her face, he quickly said, "Just an expression."

With steaming hot water running over his head, Jesse began to remember the events that had transpired in the hospital. He even remembered that he couldn't remember. That was weird. He reached for the shampoo, stopping his hand in midair. How would he know if he didn't remember something? What a screwed up mess.

Lathering shampoo over his healing head gash, Jesse realized the danger out there would continue to be real. Even if they had the car, he might still have the ability to re-create it. Of course, if everybody thought he had lost his memory, he would be safe. Or was that just naïve?

When he came out of the shower he found his clothes laid out on the bed along with some cash, a Swiss Army knife, and a cell phone. The shirt was different from the one he wore from the hospital. He pushed a button on the cell phone and nothing happened. It appeared dead. Jeans on, he dropped the cell into one pocket and the cash and knife into the other. He was sitting on the bed putting on his shoes when Juella entered the room.

"Hey, where did the cell phone and other stuff come from?" he asked.

"I washed your jeans. They were in your pockets. You having a little trouble tying your shoes?" She got down on a knee and brushed his hands away.

"I'm a little stiff on my left side." He sat upright.

"Bullet hole side, huh?" She stood up and looked at the still black-and-blue hole that had re-sealed itself. "Stand up a second and turn around."

He did as she requested.

"Why isn't there an exit hole?"

"I don't know. I don't remember anyone saying anything about it. Could they have dug it out from the front?"

He turned back around. This time she put her fingers gently on the wound and felt around. "I don't think they did any cutting here, looks like they just stitched you up."

"Why wouldn't they remove the bullet?"

"Either you were too weak for surgery at the time," she said as she probed the area near his spine, "or the bullet ended up someplace they felt was too dangerous to take the risk."

"Oh, fu—sorry—that's just great."

"I have a cure for that crabbiness." She turned and walked away, but not without taking one final glance at his bare chest. "Coffee's downstairs."

Jesse grabbed the shirt and buttoned it as he followed her to the kitchen.

"Mr. Christenson," said the old man sitting at the table. "Juella says you don't remember much about yesterday. My name is Frank, and you're welcome to stay at my ranch."

"Thank you, Frank. I'm sorry, Juella, for not saying it earlier."

"You just need some of this to make you sociable again." Juella smiled and placed a large cup of coffee in front of him.

He picked up the steaming mug and took a sip. "That's good joe. I'm feeling better already. Thanks."

"Mr. Christenson—"

"Jesse, please," he said, taking another sip.

Frank waved at a stack of papers in front of him. "I found a couple of really good websites and printed this off the computer this morning. Not one word about you being shot or missing. Just a bunch about how come your car couldn't be real."

"Oh, it's real, all right. Or was."

"I don't doubt it for a second. I'm gettin' real sick of this propaganda shit they pass off as news." Frank looked up at Juella. "You can't doubt me now, can you? He's proof of what I been saying."

Juella looked at Frank reproachfully, hands on her hips and not saying a word.

"So your idea," said Frank. "What's it based on, if not Clem's? Repulsine? Or is it a Tesla offshoot?"

"Did you tell me something about Clem yesterday? I've studied Tesla's work, but what's Repulsine?" Jesse sat back when Juella put a plate of eggs in front of him. "Thanks."

"Schauberger's Repulsine engine design was suppose to be a self-running engine that—"

"Frank," Jesse interrupted. "Did you see the videos of the car?"

"Sure, but it couldn't be that simple, right?"

"Some of this seems to be hardwired into my brain. I know I didn't go into great detail in the interviews because there were some proprietary concerns. However, the entire thing works on ordinary electromagnetic induction, with a few twists."

"Electromagnet, that's the same as an ordinary alternator. How can that be?"

Jesse stopped chewing long enough to look the old man in the eye. "Frank, they're trying to kill me so my design doesn't get out."

"What will they do? Kill me if I know?" Frank threw his head back and laughed. "What? They're going to end me before the cancer finishes me a few months from now?" Seeing Jesse's eyebrows lift, he continued. "That's right. I got pancreatic cancer. And one way or the other, I'll be dead shortly."

"Dad, don't say that. There's still hope."

"Juella, you know me. I've been an optimist my whole life, but sometimes you have to see things as they really are." Frank moved his foot over and rubbed the dog's head.

"Okay. You see them that way; I don't have to." Juella stormed out of the kitchen.

"She's just afraid to be left alone," Frank explained, looking down at the table.

Jesse looked at the top of the old man's head and said, "I'm sorry, sir, about the cancer. Fear of being alone. I can understand that."

"What most people don't understand is you come into this world alone and go out the same way. You can't take your money or your property with you. Since you can't see it or touch it, I would like to think you get to take the love you've created while you're here," Frank said.

Jesse nodded his head and took another sip of his coffee and said, "What you didn't see in the video was a small shaft sticking out at the apex of the drive belt. That half-inch shaft makes contact with the drive belt. Good friction. After the initial battery power, when the speed gets up near sixty miles per hour, it spins at twenty-eight thousand rpms. Together with generators from the other wheel, they pulse. That is, once they begin spinning. And I found a way to use centrifugal force to help initiate the critical initial spinning.

"The magnets and shaft are suspended on sealed foil bearings—the same as they use in jet engines—and in a complete vacuum with one-way check valves to prevent back flow. It's as close to frictionless as possible. When the belt pulses off they just…well…essentially coast. All the time they are creating free power. When they do start to lose rpms, the computer that's monitoring them will pulse them back up to rpms as high as the speed of the car will allow."

"I'll be damned. Don't they get hot, going that speed?"

"Did you notice the radiator still in the car? I created a water jacket around the generators and ran coolant through them back up to the radiator."

"So in that vacuum, and with them special bearings, you really don't have much friction. Kind of like coasting down a hill on a bicycle if you were on the moon."

While Frank mulled over everything he learned, Jesse got another cup of coffee and sat down to finish his breakfast.

"So, who you figure is out to…get rid of you?"

"At first it was Middle Eastern types. You know, radical Islamic

Arabs. The feds said from Iran. I guess that makes them Persians. But the woman that shot me was from the Mexican Mafia. I don't know about the guy in the hospital, but he had the same tattoo as the Mexican woman."

"Yeah, I've seen them tats. The oil companies must be paying them."

"I don't know, oil companies—"

"What, you don't know how ruthless they are? Grab your coffee and follow me."

Frank slipped his boots on and headed out the back door. Jesse squinted in the hot bright sunshine as they began walking toward a big red barn.

"Hey, Frank, where the hell am I?"

Frank laughed, "Little lost, are ya? My ranch is about thirty miles from Modesto, California. Know it?"

"Yeah, I feel like I do know it. I think I had a house just up there in the mountains…" He could barely see the foothills in the summer haze.

"See all these bags?" Frank said upon entering the barn. "It's capsaicin, from finely ground red peppers. We've been spraying it on our crops for years."

"Yeah, so?" Jesse looked around the barn filled with bags.

"Totally illegal. Most of the commercially approved insecticides are oil-based. The oil gets into the groundwater and everything gets polluted, but a one-hundred percent nature-based product that every farmer in California could make himself is illegal. And the shame of it is most Californians think we're the greenest state in the country. You still think oil companies don't control all of us?"

"How'd you come up with this?" Jesse asked.

"Kind of like you did with your car idea. My dad used to plant pepper plants around the perimeter of the garden. Claimed it kept the pests out." Frank shrugged. "I later found out that it dissolves the jugum—the back of an insect's wings—and kills 'em. You know how it is. One thing led to another."

"How do you get away with it?"

"All the state and county Ag officials know about it. They don't say anything. It's the fucking federal Department of Agriculture. Those USDA assholes get in the way of common sense. They're always trying to get us to plant more corn to turn into ethanol. Just like a bunch of pimps they are, always flashing their money. So when they show up, we always just smile and tell them next year. Idiots." Frank spat on the ground. "Feel up to a little tour?"

Frank began walking toward an old Ford pickup truck.

"Sure, haven't felt this good in a week. What did you mean 'flashing their money'?"

"You ever hear of crop subsidies? They pay us to plant what they want. Some call it Ag welfare."

Jesse nodded yes.

"You drove through Nebraska last week. Did you notice that most of the wheat fields have been replaced by corn fields? And have you noticed the price of bread lately?"

"Everything's gone up."

"Computers and cell phones ain't gone up. Government doesn't have its hands in them. Think about it."

"That's because they want you to own one so they can track you through the software."

"Well, they haven't tracked you down here." Frank opened the door of the old truck. "I got nine hundred acres. I'd be proud to show you around. There's no one out here to shoot you."

Jesse smiled at the old man. "I'm glad you didn't add *yet*."

Chapter 12

Isolated Return

Lino turned his Mercedes off the county road and onto the long curved driveway flanked by walnut trees on each side. The red barn was on his right and he couldn't help but notice a light blue Lexus SUV parked off to the side. This was the first time he had been to the ranch in seven years, and he wondered if his dad would even recognize his face.

Juella heard the car approaching and stepped out onto the front veranda. They saw each other at the same time, as Lino stopped the car. Barney gave out a few half-hearted barks and headed toward the car. His tail looked like a windshield wiper going to and fro. Lino had his door half open and was giving Barney a good rubbing.

"Lino, is that you?" Juella asked as she walked toward him.

"In the flesh."

She ran and leapt into his arms. "I've missed you so much."

"Juella! The years, they have been kind to you," Lino said, giving her a warm hug.

"I thought you were in prison. Or dead." Juella held him at arm's length and peered into his eyes as if looking for lost treasure.

"Juella, I think you've gotten taller."

"I was always taller than you—well, maybe not now. But you haven't changed; you're always trying to change the subject."

"Yeah, and you're always bustin' me."

Juella pulled him close once again. "It's so nice to see you again…the three of us were always so close."

"As long as you remember you were my girlfriend before Ronnie stole you away."

"Oh, bullshit! You dumped me for Roseanne because she put out and I didn't."

They both began to laugh.

"Your memory is still intact, as well as your directness, Juella. I think that's what kept the three of us such close friends for so many years."

Juella's eyes shone and a lone tear escaped. She turned and wiped it away. "Come on, let's sit on the porch. It's too hot out here in the sun. You want something to drink?"

"Water's good. Thanks."

Juella got her old friend a glass of ice and filled it with water. "Lino, what happened to you? I heard you finished college and then got mixed up in that awful…situation."

Lino stared at Juella, noticing how large the diamond on her left hand appeared. Which truth should he tell? Somehow, she seemed prettier now than she was when he served as the best man at her wedding.

"They charged me with the murder of my ex-girlfriend's new boyfriend, but had to drop the charges for lack of evidence. When they charge you for murder, even if you didn't do it, it never comes off your record. So I could never get a government job after that."

"You had such big dreams…FBI…CIA. You were gonna be the new secret agent superstar. You must be doing well at some job to be driving a car like the one you drove up in."

"I work for an import-export business in LA. They pay me on commission, so I do pretty well." Close enough to the truth, Lino thought.

"Import, like drugs from Mexico?"

"Juella, you know how I feel about drugs. Most of my imports are from China and Indonesia."

"Sorry, Lino. Bad joke. It really is good to see you again."

"It's cool. Where's old Frank?"

"He just took a…a guest on a tour of the ranch. You know how proud he is of the place." She walked over to the porch railing and looked out over the cool solitude of the walnut trees. When she turned back, she wore a sad expression. "You should probably know that Dad has terminal cancer."

"Oh, man, how come it's always the good ones? Is that why you're here?"

"I've taken a leave of absence from the hospital. I'm staying here to take care of him."

"Ronnie and I always said you were born to be a nurse, always fixing somebody that's broken. Who fixes you when you break?"

"I'm fine. Did you come to see your dad?" she asked, her voice flat and emotionless. "I'm sure he would love to see you again."

She reminded Lino of a rose, perfectly beautiful and delicate… with thorns attached. "Is he around? Dumb question. Where is he today? Wait a minute, it's June. So he's probably spraying for weeds, right?"

"You should have stayed here and become a rancher. You always had the touch."

"Miguel said the same thing."

"Miguel? You've seen him lately?"

Lino's eyes darted about. "Uh, I ran into him a few days ago." He stood up abruptly. "I think I'll go find Dad."

Juella grabbed Lino's arm. "I never trusted Miguel, you know? I mean, we all knew what happened to him when he was little. We all felt sorry for him, but it warped and twisted him—"

"He seems different now," Lino interrupted. "He did his time and now he's—"

"Sorry…it's okay." This time Juella interrupted. "Go say hi to your dad. I didn't mean to upset you."

"I'm just nervous. You know how my dad can be." Lino tried to put on a smile.

"You mean kind and gentle? He's always been like an uncle to me. Don't forget to stop and say goodbye on your way out."

Lino turned and began walking around the back of the house, heading for the cool shade of the walnut trees. Walking under them brought back memories of childhood days spent growing up in their shade. His father had worked at the ranch since crossing the Tijuana border at the age of sixteen. He had a small house at the other end of the ranch and had been the foreman and caretaker for forty years now. Frank was more than generous, and the two had become best buddies since then. So it was only natural that Lino and Frank's son, Ronald Reagan Garcia, would grow up to be best friends.

Ronnie had hated his name and Lino wondered how many times they had fought when he teased Ronnie by using his full name. He stopped in the slight depression where he'd stood for many hours while learning to shoot at the old oak stump. He figured there must be fifty pounds of lead in there. He walked forward and got down on one knee, sticking a finger in one of the holes. As he bent forward he was aware of his own pistol, a Glock .40, tucked into the waistband of his pants and poking him in the back.

Looking up, Lino saw an old pickup truck moving through the trees at the other end of the grove. It looked like the same old Ford, and he could make out old Frank hunched over the wheel like he'd seen him a thousand times before. Another man was riding shotgun. It wasn't his dad, though. No cowboy hat. The truck moved off in the direction of the main house, dust billowing up behind it.

When he came to end of the walnut grove, Lino saw the big green tractor slowly moving through the rows of tomatoes. He made his way to the end of the row on an intercept course to wait until the tractor came to him, just like waiting for your prey if you were out hunting. He looked up into the cab and could see a big grin on his dad's face. Lino breathed a sigh of relief.

"Lino, you stay away way too long," his father said as he opened the air-conditioned cab and climbed down to the ground. Without another word, Ernesto walked up, threw his arms around Lino, and hugged his son to his chest.

"I know, Papa, but you know how it is," Lino said, looking into the dark glowing eyes of the man who had guided him through so much of his life.

"You need to come back home and get out of that job—"

"We agreed never to talk about that, you remember?"

"I know, but you should have a family by now. At least a wife. I know, too dangerous for anything else."

"Tell me about yourself. Your health? Juella told me about old Frank."

"I'm still strong as a horse. But Frank, he don't have long."

"What's going to happen to the ranch?"

Ernesto took off his cowboy hat and wiped his brow with the red handkerchief that was always in his pocket. "He don't say, but you know him. He is very good at the business part. Walk to the house with me, Lino. It's almost lunchtime. Juanita will make you some lunch." Almost as an afterthought he said, "She will be glad to see you again."

"Papa, you've been with her for a long time now. You ever gonna marry her?"

"Your mother ended my marrying days. I'm still married to her, you know."

"I thought maybe you might have filed for divorce by now. Still no word from her then?"

"Only that note saying she needed some space. After eleven years, I still don't know what the hell it meant."

After a quick lunch, Ernesto said, "Back to work. Frank don't pay me to eat. Why don't you stay tonight?"

"I'm sorry, Papa, but business calls. I have to get back to LA."

"Lino, you need to get out—I'm sorry, son. I forget sometimes."

"Hopefully not much longer."

"Ah, a good thing. Give me a goodbye hug."

Lino watched his dad head back to the tractor. Ernesto was a proud man and would always give a hard day's work for his pay. Once again Lino found himself back in the shade of the trees and thought his dad might be right. Maybe it was time to get a real job and settle down. Lino made his way back to the front of the house and saw Juella, Frank, and a light-haired man sitting on the porch having lunch. Old Barney came over and Lino gave the dog a good rub behind the ears.

"Lino! Juella told me you dropped by. You were always like a son to me. Sit down have some lunch." Frank struggled to get to his feet and put out his hand.

Lino took the extended hand. "No thanks, Mr. Frank. I have to go. I just ate with my dad."

Jesse looked up at the well-built man and couldn't help noticing he moved with the grace of a cat. Probably ex-military.

Lino looked down at Jesse. "I can't stay. I need to be back in LA tonight. Long drive, you know."

"Oh, Lino. You just got here. Can't you stay a bit longer?" Juella asked as she got up and walked over to him.

"I'll be back. And next time I'll be able to stay longer. It's nice to see you again, Mr. Frank. You take care." Lino then looked again at the man sitting at the table and nodded to him.

Juella took Lino's hand and walked him back to his car. Jesse watched them hug. He couldn't help staring at her long legs and tight short-shorts.

Lino said something to Juella and got into his car. He drove around the circle, headed back out toward the street, and disappeared. Juella stood and looked wistfully out at the empty drive.

"Even though my son Ronnie was a year older, that boy and he were inseparable growing up, at least until after high school. Lino ended up with a scholarship to one of those high-dollar, uppity East Coast colleges."

"He looks pretty successful," Jesse said.

"Maybe now, but after he graduated from college he ended up getting arrested for murder. He got off on some kind of a technicality, but there wasn't much doubt he did it." Frank walked over and sat down heavily in his chair. He looked down at his empty glass. "Hey, you want a beer? I don't usually drink in the middle of the day but what the hell."

"Sure, why not? I'll get them." Jesse stood up quickly and had to reach out to the table for stability. He was walking toward the door when Juella saw him.

"What are you doing? Did you get light-headed when you stood up?"

"Just getting us a couple of beers," Jesse said, ignoring the rest of the question.

"I can do that. Go sit down." She walked past him into the house. Jesse followed her in and when she turned around with the beer and two frosty mugs in her hands, he was standing in front of her.

"Did I somehow insult you?" Jesse asked. "I'm sorry, whatever it was. I didn't mean to…"

Juella saw the hurt look on his face, and tears welled up in her eyes. She reached out, putting her arms around him, and softly snuggled into his neck. Not knowing what else to do, Jesse folded his arms around her and held her close. He could feel her tears on his neck.

"I'm sorry, it's just that I sometimes…I get so lonely. And sad. I don't know if I'm strong enough. And when Dad goes—"

"It's okay. Shhh." He hadn't imagined it. Her hair smelled like apricots…wonderful.

She pulled away and said, "What am I doing? I don't even know you." She set the beer and mugs down, wiped her tears, and stormed from the room like angry water from a burst dam.

Jesse watched her go. He picked up the beer and mugs and headed back to the porch. Realizing there was something going on that he didn't have the slightest clue about, he wondered if his brain just wasn't fully hooked up yet. One minute she was nice and warm, the next cold and furious.

I should know myself well enough by now, he thought, to understand that much of my enjoyment in life is inventing or imagining things. I think that's how I have always dealt with life. But exactly what am I imagining now?

Chapter 13

Known-Unknown Foes

Agent Mike Nowiki sat at his temporary desk located inside the federal office building in downtown Sacramento. He was glad he was here rather than in San Francisco. That office was stuffed with agents looking into the bombing, and besides the traffic there was always a nightmare. Since his hometown was Chicago, he was slightly bummed he wouldn't be able to catch the Giants and Cubs baseball game. Minutes ago he'd received a scanned copy of the logs from the San Francisco Police Department impound lot. He scrutinized the signature. So he was the one who authorized the removal of the Take-Us car? News to him. The form was the regulation form the FBI always used, and his signature was close, but the K was too swoopy. Someone had to have a copy of his signature to get it this accurate, which would logically mean there was someone on the inside giving out information.

With that realization, he appreciated what O'Hallohan must be up against. He had called earlier in the day to tell Nowiki there was another government agency after Christenson: the Department of Energy. Damn, that just complicated things. He consciously pushed O'Hallohan out of his thoughts. Who could he trust? Probably ninety-nine percent of the agents, but it would only take one to get Christenson killed. What was it about that guy that drew bodies like a coffin to a grave?

Had to be the oil angle. It was a more valuable commodity than gold, which was too rare for industrial purposes and really only something to ogle at. More valuable than corn, which you could eat but would eventually spoil. He wondered briefly if oil spoiled. It really didn't matter. Oil did more than lubricate an engine. It lubricated economies, and right now it seemed to be the real monetary standard for the entire world, although drugs could also be considered a commodity, especially by the underworld.

He was brought out of his thoughts by the sound of the phone buzzing. Nowiki glanced at his watch—a little after seven here on the West Coast—surprised anybody else was still working.

He picked up the receiver. "Yeah, this is Nowiki." He listened for a few seconds and then said, "I warned you she's really sharp. What happened, exactly?" Listening closely, he made a few notes. "How do you know she didn't get back on another plane?" Another pause. "She disappeared in downtown Reno, then? Yeah, in a dumpster. Okay, keep me informed."

Leena must have figured he would put tracers on some of her stuff. At least he could still trace her cell phone…if she used it. The more he thought about it, the more he knew she'd already figured that out and had a solution for it. Of course, she couldn't discard it because if Christenson's memory did return, it was probably the only way he could reach her. In the past Nowiki had always found it kind of fun being up against a smart adversary. This time it was different. She was just a pain in the ass. They would find her—probably when she wanted them to and not a minute before.

He reached over and picked up the file on the Mexican Mafia. They were located mostly in Southern California. However, they maintained a large presence in prisons nationwide, which was where they recruited new members, mostly by offering them protection while they were serving their time. He was surprised to learn that they were founded on a military system, with generals, captains, and other ranks down to ordinary foot soldiers called carnales.

They were highly organized but they didn't appear to have a head general. Each local jurisdiction had the authority to order murders of outsiders, although it took at least three high-ranking members to order the murder of a fellow gang member. He was duly impressed that those living so far outside the law had a strict set of values. They seemed to have four major rules that were punishable by death if violated: cowardice, homosexuality, becoming an informant, and disrespecting a brother gang member.

He smiled, thinking that a bunch of criminals had higher standards than much of society. They also formed allegiances with other gangs, like the all-white Aryan Brotherhood and Armenian Power. Of course, the flip side was that they had many enemies, like the all-black Guerrilla Family and the Nuestra Familia located primarily in Northern California.

Nowiki thought the Nuestras might be pissed that the hits took place in their territory. Could he use that? He jotted down some notes and continued reading.

Most of their prospective members were identified while serving a prison sentence. In order to join, they had to be sponsored. And it was this same member who would execute them if they violated any of their commandments. Once in, they were required to give the gang complete obedience, putting it before their own family or former gang affiliations. Lastly, they must deny to all that there was any such thing as the Mexican Mafia. There was only one way to get out: death.

The notorious gang enjoyed support from ordinary Mexican illegals. Since illegals were undocumented, disputes could not be reported to lawful authorities and so the gang administered its own brand of justice. For a steep price.

Nowiki found that in a weird way, for such a wayward group, they had somehow captured and brought honor to their family. He knew it was a good thing to have respect for your enemies.

It was after nine when Nowiki decided to check his email before he left. He wanted to jot a "love you" note to his wife and kids. Instead, he saw an incoming message from FBI Headquarters in D.C.

Yesterday the FBI had put up a series of websites and pressured Google to give them top rank in order to push out information on Christenson and the Take-Us car. They traced all the hits on the phony websites, most of which were from the news media. After ignoring the media hits, he saw that the remaining hits could be promising leads. There were notes next to some of the names, identifying them as convicted felons or known gang members. Nowiki considered that to be a good sign, meaning they also still sought Christenson.

He continued to peruse the list until he came upon a name noted as having been involved in an investigation in the seventies. It was unusual that there were no details about the investigation. He quickly typed in the name, Franklin R. Garcia, and found the usual personal information: date of birth, place of birth, Air Force veteran status. Garcia was apparently a witness in a suspicious death involving his neighbor in Texas, claiming it was murder. The dead man was an inventor named Robert Clem. The coroner later ruled that he died of natural causes.

On a hunch, Nowiki plugged Robert Clem into the database. No record found. Nowiki wondered how there could be a witness to a case that never existed. He typed the name into the web and what came back hit him on the nose like a sucker punch. Clem had invented a car that didn't use any gasoline, just like Christenson. And he had died suddenly under suspicious circumstances. As Nowiki continued to read, the hair on the back of his neck rose. Cover-up, the computer all but screamed.

For eighteen long years Nowiki had been an FBI agent. He knew of investigations that were politically motivated and had seen some go south badly, like Oklahoma City. Agents didn't just dive for cover after the immensity of that screw up; they dug bomb shelters. This had the same rotten smell. He knew it would be better for his career to simply close the page as if he'd never seen it.

He stood up and walked across the room, stopping to look out the window. From up here he could see the convergence of two rivers, even in the dark. If memory served, one was the Sacramento and the other was the American River. Both were made up of countless brooks, streams, and creeks. Some started with pure mountain snow and some with dirty mud puddles—and everything in between. In the end they became bigger and bigger until each was powerful in its own right.

Two into one, much like our country's political system. Such a huge diversity, but unlike the accident of nature that brought these two waters together, America chose to be one people and form a structure that allowed all to live within a simple framework of laws. Laws he'd sworn to uphold and obey. Not because it was convenient, but because it was right and good. How had everything become so convoluted?

What exactly was it that Christenson had set out to do? Break the law? No. He simply had an idea—change the type of cars we drive—and for that he got a death sentence. Nowiki felt it would be worse than shameless for him to slither away now.

He briefly wondered if he could be jumping to conclusions, but the forged form for the impounded car showed that someone in the Bureau was trying to get rid of a perceived problem. Why did it have to be inside the Bureau? They had uncovered many other government and law-enforcement organizations that were already compromised. What was it O'Hallohan said about the Energy Department guy?

He spun and walked back to his desk to reread his notes. Glancing at his watch he saw it was a little after eleven, making it past two in the morning on the East Coast. He started to pick up the phone but pulled out his cell instead, calling the cell phone number he'd stored the week before.

"Yeah, who's this?"

"It's Nowiki; is this O'Hallohan?" Nowiki could hear music in background and people laughing and talking.

"Yeah, what's up? Hang on, got to go outside to hear you. Okay, this is better."

"You been drinking?"

"That's what you do when you go to the clubs, you know."

"Clubs, yeah." It had been a long time since Nowiki was single and went out clubbing. "You sober enough to answer a question or two?"

"I'll give it a shot."

"Do you know who else is getting a copy of the reports we disseminate through your agency?"

"I know the whole idea is to bring all the information into the

Office of Operations Coordination, and they distribute information to all the different partners that could be involved in an event. My office is part of the National Operations Center and we're more hands-on. The Emergency Operations Center shares information to all the other levels through the Homeland Security Information Exchange."

"What? Damn, you're drunk as a skunk," Nowiki said. "I'll call you tomorrow."

"No, wait. True, I got a small buzz going on. Too many Jäger bombs. But I'm telling you the truth."

"Probably…at least about the Jägermeister. Can't stand it myself. Tastes like cough medicine. But with all those layers in Homeland Security, who keeps track of where the information is sent?"

"It isn't that bad. Most information is only sent to the strategic partner having a direct interest or program involved in any potential or perceived threat."

"So that's how the Energy Department was probably informed?"

"Maybe," O'Hallohan said, though he was pretty sure he'd been responsible for getting them involved. "All the different cabinet level agencies have their own security, from the Department of Agriculture to Veterans Affairs. They each have their own specific threat watch."

Nowiki's chair squeaked as he leaned back. "Exactly who decides what is a threat and what is not?"

"Oh, shit. I didn't get it." O'Hallohan waved goodbye to the shapely blonde he'd been trying to hustle for the past two hours.

"What?"

"Nothing, go ahead," O'Hallohan said, watching the blonde wiggle into a cab with some tie-wearing loser. He leaned up against the wall, now fully concentrating on the call.

"What it boils down to," said Nowiki, "is whether Christenson's car is a threat to national security or some department's own program. We both know how it is when a government agency has a pet project in its own little world."

"Maybe I have had too much to drink. What are you saying?"

"I'm saying that the D.C. game is to get a project funded. The more money, the further those in charge go up the ladder. Bigger staff, more responsibility, more pay. If that project is cut, they lose their power—or worse, lose their jobs."

"You sure you ain't been drinking, too?"

Nowiki laughed. "Sounds like it, doesn't it? Listen, I want you to look up a name on the internet. Robert Clem. That's C-L-E-M. Call me back on this cell tomorrow after you do."

Terminating the call, Nowiki closed down his computer, locked up, and headed for his hotel. While walking in the poorly lit darkness, he stepped into a puddle created by a sprinkler. He felt the weight of his pistol in its holster and glanced around, wondering if there were eyes watching him right now. He crossed the bridge over the river, still lost in thought. He was a law man, not a mud puddle. Nonetheless, he also was unwittingly the first trickle of a torrent about to be unleashed.

Day Thirteen

Day Three of the Grand Pursuit

Chapter 14

Unfathomable Discoveries

Leena took a short nap, waking just after midnight. She was still pissed about finding Agent Entersane's business card. He had violated her mother's home the same way he'd violated her apartment in Manhattan. How did he know she would show up here? More importantly, what did he want from her? Not the car; they knew she didn't have it.

Her head ached from lack of sleep, like a crummy hangover. She picked up her throwaway phone, went to recently dialed calls, and hung up when his phone transferred her to voice mail again. Dead battery, not turned on, or lying at the bottom of San Francisco Bay. It was all the same: no answer. Maybe he was still okay and would come back to her in good stead. But she had to steel herself. Perhaps a quick prayer would be better, she thought, and felt the hopelessness and doubt creep in again. No, she couldn't go there. Instead she looked at the clock. Real dark thirty. It was time to go.

Leena dressed all in black in the same type of tight-fitting clothes she'd worn just a week ago, but this time instead of painting her shoes black she'd purchased black ones. Was it really only a week ago that Jesse laughed at her for not wanting to ruin her shoes? It felt more like a lifetime.

She placed the night vision goggles over her eyes, slipped on a dark hat, and stepped out into the dark night. She stood just outside her mother's house and silently watched the night. She waited patiently for over half an hour, finally satisfied there was nothing out there but the usual night animals. She moved as silently as she could, trying to fit into the dark, but instead felt as conspicuous as a cloud moving across the moon.

She made her way through her mom's backyard and then across the field until she reached Jesse's backyard. With even more stealth, she moved from tree to tree toward her destination, the all-but-forgotten shed that the fire licked but didn't burn down.

Leena stayed behind Jesse's shed for five long minutes until, once again, she decided there was no one about. She crept around to the door of the shed. Then she reached into the waistband of her tight pants and pulled out the screwdriver she had brought along. She inserted it under the hasp and had barely applied any pressure when the hasp came off, way too easily. Someone else had already pried it off and stuck it back on.

Oh, well, either it is or it isn't, she thought as she cracked the door open and looked inside. The darkness was too much for even the night vision goggles to penetrate. She put her hand forward, moving it back and forth until it made sudden contact. Reaching under her shirt into her bra, she pulled out a small flashlight, stepped inside, and pulled the door closed behind her. Then she lifted her night vision goggles onto her forehead and risked turning the flashlight on.

The golf cart was still intact. Not really knowing what she was looking for, Leena got down on her knees and looked at the back wheel. There was the tell-tale belt attached to the back wheel and disappearing up under the rear cowl. She turned off the light and stood up. This was the first prototype Jesse built. He told her he'd moved the golf cart out of his garage to make room for the Buick when he started converting it into the Take-Us.

She risked another light. If you didn't know what to look for, this looked like all the other golf carts she had ever seen. Flicking the light off, she recalled the first time he told her about this. He said the technology was the same; only the scale was different. She had her proof, and a sudden sense of victory ran through her. It quickly dried up when she heard voices outside the shed.

"Hey, William, are you sure this is where you saw the light?" a hushed voice asked.

Leena tried to keep from turning and facing the sudden danger, afraid the noise of a sudden creak might give her away.

"I'm pretty sure it was right around here," William said in a deep quiet voice.

Leena could see light spilling into the shed from a louvered attic vent directly above the door. She hadn't noticed it before.

"Look behind the shed."

She heard steps approaching and steeled herself for action. She put the penlight back into her bra. The screwdriver would make a good weapon. Use what you have, no delusions allowed.

"Nothing back here," William said from behind the shed.

"Don't surprise me none. We searched this shed yesterday. Nothing but an old golf cart in it," said the first voice. "Let's go."

Leena slowly released the breath she didn't remember taking and wondered who was watching Jesse's burnt-up house. Even though the second man, William, was trying to keep his voice down, his deep voice seemed much louder than the squeaky voice of the first man. However, it was revealing that they didn't have foreign accents. She waited ten minutes and then added another ten minutes before her muscles ached so intensely she finally turned and pushed the door open. She looked outside and couldn't see anyone, then remembered to put her night vision goggles back on. She wondered where the two men were observing from. Probably across the street.

She slipped outside and carefully closed the door. The hasp was slightly skewed, and she put it back like it was before she arrived. She started to move around the side of the shed and couldn't understand why those guys hadn't seen the damage to the hasp.

She never saw the arc of the heavy flashlight as it descended and struck her on the side of her head, knocking her to the ground and out.

* * *

Leena stirred and slowly opened her eyes. She was on her back, looking up at the starry sky. She slowly moved her hand up to her aching head. It was tender to the touch. As she sat up, she became painfully aware of the throbbing inside her skull. The night vision goggles had slipped down around her neck. She tried to remember what happened to her. She was walking and then she woke up, no clue as to how long she was out.

The darkness was still complete, with no sign of the morning dawning. Leena slowly got to her feet, feeling disheveled and out of balance. She pulled her hat back down and placed the night vision goggles back on. In the eerie light, she started heading back the way she had come. Subconsciously she straightened her pants and began walking clumsily, not bothering to stay quiet. Too late for that now.

She slipped back into her mom's house and made her way to the back bathroom. Only then did she take off the night vision goggles and turn on the light. She reached for the Tylenol as she looked in the mirror and inspected the knot above her left ear. How had she not seen it coming?

She slipped off her shoes and began to disrobe, still thinking about what transpired. When she pulled down her tights, grass shavings fell to the floor. How did grass get into her tights? She stuck her thumbs under the tiny pair of panties and could see more grass shavings.

Oh God, no! She took a seat on the closed lid of the toilet and tried to think. Was she raped? She inspected the inside of her panties. No fluids. That was a good sign, right? But what if he had used a condom? Wouldn't she be sore, or wouldn't there be some other sign?

Her head throbbed and ached. What was that adage about how you could only feel the worst of your injuries? For a few long minutes she sat there thinking about it. No, somehow the grass got in there when she was on the ground, she concluded in certain denial. She would know if she had been raped.

A shower seemed like a good idea. She pulled the black stretch shirt over her tender head and reached back to unhook her bra. She let it fall to the floor and wrapped her arms tightly around herself. She stared at the pile of clothes on the floor. Where was the flashlight?

She started trembling. Turning, she ran and threw herself onto the bed as a silent scream metastasized into a loud shriek. Nooooo.

***

Leena twisted under the blankets. Her nipples chafed like someone tried to twist them off, and her insides ached like a battering ram had split her in half. She felt arms grabbing her and pinning her down as she struggled helplessly, once again to no avail. She fought to come out of the nightmare and force her eyes to open, head pounding. *Wake up, it's a bad dream.* But it seemed so real. What time was it now? She glanced at the clock next to the bedside.

Leena stretched and pushed herself out of bed and walked naked into the bathroom. When she saw her clothes on the floor, she knew it wasn't just a nightmare. She picked up her undies and studied them. Nothing. Glancing down, she saw small grass shavings in her neatly trimmed pubic hair. She stared into the mirror. Her eyes appeared dreary and looked lifeless this morning. The knot on her head was real, still tender to the touch.

She climbed into the shower and began scrubbing herself. When she finally finished and began drying herself off, she somehow still felt dirty. She re-entered the shower and grabbed her razor, shaving off the remainder of her visible shame.

She had to face facts. While she was unconscious last night, someone got into her pants. Did they just search her or did they… And really, what could she have hidden in her tiny floss underwear? She forced herself to acknowledge the unthinkable. They had to have touched her. Who were the bastards? She'd find them, whoever they were, and when she did…

She deliberately walked back into the bedroom and opened the closet. Reaching up on the top shelf under a folded American flag, she took the pistol her dad had put up there many years ago. It was an old Charter Arms 5-shot .38. She opened the cylinder and dropped the five cartridges into her hand, all hollow points.

"God, I swear I will find them," she said, looking up. "And then I'll know. And if you don't give them justice, I will."

She reloaded the pistol and slipped it into her robe pocket.

Chapter 15

Entangled Destinies

Another bright morning, a quick shower, and another clean set of clothes laid out on the bed. She must sit outside my door and listen for me to start moving about, Jesse thought, arriving in the kitchen and seeing the cup of coffee set out for him.

"Morning," Frank said, looking up from the newspaper.

"Good morning. You're up early. Good morning, Juella." Jesse reached for the coffee cup.

"Rancher life starts early. 'Daylight's a burning,' right, Dad?" Juella said. "Wish I had a dollar for each time I heard you say that."

"And I wish I had a dollar for every time you've said, 'I wish I had a dollar.'"

They all broke out in laughter.

"How do you like your eggs, Fruitman?" Juella asked.

"Over easy is fine."

"Juella, be nice," Frank said. "He's our guest. Fact is, it looks like you might soon have a reward on your head, Jesse, and we can collect a bounty off you." Frank smiled and spun the paper around, pointing out an article on Jesse Christenson.

"Dad has almost convinced me there's a convoluted conspiracy out there," Juella said with a crooked grin. "Almost."

As Jesse began reading, Frank got up and excused himself.

"I gotta go check on that lazy bum Ernesto this morning," he said, walking out the door. "Come on, Barney. You can ride along."

The dog got up and followed him out the door.

Jesse noticed that Juella had on a lower-cut top than she wore the day before, and some of her cleavage showed. He looked away and put the paper down when Juella brought his eggs and toast. The plate was heaped with country-fried potatoes. She brought over her cup of coffee and sat down across from him with a bright smile.

Jesse couldn't help but notice the change in her from yesterday as he plowed into his breakfast.

"This is great. Thank you," he said between bites.

"I don't know if you're for real or not, but my dad hasn't had this much energy in months. You seem to be good for him, so let me say thank you back."

"Juella, can I ask you a question?"

"Maybe," she said with a smile. "As long as it's not real personal."

"Do you always put conditions on everything?"

"That your question, Fruitman?"

"No, that's not my question. You always put a hard edge on things, but I know you're not that tough," he said, continuing quickly before she could respond. "Frank told me that the man who was here yesterday…Lino… was his son's best friend growing up on the ranch. But you said he was your husband's best friend—"

"Frank is technically my father-in-law. He and Judith, his deceased wife…" Juella took a breath. "Let me start again. Judith was my adopted mom and took me in when I was only twelve, so I grew up here just like a member of the family. When I graduated high school, I married their son, Ronnie." Jesse didn't say anything but Juella responded anyway. "No, it's not incest."

"I didn't say it was, but—"

"I was abandoned in the fields when the border patrol came and took my parents. They never came back for me. Out of the goodness of their hearts, the Garcias took me in. Ronnie and I were very honorable. We never had sex or anything. In fact it was like those romantic books where the rich king raises a ward and then the prince falls in love with her and they live happily ever after." Her eyes clouded over. "Except…"

"Except what?" Jesse asked. "Where is he now? Your husband, I mean."

"He's in Washington, D.C." Juella sat upright and looked at Jesse's face as she blinked back her tears. "Arlington National Cemetery."

Jesse's face had a look of soft understanding. He reached out and touched her hand and noticed she didn't have her wedding ring on. "Please tell me."

She didn't move her hand. "After he graduated college he enlisted in the Army; he was ROTC. I didn't want him to go, but he said it was his turn to protect and serve. His commanding officer wrote me and said Ronnie was leaving a poppy field in Afghanistan when an IED went off …exploded …and blew him out of the Humvee. He received a traumatic brain injury, and they sent him to Germany and then to Walter Reed, but by the time I got there it was too late. He had…"

"I'm very sorry—"

"No, let me say it." She took in a deep breath. "He died. There, I said it. That was seven years ago." Her eyes searched his. "It's the first time I've said those words out loud."

"I also lost my wife, some years ago. She was in—"

"A car accident with a semi-truck. I read about it on the internet. That's why I told you about Ronnie. We've both been stranded on the same small island."

"It took me a lot of years to adjust to it. The pain is less intense, but the memory will always be there," he said, draining his cup of coffee. "Maybe the worst part is the memory of the pain."

"I always thought if I didn't admit he was gone then he would stay alive inside of me. Until the end of time."

"I know. Can I get you another cup of coffee?" Jesse asked, getting up.

"Long time since anyone waited on me. Please."

He picked up her empty cup and moved across the room.

"Fruit…Jesse, I don't think it was an accident that you climbed into my dad's motor home and into our lives."

He finished pouring, placed the full cup in front of her, and sat back down. "I believe everything happens for a reason. Many unfinished things in my life seemed to have been placed in front of me. I stopped questioning a long, long time ago."

"Many unfinished things, that's what Lino said just before he left."

"Lino…the guy that was here yesterday. Why does that name sound familiar to me?"

"Yes. Your short-term memory seems to be normal." Juella moved to look at the back of his head. She parted his hair carefully and looked at the wound.

Jesse felt the tenderness in her touch. "I can't remember about the car…being in the news, I mean. I remember about the operating system—it was put into my brain in a dream, many years before I built it. But as far as taking a trip across the United States, not a thing," he said as he picked up the paper and glanced at the article telling the world he was nowhere to be found.

"Your head wound is much better; be careful not to bump it. I think your memory will eventually come back fully. Have you thought about what you're going to do next?"

"I know I should just call the cops and turn myself in, but something inside me tells me not to put my future in some stranger's hands."

"I wasn't joking this morning when I said Dad convinced me something was afoot. I always thought those conspiracy guys were just kooks. But I'm not so sure anymore. There's no hurry for you to leave. You can stay as long as you want. And if I can help, I will."

"Thanks. I feel safe here."

Frank drove by the front of the house and parked the old truck next to the barn. Soon the screen door closed and he tramped into the kitchen. "There you are. You want to go to town with me? The motor home has a tire with the tread starting to separate, and I need to get a new one. Might be good for you to get some air, I imagine. You been cooped up too damn long."

"Sure, I'd love to get out for awhile," Jesse replied.

"You too, Juella. Let's go for a little spin."

Juella drew her eyebrows together and gave Jesse a look. "He's very proud of his 'big sled' and is always looking for an excuse to get it out on the road."

"Damn right I'm proud, dropped a bundle on it. I'll get the keys," Frank said, hurrying out of the kitchen.

"I swear. What he's dropped is twenty years in the last couple of days."

"I hate to bring it up, but you don't think it's the bright-lightbulb theory, do you?" Jesse picked up both coffee cups and the dirty plate, putting them into the dishwater still in the sink and giving each a quick scrub.

"The what?"

"You know, a bulb burns brightest just before it burns out."

"You are a space case, you know. I've been around many people who have died, and that's not how it works at all." She walked over, stood next to him, and rinsed the dishes, placing them on a towel in a neat row on the counter as if they'd been doing it together for years.

"You're probably right. I am a special case, but I do know a lot about lightbulbs."

They both laughed and moved out of the kitchen. He headed out the front door as she headed up the stairs.

In the barn, Jesse watched Frank walking around the motor home like a pilot doing a preflight check. He already had the vehicle started and warming up.

"Come on in. It'll probably be a little more comfortable riding inside than underneath."

When Frank opened the door the steps slid out automatically. Jesse had never seen anything as luxurious as the inside of the coach.

"Damn, this must a cost you a pretty penny."

"Oh, yeah. Can't take it with you, you know. Speaking of that, let me thank you for taking some of Juella's pain away. She's been so sad for the last seven years it makes me feel more ill than I am, physically."

"I haven't done anything to deserve—"

"Don't matter what you want to think. I see the difference in her. Sometimes when you put up a fence to keep sadness out, it also won't allow happiness in. It gets so you kinda just go through the motions of life. Don't matter what age you are. When you stop feeling and get numb," his old eyes burrowed into Jesse, "it's the truest definition there is of hell on earth."

"What about you? Didn't you suffer, too?" Jesse asked softly.

"Of course, but I'm older and I've been around more death. I've seen many who go through the 'if only' I could have, or would have, or should have done whatever. Like they rule the world. Listen to me. God has a personal pact with each and every one of us. Everything is His will, not ours. And to say otherwise is to compete with Him."

Jesse sat silently as Frank backed the coach out of the barn and drove to the front of the house. He looked through the front windshield and saw Juella come bouncing down the front steps. She stopped and called Barney and went back up the steps to put the dog inside the house.

"Only two seats up front," Juella said as she came up the steps. "Move your butt over. You don't need the whole seat."

Christenson scooted to the edge of the seat and Juella squeezed in next to him. He couldn't help smelling the perfume she had just put on.

"You smell good."

"Like it? It's Hollister, one of my favorites." Juella looked over at Frank who was wearing a knowing smile. "What are we waiting for? Let's go."

Frank drove out the driveway and turned right onto the road, following it until it came to a tee. He turned right, again. About a mile later they came to a four-way stop. A large box van with J.D. SWIFT EDIBLES painted in two-foot letters was parked on the side of the road. The back door was open, and fresh fruits and vegetables were spread out on tables.

Frank said, "Oh, good. J.D.'s back in town. Let's get some fresh fruit." He pulled off the road, and a man with a big floppy hat and reflective sunglasses got out of a lawn chair to greet them.

"Hello, Mr. Frank. It's nice to see you again and Miss Juella—as pretty as ever," he said with a glorious every-other-tooth smile. He took Juella by the arm and led her to the table. "Come over here and try one of these black cherries—as big as your thumb and sweet, so sweet. Got 'em up north just this morning and oh, they tried to give me the smaller seconds. But no, I says, 'you always send the biggest and juiciest to the city and give us the rejects and charge us more than them city folks.'"

Jesse and Frank followed them and Frank whispered, "He's always been sweet on Juella, especially since Ronald's death. He just plain dotes on her, ever since. He's been coming to this same corner for over thirty years. Never met a man that knowed as much about fruits and veggies as him."

"Close your eyes and just feel the tenderness in your mouth," said J.D. "And then bite into it gently 'til the juice releases and you taste the sweety-tartness of it filling your mouth."

Juella did as he asked with a look of pleasure on her face.

"What do you figure she's gonna buy the whole damn truck-load," Frank said.

"Nope, not her," J.D. answered. "But if I had your money, I'd —"

"You're gonna have a bunch more money than me, 'til they haul you off to jail for not paying your taxes," Frank interrupted.

"I paid my taxes for life when I left that hellhole over across the waves. I ask for nothin' except to be left alone." J.D. stopped talking as a chassis-lowered white car slowed, and a couple of guys in the car started yelling at them in Spanish.

"Pinche culeros," J.D. shouted and gave them the finger as the car sped off. "Sorry, Miss Juella. Bunch of wannabe gang bangers."

"I don't know. They looked like a bunch of 'fucking assholes' to me, too," Juella said.

"Happen a lot?" Frank asked, shaking his head at Juella.

"More than it used to," J.D. answered. "You know, you see them sitting there with a couple of baskets of berries or oranges, and all they're doing is selling drugs right out there in the open. And the cops? Hell, they don't give a shit about it."

"Are you kidding me? I've seen them everywhere," Jesse said

with a look of incredulity. "I always wondered how much money they could make, sitting there all day with only a couple of baskets of fruit."

"Course, when you sit by the road every day you see everything that goes on and drives by. Don't take long to memorize who belongs and who don't." J.D. looked over and stared at Jesse for the first time. "Have we met?" J.D. asked.

"Sorry, but you don't stop talking long enough to get a word in," Frank said. "This is a friend of mine. Jesse."

"Thought I knew all your friends. But any friend of Frank's a friend of mine. Glad to meet you." J.D. grasped the offered hand with his hard callused hand.

"I've only known Frank a short time, but I count him a friend," Jesse said, looking back at himself in J.D.'s mirrored sunglasses. He had the feeling he was being scrutinized by the big burly man. "What did you mean about observing everyone from the side of the road? Are they that sinister?"

"They keep a watch out for the feds. You know: DEA, border patrol, and all the rest. And then they warn their buddies on their cell network. Hell, I seen a couple of them go by today already."

"Is that right?" Frank asked hurriedly. "Listen, we ain't got all day. What about those strawberries over there? They any good?"

Frank concluded his deal and after a round of goodbyes, they got back in the motor home and moved on.

After traveling a mile, there was no way they could look back and see the nondescript black car that turned onto the road they just used to leave the ranch.

Chapter 16

Credibility Issue

The internet screen came to life and directed O'Hallohan to a site he had never been on before. As he read, he understood exactly why Nowiki sounded drunk the night before. Christenson wasn't the first to invent a different way to power a car. He followed some other links and found other promising technologies that were never followed up or, for some reason, were just left out in the cold.

It was hard to tell which ideas were scams and which were truly serious. He remembered reading a few years ago about turning algae into fuel. He laughed at such a dumb idea…until the bio-refineries and bio-fuels came out to replace diesel fuel—or at least blend with it.

It seemed like the only way anything changed was if there was a crisis. And the Take-Us car was certainly creating one in its wake. Energy as we knew it would have soon been outdated.

Following Nowiki's logic, O'Hallohan wondered who in government would be most affected. For the federal government the obvious choice would be the Department of Energy.

But no single department should be accepted as "the government." Government was intended to be "of the people, by the people, and for the people." The people, therefore, should have the right to decide what was best for them. This was the first time O'Hallohan had ever thought thoroughly about who he really worked for. It might sound funny, but it truly was about the Constitution and the rights of the individual. If Clem—and now Christenson—did get in the middle of a program, shouldn't it be the program that would need to change, rather than eliminating the changers?

O'Hallohan felt an ache hitting him between the brows. He knew it wasn't from drinking too much last night. It was from coming face to face with something diseased inside the Beltway and not inside his head. He sipped his coffee. Conflicted, he wondered if he should share his thoughts with his superiors or keep them to himself.

He was reaching for the telephone when it rang on its own accord.

"O'Hallohan speaking."

"Is that the way you answer a phone according to regulations?" Nowiki asked.

"You must have you're ESP-N on."

"What?"

"I was just getting ready to call you. I read about Clem and company this morning, and have concluded that we are in the middle of a pile of shit," O'Hallohan said.

"Don't hold anything back. Just say what you need to."

O'Hallohan could hear the smile coming through the phone. "Sorry, I've been thinking through the ramifications. I mean, I'm assigned to Homeland Security. Does that mean I'm suppose to provide security for jobs, dams, buildings, energy supplies, or people? Or all the above? What we do affects thousands, and maybe even millions, of Americans. But at the same time, we really are just trying to save one."

"Better make that two. Leena gave us the slip yesterday. At least we hope she ditched us and didn't get nabbed."

"She's tough and smart. Be glad she's on our side. Where did you lose her?"

"Reno."

"She went back home," O'Hallohan said and wrote her name on the tablet he invariably kept in front of him.

"First thing we thought of, but it's hard to stake out that neighborhood. It's so quiet everything is noticeable."

"Just set up a team in the bushes. Lots of thickets around there."

"After what you learned, do you really think I should request a team?" Nowiki asked, heavy sarcasm in his voice. "Besides, I think I might know where our boy is."

O'Hallohan sat up with a start. "Where, pray tell?"

"We had a hit on one of the bogus information websites we set up, which is where I got the lead to the Clem thing. I cross-referenced it with the license plates Air Force security recorded on all the vehicles leaving the base after midnight of the night Christenson disappeared. At first, there was nothing…until I checked the ownership of a certain motor home. It's owned by a rancher in California: Franklin Garcia. Same person as the website hit."

"Is he connected to the Mexican Mafia or something?"

"Damn, I didn't think of that angle," Nowiki said. "I just figured Christenson stowed away or begged for a ride."

O'Hallohan stood up abruptly. "I'm going to get my team together and be there in about four hours. Can you wait that long?"

"Hang on a minute. I don't think a team is a good idea. I know you trust them to the hilt, but an official move…well…too many ears."

"You're right." O'Hallohan sat back down and sighed like the air slowly going out of a punching bag. "Since I'm on my own now, just kind of wrapping things up and not really reporting to anyone right now…" He stopped and took a deep breath, making up his mind. "I'll catch a commercial flight and be there as soon as I can. I'll text you the details."

* * *

Nowiki, seated in his car, spotted O'Hallohan easily. He was a head taller than almost everyone else. And his red hair made him stand out like a Norse Fire God.

O'Hallohan opened the back door and slung a large black bag onto the seat.

"What's in the bag?" Nowiki asked. "Wait a minute. I don't want to know."

"Just a small-yield nuke." O'Hallohan laughed. "Good to see you, too. Where'd you get the car?" He asked as he moved the seat to accommodate his long legs.

"Enterprise Car Rental. Figured we didn't want an agency driver to go along with us."

"Yeah, good idea, but you could have gotten a bigger model so my knees wouldn't be in my throat. What shade of green is this, anyway?"

"Puke green. Have you seen the paper?" Nowiki flipped it over to O'Hallohan. It was folded open to a picture of Christenson and the Take-Us car.

After a few minutes of reading, O'Hallohan looked up. "Who did this? Any idea?"

"Someone with some juice, that's for sure. Good news is they don't have either him or the car. Otherwise, why put this in the paper?"

"True enough. Where're we going?" O'Hallohan asked, reaching into his pocket for a pair of shades.

"Garcia owns a good-sized ranch out in the sticks, about thirty miles outside of Modesto," Nowiki said, and the two settled in for the long drive.

Two hours later, Nowiki turned the car off the road and entered the well kept lane. As the driveway finished its S-curve and came within sight of the main house, he said, "Nice joint. Doesn't look like anybody's home, though."

He began the final turn of the circle that brought him to the front of the house. O'Hallohan had the car door partly open before the car stopped and was pulling his jacket open to reach his MP5 submachine pistol.

"I wonder why the front door is half open," O'Hallohan said. He glanced over at Nowiki. "You armed?"

"Yeah, got my forty. Why?"

"Something lying in the doorway. Stay behind the car and watch my back. Oh, shit. Windows on both sides of the door."

O'Hallohan looked both ways, made his decision, and ran to the end of the porch, flattening himself against the wall. He slowly moved to edge of the window and took a peek inside but couldn't see in because the curtain was drawn. He got down on his knees and crawled along the covered porch until he reached the front door.

Inside the door a dog lay in a puddle of blood. It appeared to have been shot. He risked a quick look around the doorframe and pulled his head back. Like lightning, he moved to the other side of the door and looked in from the other angle. Turning, he signaled Nowiki to move in and stay low.

Nowiki was breathing deeply when he arrived at the door, and his eyes went wide when he looked down and saw the dog. "Now what?"

He looked at O'Hallohan, who was no longer the fun-loving guy with the forever half-smile on his face, but a cold-eyed warrior with death written all over him.

"I'm going in to the left," O'Hallohan whispered. "You stay here and watch the right side of the room, my blind side. Might be a friendly in there. Don't shoot until you know for sure, okay?"

O'Hallohan took another quick glance and slipped into the house. Efficiently he checked out and dismissed all the rooms on the first floor. Going back into the kitchen, he noted three coffee cups on a towel by the sink. When he came back into the living room, he motioned Nowiki into the house and pointed to the stairs. O'Hallohan made his way up as Nowiki positioned himself to cover him if necessary.

Nowiki was starting to get anxious when O'Hallohan's voice came drifting down the staircase.

"All clear. And it looks like our boy was here." He came into sight holding a shirt that was stiff with dried blood. He came down the stairs and handed it to Nowiki.

Nowiki put his pistol back into his shoulder holster. "Fits the description. Yeah, probably the one he wore out of the hospital. Blood but no bullet hole or knife entry. Not a lot of blood, but enough. I wonder if he was cut in the knife fight."

O'Hallohan walked over to the dog and laid his hand on him. "Still warm. Damn! We must have just missed them." He stroked the dog's fur. "Probably a good old boy. Cold motherfuckers who'd kill an old dog like this." He stood up and said, "How many people lived here?"

"I didn't want to set off any alarm bells, so I didn't research deep into this household, but I do remember the son was killed in

Afghanistan, seems like toward the beginning."

"This must be his picture here." O'Hallohan moved over to the wall and looked at the photos displayed there. "Pretty girl. Might be his sister, no must be his ex- or maybe his widow," he said, finding a wedding picture of them together.

Nowiki joined him at the wall and looked at the wedding photos of the entire wedding party. "Where have I seen this guy before?" he asked, pointing to Lino's picture.

O'Hallohan looked at the picture and shrugged. "I think it must be Mom, Dad, and Christenson here now."

"Why's that?"

"I saw three coffee cups in the kitchen." They went into the kitchen and saw the clean cups neatly arranged on the counter.

"I don't think the ones that killed the dog got them," Nowiki said.

"All right, I'll bite. Why?"

"It's what isn't here. Dead bodies. I said before the guy's a traveling morgue. The dog would have alerted him to something going on, and he would have fought his way out. He's like you, O'Hallohan. A warrior. It's his M.O."

Before O'Hallohan could respond, they heard the sound of an approaching diesel motor. They headed to the front door and looked out, seeing a bright green tractor moving toward the barn. A dark-skinned man with a cowboy hat parked the tractor and was getting down when the two agents approached him.

"Are you Franklin Garcia?" Nowiki asked, taking charge and flipping out his ID badge. "I'm Agent Nowiki, FBI."

"Me? No. I just work here," said Ernesto.

"Do you know where we might locate him?" Nowiki asked brusquely.

Ernesto looked down at his feet and didn't answer.

"Just so you know, it is imperative we speak to him," Nowiki said.

Ernesto continued to look at his feet, not saying a word.

"I'm sorry. I didn't catch your name. I'm Pat O'Hallohan," Patrick said, holding out his hand.

"My name is Ernesto. I'm the caretaker here," the man said,

puffing out his chest as he reached for the offered hand.

O'Hallohan put his hand on Ernesto's shoulder and led him away from the FBI agent, who followed at a discreet distance.

"That's great," said O'Hallohan. "And just ignore my partner there. He tends to get a little too excited. Mr. Garcia is not in any trouble. We just need to ask him a few things."

"Is this what they call a good-cop, bad-cop routine?"

O'Hallohan laughed out loud, taking the older man by surprise. "Actually I'm not a cop at all. I work for the Department of Homeland Security. And to tell you the truth, we're looking for a man named Christenson. We thought Mr. Garcia might have been letting him stay here at the ranch."

"Christenson is the…is a wanted man, then?"

"No. Well, kind of, but not in a bad way. You see, we were supposed to be protecting him, and…well, you know… shit happens. And we think he's in terrible danger."

"Is that why the other federales, were here today?"

"What other federales? What do you mean?"

"My eyes are not as good as they were, but I saw them pull in after Mr. Frank and Mr. Christenson drove off. I was spraying weeds down at the other end of the ranch," Ernesto said, pointing vaguely to his right.

"How do you know they were federal—"

"They come out here all the time," Ernesto interrupted. "They're always bothering Mr. Frank, wanting him to plant more corn, spray different insecticides, and such. Their car, it is so plain you can spot them a mile away."

"They were here. You're sure?"

"I saw them turn into the drive."

"When did they leave?"

"I didn't see them go but it must have been just before you got here."

O'Hallohan stopped walking and made a decision. "Ernesto, I need to show you something we found when we got here." He led Ernesto back to the house and up the porch steps.

"Oh, no. Barney. No," Ernesto said, tears in his eyes as he knelt to touch the dog. "Miss Juella will be very hurt when she gets back. She's had so much pain in her life."

"She's with Mr. Garcia and Mr. Christenson?"

"Yes, probably. I met Mr. Christenson as they were leaving… he is a nice man."

Ernesto stared out the driveway as two men approached. When the men saw the group on the porch they turned and fled.

"What the fuck?" Nowiki yelled.

"Probably looking for work. You guys look like cops and the illegals know it," Ernesto said.

"Did you recognize them?" O'Hallohan asked.

"My eyes, they are not so good."

"They seem pretty benign to me." O'Hallohan watched the men disappear around the bend. "All right, let me get back to Mr. Christenson. After seeing the dog, you know he is in great danger."

Ernesto nodded. "How did you find him here?"

"We believe Mr. Garcia took him from the hospital in his motor home, and essentially we ran the plates," Nowiki said, following them up to the front door. "The danger is very real. That's why we need to find them."

"Mr. Frank introduced me to him and told me to keep it my secret. If I tell you now, I am no longer trustworthy. I do not know what to do."

"You're right. I don't think you should say where Mr. Frank went," O'Hallohan said, holding his hand up to keep Nowiki from exploding. "Of course, you didn't promise Mr. Christenson anything…and since we don't really care about the Garcias…"

"You are a wily one, Mr. Pat," Ernesto said and turned to the FBI agent. "Agent Nowiki, do you know my son Lino Santana?"

Nowiki hesitated. "The rock musician?"

"No, that's Carlos," O'Hallohan said.

"Oh. No, I don't think so. Why?" asked Nowiki.

"I was just wondering, is all. I believe Mr. Christenson went in Mr. Frank's motor home to town to get a new tire."

"What time was that?" O'Hallohan asked.

Ernesto looked up at the sun. "Maybe a couple or three hours ago. They must of stopped for lunch; otherwise they should already be back. Probably be back soon."

"Thank you, Mr. Santana. We really are the good guys," O'Hallohan said with as much conviction in his voice as he could muster.

"I know. You never once threatened to deport me. By the way, I am a United States citizen." He looked down sadly at the murdered animal. "I'm going to the barn to get a wheelbarrow. I need to bury Barney."

After he departed Nowiki said, "Santana. I remembered the name from when I was researching the Mexican mob. Lino Santana's an enforcer for them."

"So you knew the musician was Carlos Santana," O'Hallohan said, seeing the smirk on Nowiki's face. "You think he was here and killed the dog? You heard him say there was a federal car here before us."

"Yeah, I was wondering if that might have been those Department of Energy guys you told me about."

"He said Agriculture."

"He just saw a government car and figured they were from the USDA. But there's no reason to think they would be involved in this," Nowiki said.

"The Department of Energy agent all but told me if they found the car they would stash it away in some dark warehouse where it would never see the light of day. I didn't think the government really did that sort of thing."

"On orders or rogue, give me a break." Nowiki rolled his eyes. "You're kinda new to this, huh? Why don't you show me where you found that bloody shirt?"

"Then what?"

"Then we sit down and wait for the Garcias and Christenson to return...unless someone got them first."

Fifteen minutes later a black government-owned car came down the driveway. Nowiki and O'Hallohan waited for it to stop before they walked toward it. The passenger window rolled down, and a little man with big glasses said, "So I take it we're too late."

"Agent Entersane." O'Hallohan glanced over at Nowiki and then continued. "Department of Energy running out of juice or what?"

"Real funny. So Christenson's gone already and you're waiting for him to come back. You really think that's going to happen?"

"Wasn't he here the first time you came by?" Nowiki asked.

"You're the FBI agent. Nowik-something. I have it written down here." Entersane looked down at a sheaf of papers on his lap.

"Nowiki's the name. So why'd you come back again?"

"Hate to disappoint you, but we just arrived. Why don't you fill us in on what's going on?"

Nowiki leaned around O'Hallohan and put his hands on the door, placing his face about six inches from Entersane, who immediately leaned away. "O'Hallohan didn't really say it, but I got the idea from him that you're a real prick."

"There's no reason—"

"And you need to know that I work for the FBI, and I don't answer to any other branch. And if you forget that, I will drag your skinny ass out of the car"—Nowiki straightened up and stepped back—"and politely remind whatever's left of you."

"I've read your reports, and I am involved in this investigation just as deeply as you are," Entersane said in a subdued voice.

"Well, you can read all about it when I file my next report then."

"Hang on," O'Hallohan said. "Maybe we're getting too excited here. Our report is going to say 'Without a doubt, Christenson was here, but now he's gone.' And we wouldn't be sitting here if we knew where he went."

"Thank you, Agent O'Hallohan. I'll be in touch." Entersane adjusted his glasses and straightened up in the seat. He spoke to the driver and they swung around the driveway, heading back out to the street.

"We're getting pretty good at this good-cop, bad-cop thing,"

O'Hallohan said. "What did you see in the car?"

"Two submachine pistols, just like yours," Nowiki said, watching the rear of the departing car. "We need to go talk to Ernesto again."

Chapter 17

Trust and Betrayal

The long drive from San Fran to LA the night before made his head feel so heavy he wanted to crawl back into bed. Lino glanced at the DVD on the counter and like a zombie started blending a protein breakfast smoothie. He should have watched it last night. Once again he thought about the extra heavy traffic coming into LA. He'd meant to come straight home from the ranch but had decided he needed to take care of some personal business first.

"God, I hate LA," he said aloud. But since he lived by himself there was no one to agree with him. Tired of being alone all of the time, his thoughts drifted to Juella. She looked good, much better than the last time. But of course that was at the funeral.

Looking back, he realized it was the day his old life ended and a new one exploded into existence. He'd sworn an oath to get even with those who'd killed his best friend. No, that wasn't right; Ronnie was much closer, more like a brother. Why didn't he follow through and join the Army after Ronnie's death? That would have been the honorable thing to do. And it would have been the easy way out if he lived through it. Do a tour and then get out. His conscience would have been clean. But Ronnie would still be just as dead. He couldn't allow those thoughts and stopped them cold. Still, Juella's eyes had life in them again.

Sighing, he picked up the DVD and placed it in the sliding drawer of the player. He saw an old car—maybe a Buick—and a hot TV babe speaking into the microphone. He didn't have the sound turned up, so he just guessed at what she was saying. The camera settled in on the driver, who was wearing a big shit-eating grin. The guy looked familiar and Lino wondered if he had seen this newscast already.

After a while Lino realized the video must have been shot over a period of days. It ended with the bomb blast in San Francisco last week. He'd watched endless hours of the coverage of that incident and must have seen the guy's face there. Something nagged at him, as if he'd seen the guy somewhere else, but couldn't place where.

He restarted the DVD, this time with the sound turned on. He was sure he'd never heard the man's voice before and began to wonder why Miguel wanted the guy dead. Almost all the hits were drug related when the gang was involved. The bottom line was always drugs, which of course was money. Even the killing in Modesto a day ago. Yeah, it was supposed to be about honor, the broken oath, but really Luis—small time Luis—had used some of the drugs and sold the rest. He kept the money and then died, another dead moron.

Lino froze the DVD near the end and studied the man's face for a long minute. He was almost sure he'd met him before, and knew he would recognize the man if he saw him again. He was about to pop out the disc when a thought occurred to him. The bomb blast. Did it have anything to do with this man?

He reached over and turned his cell phone on. It had been charging on the counter, having gone dead the day before when he'd forgotten to take his charger with him. Lino's thoughts were interrupted when his cell vibrated. Text message. He flipped it over and saw a series of ten numbers. Miguel wanted him to call.

The ten numbers were in code. Miguel was paranoid, and rightly so. He had a number of cell phones with different numbers, one-timers. Lino got out a pad of paper and wrote down the ten-digit number. Under it he wrote the date of the text numerically: month, day, and year. He subtracted the date from the number Miguel sent. Simple but effective. He decided to wait until he went to the gym before he called, so he sent a quick text.

He added some fresh strawberries to his protein smoothie, sipping it as he threw on a pair of shorts and a baggy shirt. He picked up his favorite pistol, a Glock .40 cal, and studied the small video monitor on the bar, making sure no one was hanging outside his door before heading out to the gym.

***

"Hey, Barbie, can I borrow the phone again, please?" he asked the extremely fit looking receptionist with the short dykey hair, the same one he'd been flirting with unsuccessfully for the past six months. How could she say no?

"It's Lino," he said into the phone, speaking from the glass encased office and watching Barbie hand out towels.

"Where you been? I texted you yesterday," Miguel said.

"I had to run up to the city and forgot my charger. My cell went dead." As an afterthought, he said, "Sorry."

"Yeah, it happens."

"So what's up?"

"You seen the DVD of the guy we're looking for?"

Lino reached over and picked up the DVD cover case he'd brought along and said, "Just finished it a little while ago."

"You ever seen the guy around?"

"Don't think so, but he did look kind of familiar."

"Did you go back to the ranch a day ago?"

Hearing a strange tone in Miguel's voice, Lino set down the DVD and listened intently. "Yeah, I saw my dad and Juella."

"Anybody else?" Miguel's voice was loaded with sarcasm.

"Let's see, Frank was there and another guy…Holy shit! That was him! That's where I saw him. I would have recognized his voice if he'd said anything, but he didn't say a word."

"Did he look the same?" Miguel's voice had returned to normal.

Lino thought back to Christenson's face. "Yeah, maybe a little thinner and paler. You know these gringos. They're all pale faces, some more than others."

Miguel snorted out a laugh. "You said Juella was there?"

"Yeah, she's taking care of Frank. He has terminal cancer."

"Did you see a big motor home?"

"Don't think so. But maybe it was in the barn. Why?"

"They took off and aren't at the ranch any more. They must be in the motor home."

"Maybe they took one of the cars or pickup trucks."

"No, I checked and they were all there," Miguel said. "We need to find them fast, and I mean right now. Drive back up there and talk to your dad. He knows where they are, I'm sure. And he wouldn't tell anyone else, even if they tortured him."

"True enough." Lino groaned. "Drive back up today?"

"Listen to me, Lino. This is the most important thing you can do. Drop everything else and do this."

After he hung up, Lino walked out into the gym. He had to take a shower anyway; he might as well work out some of the kinks in his back. What would one hour matter? He didn't bother with stretching, his patience gone. It probably wouldn't work anyway, as tight as he already felt.

With his mind a thousand miles away, Lino began lifting free weights. His body had changed a lot from the skinny kid he was, growing up. He'd started working out with weights during his brief prison time and was now blessed with powerful muscles. His huge arms and broad chest rippled with them, and he believed he was in the best condition he'd ever been in. He took his time with his reps, doing everything by the book. However, he hurried between sets, in this way increasing his heart rate and working his cardio at the same time.

When he had finished and showered, he ogled Barbie. She looked good—sleek and trim—and gave him a tight little smile that said I'm being nice to you because I work here. He smiled back and walked out and slithered into his Mercedes. When this was over, maybe he'd think of a way to change that smile. He drove out to "the 5" as they say in LA and settled in for the long drive north toward Modesto.

***

After talking to Lino, Miguel closed the phone and dropped it into a sink full of water. It was dead now, just like the Christenson man soon would be. He couldn't believe how his luck had turned so quickly to bad luck, finding the guy and then losing him in a matter of hours. That ranch had always been bad luck for him.

He didn't live there growing up, but he was just across the field in a migrant shack with his papa. *No,* his mind screamed, *that man was not my papa.*

Miguel barely remembered his true father. The man had left to go to the Estados Unidos when Miguel was only four. He'd found a job on a large ranchero and two years later came back to Mexico for the family.

The memories crowded back. His father, mother, two older sisters, and Miguel were walking in the desert, led by a big gringo, a "coyote" well paid to smuggle them across the border. They stopped to rest while the gringo and Miguel's father walked ahead to look around.

"Mama, I have to poop," Miguel said.

"Not here! Go up the in those rocks," Mama said to him as she sat down tiredly on the dirt trail. They had been traveling for many weeks and hundreds of miles.

He ran to a large pile of rocks and decided to explore after doing his business. He had climbed the big mound, nearing the top, when he turned around. In the distance, he saw his father, the big gringo, and another man with a big gun under his arm. They were standing by an old, beat-up truck.

Miguel was used to seeing men with guns since leaving Mexico. But suddenly the other man pointed the big gun at his father. The boom was loud even way up there and made Miguel crouch down behind the rocks. He didn't dare move.

When he finally peeked over the rocks, he saw the two men hurrying toward his mama, who was standing up now with his two sisters huddled close by. The big gringo grabbed Miguel's oldest sister, who was only twelve. He pulled her aside and in one motion ripped her blouse until her small titties were exposed.

Miguel heard both his sisters scream and watched his mama lunge toward them. The big gringo turned and slapped Mama to the ground. The man with the gun stepped forward and said something, pointing at Miguel's sisters and then at his mama, who was still lying on the ground.

The big gringo said something back, and the man with the gun made his sisters pick up their bedrolls. Then he herded the two young girls toward the truck. Mama began to rise to her feet, but the big gringo pulled a knife from under his shirt and smashed her back to the ground with the butt of the knife. He got down on one knee and ripped her skirt off. Then he cut off her underwear with the knife. Mama, still dazed, just lay there while the big gringo pulled his pants down. Then the man began humping her like Miguel had seen dogs do in his old village.

Miguel didn't know what to do. His mind told him to go and help, but his body wouldn't move. He tried to get up, but Mama had turned her head in his direction and was looking up into the rocks. He knew she was looking for him and telling him with her eyes to hide, to run away. He realized he was crying, tears running down his face, and reached up to wipe his eyes when he saw the gringo give a sudden jerk with his body.

The man slowly stood up, staring down as he pulled his pants back on. He kicked Mama in the side and gestured for Mama to get up. She was still staring toward the rocks, trying to avoid looking at the man. Then the gringo walked behind her, grabbed hold of her hair, and tugged hard, slicing the large knife across her throat.

Miguel saw the red blood squirting. When the man let Mama go she twitched and jerked on the ground and then went still. The gringo wiped his knife on Mama's skirt and turned to join the other man at the old truck.

When he got back to the truck, the big gringo waved his hand toward the mound of rocks where Miguel was hiding. The man with the gun fired off several shots, which ricocheted off the rocks, not even close to where Miguel was.

Miguel waited many hours until it was almost dark before he mustered the courage to climb back down the rock pile. Mama's eyes were open but covered with flies. She was pale, and he knew she was dead… like the chickens they slaughtered for dinner. He started crying again. Then he picked up her ripped skirt and put it over her naked bottom.

Miguel went to his father, whose face also was covered with flies. His eyes were closed like he was sleeping but somehow looked so sad. Miguel shook him and called out his name. It was then he realized that both of his parents were gone. And they both stank like dead poop.

Miguel had to get away from them. He looked down one last time, put his small hands in his pockets, and began walking. Not knowing where to go, he followed the truck's tire tracks. And when the tracks joined many more at a small dirt road, he turned toward the setting sun. He trudged on until sometime in the dark of the night, when he climbed under a bush and fell asleep, exhausted.

He didn't know if it was the sun in his eyes or the pain in his stomach that woke him. He hadn't eaten since early the day before. On top of that, he was very thirsty. He started crying again and closed his eyes to go back to sleep, but the emptiness in his stomach kept him awake. Finally, he got up and started walking in the same direction as the day before.

Around noon a dusty red Chevy Nova came around a corner behind Miguel and stopped next to him. By then he was almost ready to fall over. The dented door screeched out in protest as the man stepped out of the car. Miguel just stared at him.

"You are lost, little one?" the man asked.

Miguel tried to speak but only a small squeak came out of his parched throat.

"Here, have a drink of water," the man said, handing him a shiny canteen. Miguel drank thirstily until the man grabbed it out of his hands. "Easy! Too much is bad at first. Where do you live?"

Not knowing what to say, Miguel just pointed down the road where he had come from.

"That way, eh? That's toward Mexico. Where are your parents?" the man asked.

Miguel stared at the canteen.

"Take just a little sip this time," the man said as he handed Miguel the canteen once again.

Doing as he was told, Miguel took a small sip of water and then pointed back the same way.

"I just came from that way, and I haven't seen anyone for the last fifty miles. Are you sure?" the man asked.

"Si." Miguel choked out the single word and took another sip of water.

"What is your name?"

"Miguel," he said, his voice coming back to him.

"Miguel what?"

Miguel didn't answer, instead taking another sip of water.

"What is your last name?" the man repeated. "The last name of you papa?"

"My papa's name is Papa, and I am Miguel."

"I didn't see your papa or anybody else on the road."

"He is like the dead chickens in our village."

The man stared off into the distance and suddenly smiled. "Why don't you get in the car and I'll get you something to eat."

Something about the way the man smiled reminded Miguel of the big gringo's smile. "No, that's okay. I—"

The man slapped him across the face, grabbed him, and forced him into the car, the action so quick he didn't even have a chance to run. Tears came to his eyes as he realized how big and strong the man was. The man went to the other side of the car. He glanced about before closing the squealing door and starting the car.

"You need to start minding better. I am your papa now," the man said as he reached over to touch Miguel's stinging cheek. Then he reached into the back seat to get a paper bag with some tortillas in it.

In spite of his fear, Miguel wolfed them down.

They drove all that day, and soon Miguel forgot his fear and fell asleep. When he woke, they were stopped in the driveway of a small house. He was led into the house, still tired and hungry, but the man—his new papa—was in a hurry to go to sleep.

He pointed at Miguel and said, "Take your clothes off, all of them, and get into the bed."

Miguel took off his clothes, even his underpants, and lay under the sheet. He had never been in such a big soft bed. Then his new papa came over to the bed. He was naked and stood out like the big gringo did before he got on top of his mama.

The new papa pulled the sheet down and said, "Get on your knees."

When Miguel hesitated, his new papa cuffed him alongside his head. He started to cry but did as he was told.

"It might hurt now, but you will grow to love it," the new papa said.

Miguel whimpered as he felt his new papa's rough hands grasp and pull his butt cheeks apart. A push and then he really screamed. But not as loud as Papa screamed seven years later when Miguel was driving him back from the bar and purposely lost control of the car, running off the road and crashing into a tree. Not wearing a seatbelt, Papa hit the windshield and was stunned, giving Miguel time to retrieve a sledge hammer from the back and smash it into Papa's face. The only thing the police saw was another dead undocumented illegal Mexican that no one gave a shit about.

Miguel stirred from his memories and reached into the sink. He pulled the cell phone out of the water and threw it against the wall, where it shattered into a violent spatter of wet plastic pieces.

"Roberto, come here," Miguel yelled. A ten-year-old boy, as cute as a little brown berry, came into the room and cowered near the door.

"What is it, Papa?" the young boy asked in a quiet frightened voice.

"Come over here. Now!" Miguel ordered, undoing his belt.

Chapter 18

Extreme Ache

Leena sat on the back deck, lost in thought. Her tight smile froze as she remembered it was where she kissed her first boy and fought off his wandering hands so many long years ago. It was also where she made so many other small decisions that eventually took shape and became the tapestry of her life. She could lay claim to having a great childhood, but it was not without pitfalls. Was anyone's, truly?

Her dad had constantly kept her busy, knowing that when you kept young bodies in sports they tended not to have enough energy or time to get into trouble. Sports became her outlet, in spite of breaking her left wrist snow skiing her freshman year.

She stayed away from the druggies and losers, but not so far away that she couldn't say "Hi" and be polite. That was probably why, in such a small school with a graduating class of a couple of hundred kids, it was easy to be popular. Her election as homecoming queen proved she was. She was a good student, if you didn't count math, and her parents made sure she stayed on track with her studies, setting lofty goals. When graduation came, it paid off. She had a multiple choice of colleges.

Leena loved her dad, and he had tried his best to chaperone her, but even his eyes couldn't be everywhere at once. After the senior prom, having slammed a few pitchers of margaritas, she awoke entangled with her date, innocence lost. When she walked in that morning, her parents had been sitting out here on this same deck, and she thought for sure they could see her walking bowlegged.

It was the first and last time she lost control. Her small smile disappeared. Today her crotch didn't feel sore, but her conscience felt bowlegged and dirty. Her anger reached a murderous pitch.

She sat up suddenly when she heard a car crunching the gravel as it eased its way down the driveway toward the house. The sun had set an hour ago, and it was almost dark. Moving quickly, she stepped off the deck and concealed herself behind one of the large pine trees in the back yard. She reached under the tight black sports shirt she put on just an hour ago. Watching silently she gripped the pistol she had stashed in the waistband of her tights.

She pulled the gun out and laid it against the tree and sighted in. She glanced at her hand. It was as steady as the tree it lay against. She thumbed the trigger back, the hard click loudly audible. Her trigger finger tensed as she saw a shadowy figure walk around the corner of the house. He wouldn't get the chance to rape her again.

"Leena! You know that's Agent Nowiki, don't you?"

She spun around but didn't see anyone.

"It's me, O'Hallohan. I'm behind the tree to your left. Don't shoot me, okay?"

"Show me." Her voice sounded hoarse.

One hand appeared, then the other, and he stepped out into the weak evening light. He had a crooked smile on his face. It turned to surprise when Leena thumbed off the trigger and ran to him, throwing her arms around him and pulling him close.

At first he just stood there. Then he folded his arms around her, lifted her off her feet, and pulled her even closer. This was no weak little girl. She was a hard little body. He felt a sudden heat and was saved embarrassment when Nowiki walked up.

"Ain't this cute. I see you found our missing fugitive," Nowiki said.

"Screw you, Nowiki," said Leena, arms still around O'Hallohan and facing away from the FBI agent. "I was never placed under arrest."

"You're right, but we were using you as bait."

O'Hallohan eased her back down and Leena stepped out of his arms. She looked into Patrick's eyes. "Thanks, I needed that. But why didn't you let me shoot him first?"

"I think the neighbor's have had enough gunplay for this life-time," O'Hallohan answered.

"Thanks, buddy. It's okay to shoot a federal officer as long as you don't wake the neighbors?" Nowiki said as he continued to walk toward Leena. With a rare smile, he surprised them all when he reached out and gave her a hug in his bear-like arms. "So what kind of mischief have you gotten yourself into?" he asked, letting her go. "I haven't seen any reports of piles of dead bodies around here."

"Just when I was starting to think you were human," Leena said, but this time her voice had softened.

"Yeah, whatever. What are you doing here? And don't tell me you're visiting your mother," Nowiki said, returning to business.

"Okay, I won't," Leena said. "And just why are you here?"

Nowiki sputtered. "Is this going to be a game of you show me yours and I'll show you—"

"We're here because we found where Christenson was hiding," O'Hallohan said, interrupting.

"Is he okay?" Leena asked. "Is he back in the hospital?"

O'Hallohan put up a hand, stopping her. "He wasn't there by the time we arrived. But we think he's okay. He's on the run again."

"Tell me what you do know," Leena demanded.

"Wait a minute…first tell us what you're doing here," Nowiki said. "Look, if it will make you feel any better, neither my office nor O'Hallohan's knows what we're up to."

Leena looked up at O'Hallohan who nodded and said, "It's true. There has to be a leak."

"I told you that a week ago," Leena said. "You should've let me do the story."

"Well, the FBI knows about it, and they're searching for it right now." Nowiki turned and walked away and then spun back around. "Can we all just agree that all of us want the same thing? We want to save Christenson's life."

Leena looked intently into Nowiki's eyes. "I want more than that, but yes I agree," Leena said, walking toward the deck. "Come up here and sit."

They climbed the steps and after they sat down she said, "Please, can you tell me about him?"

Nowiki and O'Hallohan reported all they'd learned, and she thought it over silently.

"What, no questions?" Nowiki asked, eyes narrowing.

"How about, can I get you guys something to drink?" she asked cautiously.

"No thanks. But I have a question or two of my own. Why do you have the gun? And why are you dressed in black? Going somewhere?" O'Hallohan asked.

Leena looked back and forth between the men and took a deep breath. "Trust, then, it is. Sometime last year, Jesse told me he built a prototype that used the same technology as the Take-Us car. I went to his house last night to see if it was still there."

"So that's why you came back here." Nowiki nodded, watching her. "But it can't still be there. Because the place burned to the ground. We just drove by."

"I suppose you didn't notice there was a small shed next to the fence. The prototype is inside." She saw the questioning looks of both men. "It's a golf cart. Works the same way as the real thing, only it's smaller."

"And you saw this prototype golf cart last night?" Nowiki asked.

"Yes. Well, sort of," Leena said looking down and avoiding both men's gaze. "I heard a noise and ran away and, well, I think someone is watching the place."

"You guys have a team set up there?" O'Hallohan asked Nowiki.

"You mean the FBI? Not that I know of. What's to watch? A burned out house? It's the last place he would try to hide. He's not stupid," Nowiki said.

"Did anyone else know about the golf cart?" O'Hallohan asked Leena.

"I don't ever remember speaking about it. In fact, I thought it was rather silly at first," she said, a sad smile appearing for a fleeting moment.

"What was it you told me about the guy from the Department of Energy?" Nowiki asked.

"Department of Energy? Why are they sniffing around this?" Leena asked.

O'Hallohan took a deep breath and told Leena everything he had learned the past few days, not caring if it was classified or not. Then Nowiki joined in, filling in more of the blanks. After he finished he said, "I didn't tell you anything. In fact, this conversation never happened."

"The Energy Department agent has been inside both my apartment and this house," Leena said. When neither man commented, she continued. "Government within a government. It's been talked about for years."

"Maybe, but I think it's more like fiefdoms, all agencies scrambling for the same tax bucks," O'Hallohan said, standing up and walking off the deck.

"Where are you going?" Nowiki asked.

"To get my bag. I have a set of nighttime camo clothes in it. We'll find out who it is instead of sitting here speculating. Isn't that where you were going, Leena?" O'Hallohan asked over his shoulder.

Nowiki looked at Leena and said, "A man of action for sure. But what if it's not a police agency, but the Mexican mob instead?"

"I don't think so. I didn't hear a Mexican accent."

"You didn't tell us you heard any voices," Nowiki said abruptly.

Leena looked down at the table, avoiding Nowiki's eyes. For a few seconds she thought about telling him the part she left out. But her shame was too great, and she felt dirty even thinking about it. Maybe tonight she would get the answer she craved. "I told you I heard a noise. Well, the noise I heard was voices approaching."

Nowiki had been in law enforcement for most of his adult life and knew a lie when he heard it—especially from Leena, having spent so much time around her. She always appeared strong, but for the first time he sensed some kind of weariness. He looked at her thoughtfully. She looked the same. Her eyes were bright, almost blazing. But there seemed to be a hardness to them he'd not noticed before. Stress? He started to say something but decided to let it rest. For now.

O'Hallohan came around the corner with a bag slung over his shoulder. "Where can I change?"

"Come on, follow me." She showed him to her bedroom and shut the door behind him. She was waiting for him when he came out. "I'm coming with you, you know."

"I figured as much."

She looked up into his face, surprised, and picked up her night vision goggles. "Not going to try to talk me out of it?"

"Wouldn't do any good. A pair of NVDs huh? Good. You can walk point."

Leena walked past Nowiki. As he opened his mouth to speak, she said, "Remember, you're not even here."

Nowiki continued to watch her. "If I hear any fireworks, I'll drive the car down the road. Okay?"

"Try not to worry. I'll keep an eye on her." O'Hallohan checked the magazine of the MP5 that was slung over his shoulder and lengthened his stride to catch up. This was unnecessary because when Leena reached the meadow she slowed down and crept like a shadow until they came to the rear of Jesse's property. As she started to take another step, she felt O'Hallohan's hand on her shoulder.

"Where is the shed located?" he whispered, his face close to hers.

"There on the right, just in front of that brushy cedar tree," she whispered back.

The night air was heavy with the stench of the burnt house. O'Hallohan didn't have night vision but could still make out the heavy shadow in the darkness. He didn't want to scare Leena, but he had a bad feeling about crossing the clearing to move toward the shed. He squeezed her shoulder once again.

"Let's make our way around to the right. That would be the best place for them to keep watch," he whispered. He saw her nod in the darkness and she began to move slowly in the light brush. With pine needles underfoot, they made little noise as they began circling the house.

Approaching the thickest part of the surrounding brush, Leena tripped over an unseen root snaking along the ground. At the same time, O'Hallohan heard a noise and grabbed Leena around the waist, keeping her from falling. The sound of the broken twig hadn't come from them. As he stood with one hand on his MP5 and the other around her waist, he heard a soft coughing sound followed by another. Quietly he pulled Leena to the ground and half covered her with his body. He frantically ran his hand over her breasts and then down to her stomach. Leaving his hand there, he leaned into her face and whispered, "Where are you hit?"

"I'm not hit," she replied more calmly than she felt, sensing his breath on her lips. "What did you hear?"

"Silencer. Don't move."

Leena lay on her back, looking up at the stars, and felt the heat from O'Hallohan's body. He felt hard and tense. His hand snaked back across her breasts as he freed his gun, totally concentrating on the direction the sound came from. They lay like that for what seemed an hour, not daring to move, his body entangled with hers. Knowing they could be killed at any moment, still she was not troubled. In fact, she felt as safe as if she were in her own bed. When O'Hallohan finally moved off of her, she felt a twinge of sadness at the loss.

Once again he put his face next to hers. "Let me use your night vision. I'm going to crawl ahead. Get your pistol out and shoot anybody that approaches you. I'll call before I come near."

She handed him the NVDs and put her face in front of his to whisper, "Please be careful." Then she gave him a kiss for good luck. At least that's what she told herself as she pulled the gun from her waistband. It felt damp in her hand.

She started to worry when it seemed as if it had been a couple of hours since he had left. She was staring straight ahead when she saw the beam of a flashlight bobbing in front of her.

"Leena, it's me."

"I'm over here," she said standing up and walking stiffly toward him.

"Come with me," he said. "I need to show you something."

She began walking toward the small light. "What did you find?"

"Brace yourself."

He pointed the flashlight to a heavy brush pile and she could just make out a black t-shirt and—

"Oh, my God," Leena whispered and then started to retch. He'd been shot in the back of the head and the bullets had taken most of the man's face and spread it all over the ground.

"Look at all the tats he has," O'Hallohan said. "Prison or gang, you think?"

Leena had looked away but forced herself to look at the man's arms and neck. She quickly looked away again after seeing what remained of his face. "Who…who did it?" she asked, knowing in her heart that it was exactly what she had wanted to do—and might have, if O'Hallohan and Nowiki hadn't shown up.

"I don't know, but I thought I heard some kind of racket and a car start when we were lying on the ground back there. After I found him, I reconnoitered the entire area. I'm pretty sure there's no one else around."

Leena wondered how O'Hallohan had heard a car start. She'd heard nothing but her own loud thoughts. "What should we do now?"

"Let's go back and tell Nowiki. This is more his purview. But first show me this golf cart you told us about."

They walked down a short rise and across the dry creek bed, then skirted around the house until they came to the shed. O'Hallohan shined the light on the door.

"Oh, no. The lock is missing," Leena said.

"Hold this and step back." O'Hallohan handed Leena the flashlight and raised the barrel of the machine pistol. Then he yanked open the door.

Leena stepped forward and poured the flashlight's powerful beam into the empty shed. "Oh, God. It's what I feared." She hung her head and tears found their way down her face as she openly sobbed. "I lost Jesse and now the proof to keep him alive."

Sealed Truths

O'Hallohan came over and put his arms around her. She shuddered and swayed until blackness engulfed her. He held her tight as she collapsed.

Day Fourteen

Day Four of the Grand Pursuit

Chapter 19

Deception or Decision

Something awakened him, but the only sound Jesse heard was Frank's snoring, coming from the back bedroom. Jesse lay on the soft carpet, having insisted that Juella take the couch for her bed. He felt more than heard the rustling of his blanket as Juella lifted it and slid in next to him.

"I know you're awake. I can tell by your breathing," she whispered in his ear.

"What are you doing here?"

"Probably something I'll regret later."

He came more fully awake now, feeling her soft hands on his face. Her lips were moving. At first he couldn't make out what she was saying.

"Jesse, wake up. You're having a bad dream."

He startled and sat up abruptly. "Dream?"

"You were thrashing around and saying, 'No, no, no.' Don't you remember what you were dreaming about?" Juella asked.

The lie came easily to his lips, but he changed his mind. "It was sort of complex," he said and glanced down quickly at his blanket for a telltale sign. Thank goodness it was dark in the motor home.

"Complex, yeah, that would describe you well," Juella said. She moved back to the couch and scooted back under the blanket. "It's sure cold up here."

"Under the blanket?" he asked, still feeling guilty about the dream. "Oh, you mean at this altitude."

"You want to crawl under my blanket and keep me warm?" She

rolled over and put her back to him. "You should be so lucky. Go back to sleep, Fruitman."

Jesse stared at the ceiling. Like all men, he understood the universal sign of a turned back. It was okay, because something about the dream—perhaps nightmare—didn't add up. He thought about his tangled mind and wondered if some sort of memory was trying to force its way through.

One thing he did know was that once again he was on the run, this time with the help of two strangers. When Frank got the call from Ernesto about the feds waiting at the house for them, he wanted to return. But something else Ernesto said seemed to galvanize Frank into action. Abruptly leaving the tire shop, they drove away, not even bothering to get the bad tire fixed, let alone replacing the spare tire. They were now up in the High Sierras, camping—or rather hiding out—in the thick forest.

For a long while Jesse lay with his eyes open, listening to Juella's regular breathing. As she fell into a deeper sleep, her breathing became softer, more innocent. He knew he should get up and flee into the mountains and leave these two kind strangers.

His aroused senses told him that something not good was yet to come in this journey. Was he too weakened from the previous trauma to survive out in the wild by himself? Taking inventory, he determined that his side was tight but no longer burning. His head felt numb, and the ever-present headache had calmed down to a dull thump. He quietly got to his feet, still dressed. He slipped on his shoes and wrapped the blanket around him like a cocoon.

As silently as possible Jesse crept outside. Under a sky of a billion brilliant diamonds, he walked to the shore of the clear mountain lake. Mist rose from the water and swirled in a macabre dance, like ghosts gone dancing. He sat down and leaned back against a large boulder.

Ghosts. That would describe the comings and goings of the different people in his battered brain. Who were they? Real or not, alive or dead, were they some distant part of his own history or dreams like the one he'd just had of Juella? For a long time, measured in thoughts not minutes, images kept tumbling and reeling through his mind until finally sleep engulfed him.

Jesse woke at the first sound of movement and heard the motor home door close as Frank emerged from the huge RV with an old cowboy rifle under his arm. He carried two steaming mugs in his hands.

"So you're gettin' used to ranch time, eh?" Frank asked as he handed Jesse a cup of hot coffee. "My favorite time of day. Hope always rises with the sun, and everything begins anew." He glanced over at Jesse.

"I don't know about that," Jesse said, one hand wrapped around the mug and the other reaching toward the sky, stretching and yawning at the same time.

"Don't have to know it. Just have to live it."

Jesse sat up and watched as Juella came out of the motor home, almost floating down the steps. He let out another yawn as she approached.

"He's probably tired from having nightmares about me all night," Juella said to Frank.

"Oh, you two have something to tell me this morning?" Frank asked with a lopsided grin on his grizzled unshaven face.

"Oh, Dad, knock it off," Juella replied. Brush in hand, she moved off toward the lake.

Jesse looked at the old man. "She's kind of right. I did think about her last night," he said. "And also about you. They weren't pleasant thoughts or dreams."

"You want to skedaddle, huh? Figured you'd get around to it sooner or later." Frank walked over and leaned the old lever-action rifle against a small stunted tree. "I'd probably think the same thing myself."

"Then you realize how dangerous things are likely to get, unless I can find a place to shelter until I fully heal."

"Yep. I would think that, too. But what if they don't give you the time to heal up?" Frank lifted his foot up and placed it on the rock Jesse was leaning against. "But maybe the bigger question is, where? You agree?"

"So right away you found the weak link in my plan," Jesse said, shaking his head.

"What weak link?" Juella asked, stepping around the rock. She had brushed out her long wavy hair, and it flowed over her shoulders. It looked radiant as the early sun's first light filtered through.

"He thinks he needs to get away from us and hide out," Frank replied.

"Yeah, that worked real well at the ranch. In case you didn't notice, it's not exactly on a major tourist route like this is." She waved her arms about, staring at Jesse.

Frank warily looked around in the early morning light. "Come on. Let's get back into the coach and get another cup of joe." He picked up and cradled the rifle.

Inside the motor home, Frank turned on a stove burner under a loaded camping coffeepot. "I know I could fire up the generator and use the coffee maker, but something about cowboy coffee is the best."

"You won't hear me arguing," Jesse said. "I must have loved coffee in my previous life, too." He looked first at Juella and then slowly back to Frank.

"You seem better today," Juella said gently as the coffeepot started to perk.

Her tenderness made Jesse suddenly snap. "Listen to me," he said, the words rushing out. "I...I don't know how to say this, but they've already tried to kill me once, or a couple, or—damn...a bunch of times. They aren't going to stop now! And it's not your fight."

Frank started to say something but Juella spoke first, the words exploding out of her mouth. "Not our fight? Are you freaking nuts? My husband gave his life for our country. In Afghanistan. Why? To give them a chance to vote? I think not. It was for that black crap. Oil. That's what the war is...and...and always was about. Don't tell us we aren't in this fight. And don't tell me what I can or can't do, Fruitman." She stormed over and started to fold the blankets on the couch.

Frank wore a sad smile as he looked over at Jesse, who was staring at Juella's long dark hair while she was straightening the pillows. "Ready for another cup of coffee now?"

Jesse pried his eyes away and said. "Whoa, something's going on behind those dark eyes."

Juella turned and stared at Jesse. "Don't you dare belittle me, Jesse Christenson," She said with ice in her voice.

"Oh boy, better make it a double," he said as Frank filled his cup.

Frank sighed and sat down across from Jesse. "Juella, come over here and sit down. We need to talk this whole thing out and gather up a plan."

Juella had her hands on her hips and after a deadly look at Jesse, sat down next to him. She took a sip from the coffee set out in front of her.

"The way I see it, is this," Frank said. "If they get rid of you and the car, everything can return to the way it's always been. We can't do nothing about the car, but we have to get you to a safe place."

Jesse started to say something, but Frank held up his hand. "Juella doesn't want to hear this, but I know I have terminal cancer. And I don't have that long to go." He shrugged his shoulders. "And so, what's a couple of months more or less? I want you to grant my wish to continue on with you."

Juella looked fondly at the old man, her anger dissipating, and said, "I won't leave your side. Don't you see you're the only family I have left?" She turned to Jesse and said, "Let's be practical for a minute. I am a nurse. As much of a bullet magnet as you seem to be, you need me, too." She looked up into his deep blue eyes. "This is something I'll probably regret later"

"Frank, I understand your wish. But, Juella," he said as tenderly as he could manage, "you're young, and your life has barely begun. You'll get through all of this and build a—"

"Why do you dismiss me?" she interrupted. "Hear me loud and clear. I am in charge of me and don't owe you anything. I'm coming along, and you have no say in it."

A bird began chirping outside the window. It seemed to add a measure of life back into Jesse. "You spoke of déjà vu earlier, Frank, back when you first met me. Something about this seems like déjà vu to me, too. I have a foggy memory, and I'm not sure why, but it seems I have a hard time getting rid of people who want to help me." He shrugged and looked around. "I wonder why I said that. Oh well, doesn't matter. Thank you both for your help. I don't have a clue where to go or what to do, but if need be, I will give my life to protect you both."

"Once a soldier, always a soldier." Frank took another sip of coffee and said, "I know a place that might work. It's got water and electricity; and it's very secluded."

"That's a good thing," Jesse said.

"Problem is, it's a long way away."

"How far is it?" Jesse asked.

"It's in West Texas. Two days, easy, maybe one if we drive straight through," Frank replied.

"West Texas?" Juella asked. "You mean the ranch with the abandoned airport you inherited from Grandma's side of the family? I didn't know you still owned that old place."

"I folded it into the business, years back. Someone would have to look pretty hard to trace it to me, since the deed is still in your mom's maiden name."

"I remember when you loaded all us ranch kids into your old motor home and took us there. That must have been fifteen years ago," Juella said, looking into Frank's sad face. "It wasn't just secluded. More like desolate."

"Motor home." Jesse spun his empty coffee cup a few times and then said, "I thought about how they found me at your ranch. They must have traced this motor home from the hospital."

"They probably take a picture of every license plate going in or out," Frank said. "I was thinking the same thing. They're going to be looking for this rig, and it's gonna be hard to hide something this size."

"Who are they?" Juella asked. "I mean, if the Mexican Mafia knew you were there and the FBI—could there be a chasm wider than that—who's telling who what?"

For a few quiet moments, both men looked at Juella.

"You know, that's a great question," Jesse replied, suddenly banging his fist down on the table. "And I wonder who else has me in their crosshairs."

Chapter 20

Persuasive Engineering

Miguel twisted the pistol slowly to his left, grinding the barrel as deep into the punk's neck as he could. "One last time, where'd you drop the car?"

"Man, I told you! It was the third building on the right after you cross—"

"That's an empty building," Miguel said, easing up on the pressure a little.

"Those two dudes were waiting for me out back. I backed into the building, dropped the car, and split."

"You said a black dude and a skinny white gringo?"

"Yeah, tall black guy. The skinny guy, he signed my slip. Paid me cash and even gave me a twenty dollar tip. And I hauled ass home. Look, it was almost dark on a Saturday night and I had some action lined up. Come on, man, let me go."

"What were they wearing?"

"Clothes. Ouch! Fuck, that hurts," he said, feeling the grinding pistol once again. "I don't know, just—"

"Were they wearing suits and ties?" Miguel asked, interrupting again.

"I don't think so. Otherwise I would have thought they were cops." He tried to stay as still as possible.

Miguel stopped twisting the gun and stood up, holding the pistol in a loose grip. "You talk to any cops about this yet?"

"No, I ain't seen nobody. It was just another tow."

"Well, they're going to find you soon. And when they do, they'll ask you the same thing we did. Maybe I should shut you up right now." Miguel pulled the hammer back on the pistol.

"Come on, man, I ain't never crossed you guys. I been respectful and all." The punk sat up, staring into the long dark barrel.

Miguel looked down at the punk. He had enough tattoos to have been in the joint. Or maybe he was one of the new wannabes. Probably not a good idea to splatter him here.

"Where'd you do your time?"

"Mule Creek."

"Thought so. Hey, Pedro. Load this dude up with a kilo to drop off in Santa Cruz. He needs to take a vacation for a week or so. What do you say, mule?"

The punk stared at the pistol pointed at him. He dropped his head and simply nodded.

"You cross us, it won't be just you. We'll kill your whole family."

Miguel walked over to the car and got into the front passenger seat, waiting while Pedro took care of the deal. They had already stopped at the empty building on their way here. Whoever took possession of the Take-Us car had picked a good spot. It was hemmed in with complete privacy. Miguel had noticed the lock was broken, and they'd forced it again. When Pedro and he went inside, the building was empty except for some tire tracks on the floor.

A black guy and a white guy. Well at least the rag-heads didn't have it. But it wasn't another gang either. They would never leave a tip. Miguel started to get pissed and wondered what he was doing. He hated the fucking cops and now he was acting like one. All he had to do was take the car and kill the guy. But he couldn't find either one. Maybe he would just wait for both to surface, steal the car, and kill the gringo then.

Pedro opened the driver's door and got in behind the wheel. "Where to?"

"Hey Pedro, if you just stole a car from the cops own storage yard, what would you do with it?"

"You'd have to know they'd be on the lookout for it, so—"

"Yeah, yeah. Real hot."

"I'd have it delivered to my own neighborhood, but not my house. And it would have been dark soon, so I'd wait and then drive it into my garage. My pit bulls keep anybody from sniffing around."

"Yeah. You don't go far. That way nobody sees. Drive me back over to the building."

When they arrived, Miguel looked around and figured they wouldn't want to cross the busy street, so they would have turned...

"Turn right and go that way," he said, pointing. Pedro followed the street to the end, only about a quarter mile or so. And there was a building with a chain-link fence surrounding it.

"Stop here." Miguel walked over to the fence and read the sign. No Trespassing. U.S. Government Property. He knew now where the Take-Us car was hidden.

He got back into the car and said, "Jesus Christ! The government stole the car."

As they prepared to drive off, a skinny white guy and a tall black man walked from the building to their black government car, got in, and drove past them.

Miguel and Pedro watched as the black car disappeared from sight and a white van with Commercial Cleaning Services painted on the door drove into the parking lot. Two Mexican men got out, each taking two buckets of cleaning materials from the back. At the front door, one of the men pulled out a string of keys and unlocked the door.

Miguel smiled at Pedro. "This is going to be easier than I thought. Make some calls and get some more guys on this. Follow the man with the keys when he goes home and then roust him tonight and ask him if the car is in there. Be polite."

"Like we just were with the tow truck driver." Pedro grinned.

"Of course. If the car is in there, drag him back to unlock the door. There's probably a security code or something. Keep one man with his family and tell him if the alarm goes off they die. Do you know where we can get one of those car trailers like the weekend racers have?"

"I think so."

"Good. Get one and stash the car in it. Park it in one of those RV storage lots that are everywhere. No one will think shit about it. After things cool down, an easy trip to wherever the Venezuelans want it and we've got a guaranteed pipeline."

"Good plan, Miguel."

"That's why I'm El General," Miguel said, reaching under his shirt and pulling out his pistol to check the safety. "And Pedro, don't fuck this up."

Chapter 21

Passionate Resolve

Leena woke up in her own bed, the inside of her head pounding like the drums of a rock and roll band. Wait! That *is* rock music, she realized, and sat up. The sound was coming from the radio alarm clock sitting on the nightstand in her bedroom. She reached over the sleeping O'Hallohan, moved an empty wine bottle, and pushed the snooze button. She lay back down, her head feeling like a ripe watermelon about to split open from lack of sleep.

Oh, God, why oh why oh why? But hadn't she learned years ago that instead of asking God why, it was better to ask how? Her mind cried out, *not now, let me just…just what?*

In five short minutes the music started again, and this time she dragged herself up and turned it off. Not sure if she wanted to or not, she planted her bare feet on the deep carpet, strode over to the closet, and pulled out an old robe, draping it around her shoulders. Why, when you thought with your tenement of clay instead of your soul, did things always seem so hopeless?

Leena looked out the bathroom window and saw that it was cloudy. She couldn't seem to shake the blues. Dropping the robe to the floor, she stepped into the shower and scrubbed until her skin turned pink. But the water still couldn't wash off the filth she felt inside. She reminded herself to vacuum the telltale grass shavings off the floor as she put the robe on once again. Wrapping a towel around her wet hair, she took a deep breath and walked through her bedroom to the deck.

"Hey, good morning," O'Hallohan said, smiling widely. He was already out on the deck and had an old rag spread on top of the table, his gun apart for cleaning. "Coffee's ready."

"I don't want to talk about it," she said, her voice flat and unconvincing. "What are you still doing here? Didn't you get what you came for?"

"Okay, I see your point. That guy was pretty gruesome."

"What?" She filled a cup and went to the other end of the table to sit.

"Well, Nowiki and I thought it might be a good idea for me to hang out and keep you safe."

"Where is Nowiki?"

"He called in the cavalry and they're at Jesse's property doing whatever it is they do." He looked up from his gun and asked, "Are you okay? You seem, uh, downhearted."

Leena didn't respond but continued to gaze into her cup as if there were tea leaves on the bottom that would yield some kind of answer.

He placed the barrel down on the table and said, "When I was in Iraq in the Special Forces, we were assigned many missions deep in 'Injun' country. More times than I care to remember, things seemed pretty hopeless. But I came to understand that as long as I'm still alive, there's always a chance.

"You sound like…him."

"Anybody that served in the shit and came out alive pretty much gets a clue." O'Hallohan began snapping the gun back together. "What are you going to do now?"

"That's the strange thing." She was still looking into her coffee cup. "I've always been able to stay one step ahead of the curve. In control. The car's gone, Jesse's gone, my story is gone, and now," she sighed, looking at him but avoiding his eyes, "the last vestige of evidence that there ever was a working theory is gone."

"It seems to me that if I was smart enough to invent something like this car, I would have made a copy or two of the plans or software or something and sent a copy to somebody. You know, just in case."

"Maybe." She glanced back down at her cup. "This coffee is horrible. Did you make it?"

"Yeah, I kind of just guessed how much to put in."

"You're right, you know. Not the coffee," she said as she walked to the edge of the deck and pitched the coffee into the yard. "Jesse would have made copies and sent them off or stored them someplace. But where? Time is of the essence, because the propaganda war has already begun. And once people believe it, it's hard to change their opinions."

They looked up as they heard a car coming down the driveway. Nowiki. He saw them, smiled, and quickly walked over.

"Gangbanger all right, took two to the back of the skull." Neither O'Hallohan nor Leena said anything. "Hey! That's great news. If they're still looking, it means they don't have our boy."

"Who did it?" Leena asked.

"Don't know, but they saved the taxpayers some bucks. There was a warrant out for the little puke, jumped bail on a drug charge and accessory to murder. Got any coffee?"

"I'll make some." Leena moved toward the house, but stopped and asked, "Why was he there, do you think?"

"Probably the same reason you came back here. Figured Christenson or you might show up at his home," Nowiki said as another car pulled in behind his. "It's Agent Entersane," Nowiki said, seeing a questioning look on her face. "Department of Energy. What can I say? He pulled some strings and we're supposed to co-operate. He wants to talk to you, Leena."

"Screw him. I don't want to talk—"

"Hear him out, might learn something," Nowiki said.

She watched the little man approach and said, "Have a seat. I'll make coffee."

Leena went in to start a new pot of coffee and then went into her bedroom to get dressed. She stuffed the pistol into her waistband. Taking her time, she dried her hair. They each had a cup of coffee in front of them by the time she came back outside.

"Entersane, interesting name," Leena began.

"I'm not your enemy, Miss Delaney." The little man stood and held out his hand. "We at the DOE want the same thing you want, to keep Mr. Christenson safe, if possible."

Leena reached out and shook his hand and then glanced down at her own, almost as if she was counting her fingers to see if one was missing. "We agree on that, then. Do you know where he is?"

"Alas, no. And I can see you don't either. I doubt that you will ever stop looking. If I were you, I know I wouldn't. However, if you do find him," Agent Entersane said, looking directly into her eyes, "we would just like to have a small chat with him."

"More like make him disappear," Leena said sitting down across from him.

"Miss Delaney, do you really think he has a choice?" Agent Entersane asked, taking a sip of his coffee. "It will be with our help or he will die."

"You would kill him, is that what you're saying?" Leena asked.

Not answering, Agent Entersane continued. "What do you know about big oil?"

"Mostly that they rob me every time I buy a gallon of gas." She leaned forward, her reporter instincts aroused.

"Do you know how gasoline is made?"

"Of course. It's refined from crude oil."

Agent Entersane looked toward the house. "Nice house. About… twenty, twenty-five years old?" Not waiting for an answer he continued. "Wood frame on a concrete foundation, asphalt shingle roof. Pretty typical, as almost every building is made of a combination of one of four materials. The first is rock, which is where sand and eventually cement or concrete comes from. And then there's the second, wood. This house is probably Douglas fir framing and sheathing plywood, which is thinly sliced wood glued together. Third is metal, mostly steel, copper, or aluminum, which is more common in commercial buildings. Probably steel in the foundation and the fasteners holding this house together."

"Your point, Agent Entersane?" Leena asked.

"The roofing is made by mixing asphalt and sand together," Agent Entersane continued. "This deck we're sitting on is a composite made by mixing wood and plastic. This house is old enough it probably has copper pipes, but newer houses use plastic pipes. And why not? They are cheaper to install and won't burst in a freeze unless it drops to fifty below. Probably doesn't get that cold here, correct?"

"No, it doesn't get that cold here. If it did, I would put you out into it. Do you have a point?" Leena asked.

"Like it or not, plastic has become the fastest growing building material. And as a matter of fact it's a better choice than most of the traditional materials used in just about everything. You know where it all comes from, correct?"

"You're talking about petrochemicals, I presume?" Leena said, a little indignant. "Just about everybody knows petrochemicals are a by-product of making gasoline."

Agent Entersane sat back in his chair and removed his glasses. "As my fourteen-year-old daughter would say, 'that is soooo yesterday.' Look around you, Miss Delaney. Those grips on the gun, the tires on the car, the glue in the plywood. Even these lenses in my glasses. Everything is now made from petrochemicals. You see, gasoline has now become the by-product of making petrochemicals, which have become indispensable. My goodness, the stealth bomber is made from them. And if we didn't burn gasoline in our automobiles, what would we do with it all?"

Leena sat back, dumfounded, and looked over at O'Hallohan and then Nowiki. "Why are you telling me this?" Leena asked.

"Do you remember when NutraSweet came on the market?" Agent Entersane asked.

"What? I don't know. Maybe twenty years ago?" Leena replied.

"It was actually invented about forty years ago, but it wasn't allowed onto the world market at that time. Our government felt that entire economies of countries that grew sugar, many of whom were our allies, would collapse—leaving us with, let's just say, a less stable world. And so NutraSweet was bureaucratically held up to allow those countries to find other products or means to keep their economies afloat."

"So what you're telling me, or rather us, is that the federal government is not going to allow a car like the Take-Us to come onto the market at this time," Leena said angrily.

"I don't recall saying any such thing," Agent Entersane replied, putting his glasses back on as a small smile appeared. "Do you think your Jesse Christenson is the first person to think of a new or different automotive power plant design?"

Nowiki's cell phone quietly buzzed, and he walked over to the rail to answer it.

"If—and more than likely, when—we find him," Entersane continued, "assuming, of course, that he's not already dead, we'll take care of him and keep him safe. A new identity, new address, whatever it takes."

"Aren't you forgetting the website with all the data?"

"That's interesting, because the other day when I went into it to check for clues as to where he might be, it had been scrubbed. All gone," Entersane said, not missing a beat. "Strange… it would take a Cray supercomputer to break that encryption. I wonder who has one of those?"

Leena took her eyes off the loathsome DOE agent and looked over his shoulder at Nowiki. He gave her a strange look and wiggled his fingers as if to say goodbye.

"Agent Entersane, you are correct about one thing," said Leena. "I won't ever stop looking for him. And incidentally, it has nothing to do with my profession." She stopped speaking and let that sink in. "But in all fairness, I will pass on your offer. I doubt he will accept it. You see, he doesn't trust the government anymore, and quite frankly neither do I. I'm sure you can understand why. When I made a deal with these two agents, they violated my trust by bringing you over here." She stepped back, hands on her hips. "And so, gentlemen, I will say goodbye to all of you. Now. Please leave."

"Certainly, Miss Delaney, but if he does make contact, you have my card. I'm sure you've been told he's fleeing in a large motor home. It's simply a matter of time before we—or others who are not as trustworthy—catch up to him."

Chapter 22

Tightening Bonds

Five highways traverse the Sierra Mountains south of Lake Tahoe, three of them only partially open during the harsh winters. All of them have one thing in common, it being that the east slopes of the Sierras are more barren and sparse than the thickly forested west slopes, and the views into Nevada are therefore breathtaking in their abundance.

The motor home headed slowly down the twisting mountain road on the eastern slope. Jesse could hear and feel the rumble of the exhaust brake of the big diesel engine. Even the stunted trees on either side of the road seemed to want to run from the racket.

They had waited most of the morning and at noon decided to make their run. Jesse shared the passenger seat with Juella and both gripped the armrests as Frank steered the big beast through another hairpin curve. Neither of them wanted to sit on the couch because of the seasick feeling they got when they couldn't see out the front windshield. The sharp turns pushed them together, and Jesse was conscious of Juella's breast against his arm. He reluctantly moved his arm and put it around her, grasping the other armrest to better support them both.

"What's in your pocket? It keeps poking me," Juella said, trying unsuccessfully to shift her leg away from his.

"That's my cell phone," he said.

"It might come in handy. I left mine at the house."

"Don't think so. It's dead."

"Let me see it. It might be the same as mine." She moved forward and he reached into his pocket and handed it to her. She pressed a button on the front. When nothing happened, she held another button for a short while. "Probably needs a charge. Hey, Dad, do we still have the cell phone charger in here?" She stood up.

Frank concentrated on his driving as they negotiated another sharp bend. "It's in the back by the dining table."

Juella lost her balance and fell into Jesse's lap as he reached out to catch her.

"Careful! You okay?" he asked.

"Yes, sorry." She climbed out of his lap and headed toward the back. Finding the cord, she tried to plug it into the cell phone.

"Wrong connector." She handed Jesse his phone and he stuck it back in his pocket, this time on the other side. "I plugged yours back in to recharge, Dad."

"Thank you, dear," Frank said as they came to the bottom of the mountain.

Turning onto another highway, they had traveled another hour when the motor home started vibrating badly.

"Oh, crap! I bet it's that damn tire." Frank pulled off the highway next to a pine forest. He got out to check the tire, and Jesse got to his feet to stretch.

Frank was back in a moment. "It has a bulge in the sidewall. Too dangerous to go on."

Juella walked forward and said, "I checked the cell phone, and there's no service out here."

"That's okay, watch this. Satellite." Frank pushed the OnStar button and a female voice asked about their problem. She promised to send help their way.

"That wiggly road kind of wore me out a hair. I think I'll take a little break," Frank said, walking back and lying down on the couch.

"Are you okay?" Jesse asked.

"Sure, I'll be fine in a couple minutes."

"I think I'll go for a walk and leave you in peace, then," Juella said, opening the door and walking down the steps.

"Hang on, I'll come with you," Jesse said.

"Jesse, wait. Take this rifle with you." Seeing the look on Jesse's face, Frank added, "You never know."

"You're right. You never know." Jesse closed the door and went down the steps, turning to watch as the steps automatically retracted.

He followed Juella as she slogged up a steep rise into the pines. After a few minutes, they lost sight of the parked motor home, and he had to stop next to a large boulder to catch his breath.

"He's starting to get really weak. That little drive wore him out," Juella said. "How about you?"

"Me? I'm fine. But he did look a little pale."

"He'll never make it to the old airfield unless you drive and he rests in the back."

"If we can talk him into it. He seems to be pretty stubborn, but you have a way with him. I'm sure you'll talk him into it."

"A way with him, yeah. I'm pretty persuasive when I set my mind to it." She began walking again and he chased behind her. They wandered among the trees and jumbled boulders, winding up the slope until they caught a glimpse of the road below.

"Look there," she said, stopping abruptly.

Jesse looked down and his stomach turned when he saw the flashing red and blue lights of a police car pulling up behind the motor home. "Oh, sh— ah crap."

"No, Jesse. It's 'Oh, shit!' Shit! Shit! Shit!" She turned on him. "Now what?"

"It's probably just a routine traffic check or something." His voice trailed off unconvincingly.

"And if it's not?" she asked, her eyes fixated on the flashing lights.

"Well…" He patted his jeans pockets one at a time, taking inventory. "I have a dead cell phone, an all-but-useless pocket knife, a couple hundred bucks, and this rifle—"

"I am not going to be your Bonnie. And as a matter of fact, you're no Clyde. I won't do anything illegal for or with you."

"No, of course not. Come on, let's head back to where we climbed up."

He turned and began retracing their steps. When they got to

the spot overlooking the motor home they were just in time to see another police car and a tow truck pull in, overheads flashing.

"Well, so much for the routine traffic whatever," Juella said.

Jesse didn't say anything, although his brain was thinking of all the reasons they should just walk down the hill. But something deep inside of him was flashing as brightly as the lights below them, telling him not to do it.

"You need to go down there and be with your dad."

"I've already thought about it. There is no way Dad would tell them we're up here. But if I walk down there, a single girl coming out of the woods…" She walked up to him and even in the long dusk of the desert he could see her dark eyes glowing. "No way. They'd know you were out here somewhere."

"True, but if you go with me and I'm wanted, then you are breaking the law. Even if I'm no Clyde."

"Technically, we don't know if you're wanted. So no big deal. What's the plan?"

He didn't understand why, but somehow he was relieved that she was staying with him. "Why would you think I have a plan?"

She looked pretty standing there, her dark hair flowing over her shoulders, a slight smile on her lips, and her hands on her hips. "Well, do you have one?"

"Yeah." He abandoned the moment. "We stay on top of this hill line and keep the road in sight as much as we can. If they do let Frank go, he'll probably cruise back and forth until we can descend and flag him down."

"And if they don't let him go?"

"That would be Plan B," he said, looking into her eyes as she stood waiting. "I'll work on Plan B as we're walking. Come on."

Juella gave a final look at the flashing lights and then turned to follow Jesse. "It's not even like 'maybe.' I know I'm going to regret this later."

Jesse set a brisk pace but with her long legs Juella kept up easily. When they started up a particularly steep slope she was walking next to him and soon passed him, leading as he began to tire. The recently repaired bullet hole in his side began to scream for mercy as he dragged himself up the hillside. He was struggling to catch his breath when he looked up and noticed she had stopped fifty yards ahead, waiting for him.

"How bad does it hurt? And don't lie."

"I'll be okay, just a little on the weak side." He tried to smile but had the feeling it came off as more of a grimace. "We've only been walking for a couple of hours. I must be out of shape."

"I told you not to lie to me. As a nurse, I'm trained to spot pain. You've had so many traumas in the last few weeks it's amazing you can even walk."

He leaned on the rifle, using it as a crutch. "I do feel some pain, but I can still go on for awhile."

She shook her head. "Okay, Fruit…Hero. Which way now?"

They were on top of the rise and he could see the road curving around a small valley to their left. If they descended here they would have to climb back up the other side of the valley. But if they stayed on top of the ridge it would curve back around. It might be a little longer, but at least they would not have to climb the hill again.

"We still have a couple hours until it gets dark. Let's stay on the ridge."

Distances in the desert can be deceiving, and it took them two hours to go around the deep valley. When they finally arrived on the other side, he saw that the road had unexpectedly veered away from them. Worse, they had a steep cliff to go down unless they followed the ridge line further away from their desired course.

Jesse looked down into the next valley and could see a wide straight road cutting the valley in half. It was quite a distance, but he thought he could see some buildings at the other end.

"Might be a ranch down there," he said, his throat parched "I'm going to need some water soon."

"Me too, but I think I can make it that far just fine." She walked up to his side. "You seem to be struggling a bit. I know, you're fine, right? But let's rest here for a bit."

"No, not here. We're going to lose daylight soon. Let's try to get down to that road first." He pointed weakly.

"All right, but let me carry the gun for a while." She reached over and snatched it from him and started down a narrow deer trail.

It was dark when they reached the bottom. Jesse stumbled along, weaving between the small bushes and sage. Finally, they arrived at the straight wide road they had seen from above. Juella propped up the rifle and sat down with her back against a boulder. Jesse collapsed next to her.

"You would keep walking until you died, wouldn't you?" she asked. Her voice sounded deep and hoarse and—in spite of how tired he was—kind of sexy.

"I don't know. Probably. But I need to rest here a minute or two."

He leaned back and in less than a minute his head slumped over onto her shoulder. His deep breathing relaxed her and she also fell asleep.

* * *

A bright light startled Juella awake several hours later.

"Jesse, wake up! Look."

Jesse came awake, his head in Juella's lap. He slowly sat up. "Leena?"

"No. Look! What is that?" Juella asked.

He tried to focus on the rapidly approaching light. He sat up straight, with Juella still at his side. They didn't have long to wait.

"Airplane, coming in low and fast."

It whizzed by them. Juella stood up, watching. But when Jesse tried to stand he fell to his knees. He lowered his head against the rock, which felt cool to him.

"What's wrong?" she asked, and put a hand down in the dark, feeling for his forehead. "You're burning up. You need some water."

"I'll be—"

"No! You won't be all right," Juella said. "There must be a ranch up that road. It can't be far. I'm going to get you some water. Don't move. I won't have you die on me."

Juella walked to the road and followed the direction of the plane.

Jesse wondered what kind of rancher landed a plane in the middle of the night in the secluded desert. He could only come up with one answer. He anxiously got to his feet, wobbling a little. Juella had said he would walk until he died, and she was probably right. He snatched up the rifle and stumbled off after Juella, praying he wasn't too late.

* * *

Juella heard a motor running as she came to the edge of the light. She could make out an open building where the airplane was parked facing back toward the runway. A man stood atop a stepladder with a hose stuck into the top of the wing. A white minivan was parked behind the plane and Juella saw a shorter man loading something into it. She stopped abruptly.

The man came down from the wing and moved his stepladder over to the other wing as the shorter man went to the door of the airplane to get another plastic shrink-wrapped bundle. Juella slowly started to back away.

"What do we have here, a little chocha?"

Juella spun around to see a big man with a gun pointed at her. She stood still and didn't say a word.

"Now what would a girl be doing wandering around in the middle of nowhere?" he asked aloud when she still didn't answer. He reached out a hand and pushed her into the light, toward the airplane.

"Hey, look what I found," he yelled to his two compatriots. He pushed her again and she turned and walked toward the other men, who stopped and watched her approach.

"Where'd ya find her?" The pilot stopped refueling the airplane and started walking toward them.

"Standing right there in the road," the big man said. "She looks Mexican. Hey, Armando, she won't talk to me. You ask her what she's doing here."

The squat little man who had been loading the van came up to Juella and asked a question in Spanish. Juella answered in a soft respectful tone.

"She says she was being led up here from Mexico, and her coyote ditched her."

"Maybe she's not alone, and they're here to take the shipment." The pilot pulled a pistol out of his belt. "Man, I'm getting out of here." He spun and started back to the plane.

"I watched her walk up. She's by herself," the big man said. "You need to stop smoking so much weed. You're getting too paranoid."

"I've been flying the slot for five years; you do that and see how freaked out you get," the pilot said but turned around to look at Juella.

The big man reached out and cupped one of Juella's breasts, pinching her nipple hard. She didn't flinch.

"Oh, you like that, huh? Hey, Armando! What do you say we have a little fun with her?"

"Sure, why not?" The short man snorted out a laugh. "Boss ain't here yet."

"Oh, yeah! She's got some nice titties." He observed and then reached his hand down between her legs to grab a handful. So quickly the big man didn't see it coming, Juella drove her knee into his crotch and punched him in the face. It knocked him to the ground and she ran toward the safety of the darkness.

The other two men started laughing.

"You fuckin' bitch!" The big man stood up and sighted his gun at the middle of her back. A single shot rang out.

The 30-30 Power-Point 150-grain bullet entered the chest cavity and blew the spine in half, punching a huge hole out his back. It took bone and tissue as it exited, blasting the big man off his feet.

The pilot, who had stopped halfway to the plane to watch the action, pointed his pistol to where he'd seen the flash and began wildly firing away. The next shot from the darkness was a duplicate of the first, pitching the pilot onto his back. The third man, Armando, dropped to his knees after pissing his pants and started praying aloud in Spanish.

Jesse walked forward to the kneeling man and croaked out in a hoarse voice, "On your belly!"

When the man didn't respond, Jesse walked behind him and

hit him in the back of the head with the butt of the rifle, knocking him forward. Jesse reached down and searched the man quickly, relieving him of a nine millimeter automatic which he shoved into his back pocket.

"He didn't do anything to me; leave him alone," Juella said, walking back into the light.

"You wouldn't be saying that if I didn't come find you. Instead you'd be spread-eagled on the ground with this little asshole grunting into you."

He looked down at the smallish man, keeping the rifle pressed up against the back of the man's head.

"But I'm not, and he's not. Jesse, listen to me. With the other two, you were protecting me. Shooting this man would be murder. Please don't do it."

Juella's voice was soft in his ears. She seemed to understand the bloodlust that came over men when they were forced to defend those entrusted to their care. Rather than shout at him, she disarmed him with her quiet demeanor. Jesse took a long breath and let the red rage pass through him and back into the primordial earth it came from. His eyes seem to refocus.

"Yes, of course," he said, his voice still hoarse. "Juella, see if you can find me something to drink. Please."

"Sure you're okay?" she asked, reluctant to leave.

He withdrew the rifle from the man's head, shook his head, and slowly walked over to the big man's body to search him as Juella hurried toward the minivan. Jesse took the big revolver, a .44 Magnum that the dead man still clutched in his hand, and then moved over to the pilot's body, taking his gun as well. He started to throw the guns into the night but then thought better of it and stashed the Magnum in his waistband.

Juella came back with three cans of Budweiser. "Sorry, this is all they have in the cooler."

He took one, opened it, and slammed it. Then he took the second, chugging it down a little slower. She started to admonish him but stopped and made a face as she downed the remaining can of beer.

He handed her the pilot's pistol, another nine millimeter. "Can you use one of these?"

"Of course. I was raised on a ranch. But I really think we need to leave," she said. "This place is making me sick to my stomach."

Jesse noticed for the first time that her hands were shaking. Her eyes were wide, and she seemed somehow very vulnerable. He wanted to reach over and pull her close.

Instead, he simply said, "Good idea."

His voice sounded better but he still hadn't fully recovered. The beer, little more than water and carbs, seemed to give him some energy. Of course, it could still be the hot fire of pure hate tearing through his veins.

They had started walking toward the minivan when they heard running footsteps. Armando was heading toward the darkness that encircled them. Jesse had started to raise the rifle when Juella put a hand over the barrel.

"Please don't," she said, tears in her eyes. "Let him go. It's over."

He lowered the rifle but continued to look down the road. "Do you see what I see?"

Juella had to wipe her eyes. "Headlights?"

"Yeah, I think so; must be a couple miles away."

"Oh, no. They said something about their boss coming," Juella said. "Come on, let's get out of here."

They moved quickly to the minivan and Jesse ran around it, slamming doors as he went. He arrived at the driver's side, jumped in, and reached down to start the engine. Juella was seated, drinking another beer, when he bellowed, "There's no key!"

He searched frantically on the floor as she explored the dash. He ran around to the closed doors and peered at the locks as she did the same. They both looked at the approaching headlights, closer now.

"He must have them," Jesse said, gesturing toward the dark.

Juella picked up the cooler. "We'll go back into the desert."

Jesse looked out past the airplane at the still approaching headlights.

"Come on, Jesse. Please. You can't fight them all." She tugged at his arm.

"Of course not. Hurry, get into the airplane." His voice was calm as he moved quickly forward, her hand still on his arm.

"You know how to fly?"

"I think so…kind of. Here take this." He handed her the rifle. Then he climbed the stepladder and pulled the refueling hose out of the tank, placing the fuel cap back on. He pitched the ladder out of the way, ran over to the pilot's door, and hauled himself up and in. Juella was sitting in the other seat, and he took a quick look backwards. Except for the cooler, he could see nothing else in the plane.

"They stripped it for hauling drugs," he said.

"Are you sure you know how to fly? And what does 'kind of' mean?"

"Yes, I'm a pilot. No, I've never flown this particular type of airplane before. Put your seat belt on." He turned the key and pushed one of the knobs, the red one, full forward, while he eased the throttle a pinch forward.

"I can't find the seat belt. I don't think there is one," Juella said twisting in her seat.

Jesse jabbed the start button and immediately the propeller began to windmill. The engine caught quickly, roaring to life.

"Put your hands on the console and hang on. Trust me, it's going to be okay." He looked up and saw the headlights approaching fast. "Damn, this is going to be close."

He pushed the throttle slowly until it was fully forward. Steering with his feet, he lined up the car's headlights in the center of the windshield and reached down to pull up a lever, adding in a little flaps for a short field take-off. Because the airplane was stripped to carry drugs, it was light and accelerated quickly.

Jesse and Juella watched the headlights relentlessly getting closer. The driver of the car seemed oblivious to the airplane he was about to collide with. Jesse aimed the plane at the approaching lights and hoped the car was staying in the middle of the road. He couldn't see the edge of the runway and didn't have time to find the landing lights they'd seen earlier.

Full of adrenaline, Jesse was all instinct now, with no clue as to how fast they were going. He pulled back on the yoke, willing the fragile airplane to lift itself into the air. The headlights shot beneath them as they cleared the speeding car with barely inches to spare.

Jesse kept the plane low, picking up speed. Reaching out he flipped a switch, and the landings lights came on. He quickly turned them off and tried another switch. His effort was rewarded when the instruments lit up. He glanced downward as they flew over the main road and saw a lonely pair of headlights passing a couple hundred feet below them as they began the long climb out of the valley.

After clearing the flaps, Jesse looked over at Juella. She was sitting very still and looking straight ahead, a death grip on the front panel. He kept glancing down at the instruments, trying to see if all was well. There was a red glow around them and it seemed there were more panel lights than normal. The plane must have been set up for night flying.

The panel was basic and sparse, at best. There were missing instruments, like the artificial horizon and other navigational aids that would be used in instrument flying. And only one radio, not nearly as many as was customary. It seemed that all non-essential weight had been removed.

Juella's soft voice floated over the barely discernible noise of the engine. "I was wrong about you. You are a Clyde." She leaned over and kissed him on the lips. "Thank you for saving my life. In my culture, my life now belongs to you."

Jesse didn't know how to respond. "That thank you might be a little hasty." He reached down and dialed in a little trim, increasing their rate of climb. "We have no idea where we are. We are most certainly in big mountain country and we probably won't see them until we smack into them."

She put her head on his shoulder and spoke into his ear. "Whatever you do, you will save us. I have faith in you."

Jesse smelled the sweetness of her hair and for a second he—

Fighting the emotion, he concentrated on flying. Jesse realized it had been many years since he had flown, although he was a good pilot and had flown through this area before. He strained to see ahead and knew he needed to turn southeast… if they didn't hit a mountain first. He couldn't remember exactly, but it seemed to him that if they climbed to twelve thousand feet they would clear most of the taller peaks.

"I forgot to ask in all of the excitement. Are you okay? No bullet holes?"

"I'm all right; I didn't get shot." Juella spoke so softly it was hard to hear her. "Well…I don't know. I do feel woozy."

Jesse checked the altimeter as they passed through ten thousand feet. "Did you drink the whole beer?"

"Um, th-three. I don't drink alcohol, and they tasted terrible, but I was so thirsty…"

Jesse let out a little laugh, feeling some of the tension release. It was the first laugh in a long, long time.

"The alcohol in your system, on an empty stomach, and at this altitude? The effect multiplies. You've got a beer buzz going."

"All I know is your shoulder feels real good."

"I'm probably going to need it soon. Why don't you see if your seat cranks back? You can take a little snooze."

She moved her head reluctantly off his shoulder but not before she kissed him on the neck. "Spoilsport. You can have me anytime you want." She put her head back, found a lever, and reclined her seat.

Jesse glanced at the altimeter once again. They had climbed to twelve thousand feet. He lowered the nose, leveling off, and pulled the throttle back and then the mixture. He watched the exhaust gas temperature gauge as he leaned out the motor. The airplane had a constant speed prop. He twisted the knob, but realized he didn't know the proper power settings anyway, so he just played it by ear.

Jesse looked over at Juella, who seemed to be fast asleep or maybe passed out. Looking beyond her, he didn't see any mountains and started a long slow turn. He set a course southeast in the direction of Texas, which seemed as good a destination as any. Then he fiddled with the trim wheel until the airplane was pretty much flying itself. He looked down and could see patches of light and dark. Ahead, he could see nothing.

The sun would be up in a few hours, and they should be okay as long as they didn't run into any clouds. He shifted in his seat uncomfortably. If they did run into clouds, in the dark and surrounded by tall unseen mountains, they were dead.

Chapter 23

Unlikely Alliance

Leena waited silently on the back deck at her mom's house in the near darkness. It reminded her of a couple of days before when she prepared to…what? Get raped? She brought her hand down hard on the deck rail. Why? Why did she keep having these intrusive thoughts? She didn't know if she was raped and probably would never know. *God, please let me…somehow I've got to move beyond this whole episode.* She was so engrossed in her private thoughts she never heard O'Hallohan until he spoke to her.

"Remind me never to post you on guard duty," he said.

She flinched and spun around. "I…I heard you a mile away."

Leena walked down the steps and slipped into the backpack she'd prepared in advance.

"Yeah, right. We need to hurry. Nowiki's driving up the hill and should be here any minute now."

"Tell me what's up."

"Wait until we get in the car. You never know, the mountains might have ears," O'Hallohan said, his eyes restlessly moving, quietly seeking targets as they slunk through the forest.

They arrived at the narrow road just as a car crept past and put on its brakes, coming to a complete stop. They ran out and opened the doors, getting into the car as Nowiki drove off.

Leena couldn't hold her tongue. "What is it? What's going on?"

"Yeah, yeah, glad to see you again, too." When there was no response, Nowiki continued. "We've got the motor home and the guy that took Christenson from the hospital."

"But not Jesse?" Leena sagged against the door.

"Not yet. The owner of the motor home isn't talking."

"So where are we going?" Leena asked as the FBI agent flipped his turn signal on.

"Where else? To interview him ourselves." Nowiki turned the car, heading toward the high country over the mountains. "I spoke to the sheriff in confidence and asked them to hold the motor home owner at the scene. And hold off putting any information over the net."

Leena looked over at Nowiki, raising her eyebrows. "And?"

"We have until morning to get him to talk before the remainder of the law enforcement community knows we have him. Seems like we can't keep a secret anymore." He peeked over at Leena. "Okay, you were right, I admit it."

"Has the driver told us what happened to Jesse?" Leena asked so quietly Nowiki had to strain to hear her.

"Apparently, he's one of those anti-government, conspiracy-theory types. Refused to answer any questions."

"Then why are we going?"

"Because you're not one of us," Nowiki said. "Besides, I know you much better now and know you have a certain—shall we call it a knack—for getting people to talk."

"And you think I'll share what he tells me with you," Leena said.

"Your instincts are just as sharp as mine, and I'm sure you also feel the net closing in on him."

Leena reached over and put her seat belt on with a resounding click.

As if they were talked out, they remained quiet for most of the three-hour drive to the motor home, located a few miles beyond the Nevada state line. It was a little after midnight when they arrived. The clouds from earlier that day had moved eastward and the clear night sky was alight with a million stars.

They parked behind the patrol car, where a young sheriff's deputy awaited them. Nowiki took him aside and they went into the motor home together, while Leena and O'Hallohan waited patiently in the car. The deputy went back to his squad car and pulled out onto the deserted road, soon disappearing from sight. Leena and O'Hallohan got out and walked to the door of the motor home, which was standing ajar.

"Knock, knock," Leena said, falling back to her best upbeat TV voice. "Can we come in?"

"Do I got a choice?" Frank asked. "Frickin' Gestapo!"

Leena went up the few short steps and walked directly over to Frank, her hand out.

"I couldn't agree more. Hi, my name is Leena Delaney. I'm a news reporter."

Frank looked at her and opened his mouth to say something, but reached out his hand instead.

"Nice to meet you," he mumbled and looked beyond her before sitting down.

"I'm sorry. I didn't catch your name?" Leena said, smiling sweetly.

"Frank. Well, it's really Franklin Garcia."

"Frank, I'd like you to meet Agent O'Hallohan of Homeland Security. And you've probably been introduced to Agent Nowiki from the FBI." Frank nodded. "So you probably want to know what the three of us are doing here, right?" He didn't answer, but Leena could tell his curiosity was aroused. "First of all, the last thing I'm here to do is ask you where Jesse Christenson is. Can I sit here?" she asked, pointing to a spot on the couch next to where he was sitting.

"Last thing you will do...I know how that works, you know," Frank said, gesturing for her to sit down.

Leena laughed aloud, and that seemed to break some of the tension in the air. "Know that one, huh? All right, how about I tell you a story, then."

Not waiting for him to comment, she told the story of how she met Christenson, the building of the car, and the journey from New York to San Francisco, ending with Jesse's disappearance from the hospital. When she had finished she looked deep into Frank's eyes.

"Interesting, but why get so involved in what was just a good news story?" Frank asked.

"I left out the part where he sold me on his dream. He did it so well that it somehow became my dream, too. Maybe more of nightmare, really." Leena's eyes filled with large tears that slowly ran down her face.

"I've heard about you Hollywood types that can cry on cue," Frank said, leaning back.

"Screw you," Leena said, standing up. "I'll find him without your help."

"Here, little lady. Take this." Frank reached into his back pocket and pulled out an old brown hankie. "It's mostly clean."

Leena sat back down and dabbed at her eyes. "Sorry. Is my mascara running?"

"You kind of look like a ghoul," Frank said a broad smile. "I didn't even know he was hiding in the coach until I got home and he came out from the underneath storage compartment."

"How was he? He was just starting to recover in the hospital."

"Well, my daughter thought he was getting better. She was right there when he crawled out. Scared the crap out of her, and it's lucky she didn't brain him with the shovel. I came over and recognized him right away, just like I recognized you…from the newscast."

"Is that your daughter in the picture in your living room?" O'Hallohan asked.

Frank looked over at the two agents and really saw them for the first time. "You were the two in my home, then?"

"Agent Nowiki and I were there, but it was apparent we weren't the first to arrive that day."

Frank nodded. "Ernesto called and told me about you two and my old dog. That's when we took off from the tire repair place."

"So what happened to Jesse?" Leena asked.

"What's going to become of him if I tell you where they're at?"

"What do you mean, they?" Leena asked.

"Pretty obvious, isn't it?" O'Hallohan asked. "Frank's daughter is with him."

"Actually, she's my daughter-in-law. It's kind of complicated," Frank said.

"I read about it. Your son was, uh…lost in the war. I'm sorry for your loss, sir." Nowiki said.

Frank looked up at Nowiki and shook his head. "Juella—that's my daughter-in-law—took it real hard, blaming herself for not getting to the hospital in time to save him. She's a nurse. He had an awful head injury, a traumatic brain injury. For some reason, she thought if she had been there, she could have saved his life. I think when she met Jesse, who had a head wound, she transferred those feelings to him."

"I can understand that, the poor thing," Leena said, reaching up and squeezing Frank's shoulder.

"The thing is, it's the first time she's come out of her shell in seven years. It was heartwarming to see her smile again." Frank sat forward and looked at each of them in turn. "But you still didn't answer my question. What are you going to do when you find them?"

"I chased Christenson and her," Nowiki said, pointing at Leena, "all across the country. And in spite of all the carnage they left behind, all I could come up with was an illegal weapons possession charge. In light of some concrete national security concerns, those charges will never be brought forward."

Nowiki glanced at Leena, who sat perfectly still with a knowing smile on her face.

"What about you, Mr. Homeland Security?"

"The last orders I received were to keep Mr. Christenson safe," O'Hallohan answered. Directing his gaze toward Leena, he said, "And quite honestly, I've become personally involved enough that as a matter of conscience, I could do nothing else."

Frank squirmed in his seat and said, "You may not know this, but I'm a sick man. And I don't know if I can do this on my own. Today—"

"Mr. Garcia, I do know about your terminal cancer prognosis. You'd be surprised at how thick your file has grown," Agent Nowiki said. "And since this is an official investigation, I need to report everything you say to me. So I hope you'll excuse me while I go outside and take a leak."

After Nowiki departed, Frank said, "He's a good one, huh? Kind of reminds me of me, in a way."

Leena's voice was soft. "Where are they, Franklin?

The old man smiled. "You did say the last thing you were here to do was ask where Jesse Christenson is." He glanced out the window into the darkness. "It's been quite a few hours, but they headed up that hill right there outside the door."

O'Hallohan walked over to the door and looked out into the complete darkness.

"Do you think they're still up there?" Leena asked, trying to push down her excitement.

"Nope, he's too smart a cookie. Knows they would either haul me off or let me go. Either way, he'd probably figure the feds would be out scouring that hill at first light tomorrow morning."

"He's right. It would be all but impossible to track him tonight without the proper equipment. By the time I received it, it would be light anyway," O'Hallohan said.

"So what would you do then, if it was you?" Frank asked.

"First thing would be to send your daughter—is it Hway-ella?—back down the hill here," O'Hallohan said, while Frank nodded.

"But after what you told us about her, there's no way she would leave him out there by himself," Leena said, looking at Frank who continued to nod.

"Okay then," O'Hallohan said, rubbing his hands together and warming to the subject. "I don't know exactly where we are, but it seems like we're way out in the boonies. So I would head out, trying to keep the road in view so as not to get hopelessly lost, and eventually circle back to the highway." He looked over at Frank who was now smiling. "In case you were let go, you would cruise back and forth on the road waiting for them to show up."

"That's about how I have it figured, too," Frank said.

"That sounds plausible, but I need one small favor from you, Frank." Leena turned to O'Hallohan and said, "Patrick, can you go get Agent Nowiki for me?"

As soon as he stepped outside, Leena said, "They still have to do their jobs, and we know there is a high-level leak." Frank eyebrows rose. "I need you to tell Agent Nowiki that your daughter took Jesse into the nearest big town and dropped him off."

"A leak, huh? I ain't no liar, Miss Leena, but I suppose if it will protect these two boys…" Frank rubbed the stubble of his beard. "Not to mention the other two. You figure they're worth it."

"Yes, I do," she said as Nowiki entered the motor home.

She walked outside and stood silently beside O'Hallohan, staring up the hill and beyond, into the unknown darkness of space.

"Do you hear that?" O'Hallohan asked.

"What? No."

"There's another one, sounds like gunfire. Long way off."

They listened in silence for long minutes, interrupted only when a car went whizzing past.

"I don't hear anything else," O'Hallohan admitted.

Nowiki came back outside. "Mr. Garcia told me his daughter took Christenson into Modesto a couple of days ago. So I'll file my report and begin the search. Mr. Garcia is free to go and is happy to take you both as far as Las Vegas. Keep in touch if you find out anything useful."

They followed Nowiki back to the rental car where Leena grabbed her backpack and O'Hallohan got his. Leena wrapped her arms around Nowiki and gave him a kiss on the cheek. "I promise I'll keep in touch."

Nowiki grasped O'Hallohan's hand. "Keep her safe, cowboy."

"You can count on it," O'Hallohan said, letting go of his hand and watching as Nowiki got into the rental car and drove off.

They put their gear in the back as Frank fired up the motor home and said, "You know, we would never have stopped here if I didn't have a tire come apart. The deputy called road service and they replaced the tires this afternoon. Kind of funny how fate steps in. Just a few short hours ago, Jesse and Juella were sittin' where you two are now."

"Let's hope they did what you two suggested," Leena said, conscious of O'Hallohan's presence.

As they drove ahead into the dark, lit only by the motor home's headlights, Frank asked, "So, Agent O'Hallohan, how far you figure they got?"

"Hard to tell. Healthy and in shape, an easy ten or twelve miles. Hurt like he is, maybe five."

Frank noted the odometer and after five miles slowed down. Every so often he flashed the lights on and off. If Jesse and Juella were watching the deserted road, they would notice the signal. He continued driving this way for several miles, all of them staring out the windshield.

In the headlights, Leena saw they were going down a steep hill, beginning to cross a valley. In the darkness she noticed a dirt road off to their right. Looking down the lane, she saw bright lights flash on and quickly go out.

"Did you see that?" she asked with a sudden longing ache.

"No. What was it?" O'Hallohan asked.

Frank slowed the motor home, and they heard the muffled sound of an airplane directly above them. The sound reminded Leena of shushed footsteps on a grave.

Day Fifteen

Day Five of the Grand Pursuit

Chapter 24

Altitude Sanctification

Jesse felt a sense of relief as the early morning light spread below them. He could make out some mountain tops protruding through the lower cloud layer. Since they hadn't run into any mountains throughout the night, he realized how much they had been blessed, flying in and around them the last few hours. He reached out and tapped the gas gauge again, hoping it would start registering something. He put his hand over his mouth and stifled a yawn.

Feeling her eyes upon him, he glanced over at Juella. "Oh, good. You're awake."

She sat up and stretched in the small space and then touched his face.

"You could use a razor," she said, caressing his face with the back of her hand. "Your eyes look tired. Or is that your worried look?"

"Both. We have a few small problems."

"Like my headache?" She looked out the window. "Where are we?"

"That's one of the problems. I don't know where we are. That might be the Grand Canyon over there on the right."

"There are clouds down there and it's kind of hard to see in this light. Maybe in a few more minutes we'll be able to tell." She peered out and down.

"That's problem number two. The gas gauge doesn't work and I don't know how much longer this crate's going to stay in the air."

"How long have we been flying?"

"You must be a mind reader. That's question three. There is no clock in here. In fact, they've stripped this plane of all unnecessary weight. It only has the bare essentials. And have you noticed how quiet it is? The smugglers must've installed mufflers to keep it quieter than a normal airplane."

"You pulled some type of hose from the top of the wing. Wasn't that gas?" Juella asked, looking at the gas gauge as he reached forward and flicked it for the hundredth time.

"Yes, but I don't know if the tanks were full or not. When I realized the gauge didn't work, I slowed the plane down and tried to conserve as best I could."

"How long do these airplanes fly on a full tank?"

"Five or six hours, probably. And the best I can figure, it's got to be getting close to that." Before she could worry any more he added. "I've never been in an airplane where there weren't any charts...air maps. See if you can find any in your side pocket or maybe in the back."

"I don't have a side pocket. They must have stripped that, too. Hey, there's a briefcase behind your seat," Juella said, reaching behind him and setting it on her lap.

"Good, must be his flight bag."

She tried to slide the buttons to open it. "It's locked."

"Not sure how I know this, but I think I owned a similar one. Try setting all the numbers to zero."

"They're already at zero."

"Oh. Got to be something simple," he said, watching her spinning the numbers to different combinations. "Maybe we can pry it open and—"

"Got it, one-two-three and four-five-six," she said, lifting up the top. "Holy crap!"

He looked over. "More like holy shit."

"How much money do you think this is?" Juella asked lifting up neatly stacked piles of hundred dollar bills.

"I remember reading that a half inch of hundreds equals ten grand. Those piles are about four inches thick, so that's eighty grand each. And there are, what...fourteen—"

"You're so analytical. How about a million bucks." In her hands she had piles of money that she slapped against her face as she looked over to him. "At least we got gas money."

His smile quickly faded. "Gas. I suppose there aren't any charts in there," he said, once more scanning outside the windshield.

"All this money and it doesn't do us any good," she said, her smile also disappearing as she pulled out more stacks of cash, looking for a map.

"Something about the briefcase…I can't remember, but that's a fortune to just let—"

"Go without a trace," she said, finishing his sentence. "I saw that once in a movie…what should we do now?"

"Empty the case and throw it out the window." He studied the window of the airplane. "Uh, won't fit. Better make that 'door.' Of course, if we don't find an airport up ahead, I guess it will still hit the ground."

Juella emptied the case, stashing the money behind his seat. She kept the last slab of bills in her lap and flipped through it. "Do you think it's illegal to keep this money?"

"Isn't everything illegal anymore?"

"No, seriously. If it's drug money, wouldn't that be like, I don't know, finding gold or something?"

"Hey, you've got a point. But wouldn't it be more like finding pirate booty? You know, like a buried treasure chest."

"Yeah, like that." Juella took the band off the money and shuffled through it.

"I don't know. We did sort of commandeer the pirate ship, but I've heard that most of the planes these drug runners use are stolen anyway."

"See? There you go, Clyde. You rationalized it away, and in the process you turned me into your Bonnie." She searched his face and then reached over and took his hand and put it on her breast. "Guess I come with the treasure. Like I told you last night, I'm yours. You can have me anytime you want."

"No, Juella. It's just the stress and being put into such a small box, with only the two of us to comfort each other." He removed his hand from her breast and put it back on the yoke.

"I've thought about it a lot since you first showed up, and it can't be just coincidence, us being together. Fate. You with your wife gone and me with my husband…well, he's gone and I'm still here. And maybe I haven't admitted it, but I am lonely."

Her face had such a pained look, Jesse wanted to reach over and soothe her, but he kept his hands on both handles of the yoke.

"I want to talk this out with you," he said as kindly as he could. "But right now I need to concentrate. Without a map to find out where we are when we have to go down through the clouds…I'm sorry, Juella, but there might not be a future. It's as close to suicide as I've ever—"

"I told you before I have complete trust in you. Someday you will believe in me, also."

"I believe in you already. In fact, I need you to take the yoke—the, uh, steering wheel—in front of you and steer the plane for a minute," he said uncomfortably, trying to refocus and change the subject.

"No! You want me to what? I don't know how to fly."

"It's not really flying…more like driving a car," he said, looking back over at her. "Just place your hands on the yoke. Come on. It looks like half of a steering wheel. I'll keep mine on, also."

She reached out gingerly, as if it were a snake that would bite her, and placed her hands on the yoke.

"Okay, quick lesson," Jesse said. "If you pull back, we go up." And they did. "Push forward and we go down."

She pushed down too quickly and the aircraft lurched downward.

"Easy, easy. Everything in slow motion," he said.

"No, you do it. It scares me." Juella removed her hands.

He quickly leveled off the plane and said, "I need to look at that briefcase, Juella. Please put your hands back on the yoke. All you have to do is hold the wheel straight and kind of aim to the right of that approaching mountain top."

Carefully, she placed her hands back on the yoke. Jesse reached over and took the case off her lap. He looked closely at the inside of the latch. Sure enough, there was a wire soldered onto it. He glanced at Juella, who had a death grip on the steering wheel. Reaching into his pocket, he pulled out a small Swiss Army knife and wondered briefly when he got it. He opened the small knife blade and tried to cut away the lining of the case. It was difficult with such a tiny blade, so he started to grab it and rip it out.

"Can't you hurry? I don't like this."

He looked up and turned the steering wheel slightly to the right. "You're doing just fine."

"What are you doing?"

"Checking to see if they put a bug in this."

"What if they booby-trapped it with a bomb or something?"

Jesse stopped and looked over at her, wondering why this reminded him of something else. "You're right. There might be something in there. Here, take the knife. I've got the yoke again." He reached up and pulled the throttle back, slowing the plane.

The sudden quiet frightened Juella. "What are you doing?"

"I need to slow the plane down so that I can open my door and throw the briefcase out." He pulled the nose up and slowed the airplane to just above stall speed then began trimming the plane. You need to take the steering wheel again so I can throw this out."

She made no move, and he said, "If you don't steer the plane, then you'll have to open your door and throw it out."

"I don't have a seat belt on." She was pale and wide-eyed. "Okay, I'll steer."

Jesse put his shoulder to the door and slid the closed briefcase to the crack, then pushed the door open, filling the airplane with a sudden rush of cold air. Taking the handle, he reached down as far as he could before releasing the briefcase so it wouldn't strike the small tail wing. He closed and latched the door and took the yoke again, adding some power. Then he changed his mind and began a long shallow dive.

Juella picked up the knife he had given her, looking at it for the first time. "Where did you get this knife?"

"It was in my jeans pocket."

"Yes, I know that, but where did you get it before?"

"I don't remember. Why?" He looked over at it.

"I've never seen a Swiss Army knife like this one," she said as she opened it. "This is very clever. It has a one-gigabyte flash drive built into it. See?"

When he looked over, blurry visions of a past life started to come to him. What did it mean? He consciously stopped the thoughts and concentrated on flying the airplane again. Taking a quick scan of the instrument panel, he glanced outside before looking at the knife again. "I'm not sure."

"I think this is one of the reasons everybody is after you. I bet this has all the car stuff encoded on it." She closed it up and slid it into her front pocket. "They'll never suspect me of having it. Might keep you safe if I hold onto it."

He started to tell her it wasn't her battle but instead read the look on her face. "Very well…for now. However, it's now light enough outside. We need to find a hole in the clouds so we can see what's below them. I'm sorry, Juella, but all my senses tell me we don't have much fuel or time left, and it's better we try to get under these clouds now than run out of gas and have to glide through them with no engine."

"I understand. Is that a hole there?" she asked.

"Kind of, but we need to be able to see the ground."

Jesse kept flying, and with every second he could feel his stomach beginning to burn. They strained to find an exit from their soon-to-be certain death. In frustration, he smacked the fuel gauge, again to no avail. Noticing the clouds rising above them up ahead, Jesse reached for the throttle to climb over them, wondering if he had the fuel for such a climb.

At that moment, Juella said, "Look, I see the ground."

"Where?" he asked, much louder than he meant to.

"Over on my side."

He banked the plane sharply onto its side, pulling Juella into him. "Got it. Hang on; this is going to be tight."

Wisps of cloud went sliding past. He cut the power and began spiraling down into the hole between the clouds. He could see the rapidly approaching earth below. The altimeter spun backwards, indicating they were just over 7,700 feet above sea level. That left maybe 2,000 feet to the ground. He kept banking and came bursting out of the clouds only a few hundred feet above the ground.

"Yes," he yelled aloud, breaking the smothering tension.

Juella threw her arms around him and gave him a kiss. "I told you, you'd save us." She moved back over to her seat. "But aren't we kind of close to that mountain?"

"Oops." Jesse quickly turned the wheel to the left and began moving away from the mountain that had been concealed in the cloud. If they had been just a half mile further south, they would have crashed into it on the way down. "Check that out, my darling," he said, pointing and then pumping his fist into the air.

"Where? What is it?"

"That's an airport." He turned and flew directly over it, looking for the wind sock. He found it and noted the wind direction, glanced around in all directions, and entered the pattern for his final approach.

"Aren't you supposed to call somebody and get permission to land?" Juella asked.

"Jornada is the name of the airport, written right there on the runway. It's a small uncontrolled airport. Yeah, you're suppose to announce your intentions, but we don't know where we are, who we are—that would be our call sign—or even the radio frequency we're supposed to be using. Incidentally, I can't get the radio to work either, so what do you say we just fake it?"

Jesse set the airplane for landing and dialed in full flaps. He was a little fast coming in over the large numbers painted on the runway. Better fast with no gas, than dead slow. He greased it in for a pretty good landing and braked gently. Soon, they turned off the runway, heading toward the hangars and another building. He felt the tension drain from him as if it was bedtime, although in actuality it was early morning. He didn't see anyone as he taxied the plane between the hangers. At the far end, he executed a one-eighty, facing back the way he'd come and leaned out the engine until it starved for lack of fuel and died.

In the ensuing silence, Jesse said, "I guess we made it." He reached up and turned off the key.

Juella was smiling. "Not bad, Clyde."

He turned in his seat and for the first time really looked into the back of the airplane. The stacks of money Juella had placed on the floor behind his seat had slid around, and the entire back of the plane looked like the interior of an armored car that had crashed.

"I think I'll have a beer for breakfast," he announced, reaching into the cooler. "Care to join me?"

"I think I'll find the little girls' room first." She opened her door and wrapped her arms around herself. "It's cold out here."

"It's the elevation, almost fifty-five hundred feet," he said, but she had already walked away before he finished speaking. His thirst returned, and he slammed the beer, opening another and taking a healthy swig.

Unlatching his door, Jesse stepped outside. It was the first time he'd really seen the airplane. It was painted dull flat black. As he walked toward the tail, he saw the registration numbers painted in dark red, almost invisible. Probably fake or maybe taken off a legal airplane registered somewhere else in the country.

He walked back around, opened the small luggage door behind the main cabin, and found a couple of blankets, a pillow that had seen better days, and a few other items—tools, a fuel tester, and an extra quart of oil. He took the blankets and pillow and climbed back up into the rear of the plane. Taking the pillowcase off the pillow, he began gathering and putting the money into the pillowcase. He finished his beer and got another from the cooler.

The door opened and Juella joined him in the back. "What are you doing?"

"Making sure there's nothing hidden in these stacks of bills," he said, flipping through another stack. She joined him until she had the last stack of bills. Tearing of the band, she took a handful of bills, folding them and putting them into her pocket.

Jesse watched her, and when she looked up he looked into her dark mysterious eyes. He didn't say a word, but something inside told him it wasn't right.

"What? They were going to rape me and then kill me—or maybe worse, put me in a whore house, hook me on drugs, and work me as a coke whore for the rest of my life," Juella said with a clenched jaw. "Look at this money. Where do you think it came from? Probably some rich addicted stockbroker on Wall Street."

"Still we should—" he said, looking away.

"You look at me, Jesse Christenson," Juella interrupted. Her dark eyes were blazing. "This is our money! We earned it. The world has changed. It isn't for the weak and humble anymore."

Worn out, he nodded, opened the door, and put the pillowcase full of money into the cargo compartment. Then he decided to walk over and visit a tree. When he came back, Juella had spread one of the blankets on the floor and was holding a beer while covering herself with the other blanket.

"Come on in," she said. "We can keep each other warm."

He was too cold and tired to argue. Besides, she was fully clothed and he figured it would probably be a cold day in hell before he ever won an argument with her.

"I thought you didn't drink," he said.

"There's nothing else but beer, and this one's not as bad as last night's." She made a face and he laughed aloud.

He finished his and put his head on the shared pillow. She felt warm beside him, and within minutes he was sound asleep.

His dreams were a strange mixture of gunfire and passion. One minute he was shooting, being shot at, and almost dying. The next he felt himself screaming in a sudden violent spasm of pure joy. In his dream he felt warm and secure as he slowly ran his hand down over naked breasts and across a flat stomach, moving down until his fingers became entangled in thick pubic hair.

When at last he came fully awake, he opened his eyes to see the ceiling of an airplane, and remembered where he was.

"Leena?" He turned his head and saw Juella's dark sparkling eyes. Juella looked back at him from the crook of his arm. "That's twice you've called me by your wife's name."

She moved to kiss him and he flinched when he realized his fingers were buried in her pubic hair.

"It's okay," she said. "It will take some time for both of us to get used to it."

She kissed him passionately on his dry open mouth, and he didn't know how to respond or what to do. He wondered if this was still a dream. If it was, he didn't want to wake up. Then he felt her hands and knew this was for real as his body responded for him. Even so, he still didn't want it to end.

Chapter 25

Retracing a New Path

The dawn light was just beginning to chase away the darkness as Leena and O'Hallohan hiked up the sparsely treed hill, where a day before Juella and Jesse had disappeared. For most of the previous night they had driven up and down the highway, hoping Jesse would flag them down. O'Hallohan had decided that if they didn't show up, he would try to retrace their steps and find them.

It was a good plan, but Leena would have none of it, insisting she was as fit as he was and would go along. They started off up the hill, each wearing backpacks and carrying water, food, and a first aid kit just in case. Right away, O'Hallohan found the rock where Jesse and Juella had spent some time. After looking at the confusion of footprints going both right and left, he decided they had gone first one way and then backtracked the other way.

O'Hallohan and Leena set out briskly after them. There was an obvious animal trail and it seemed they had followed it, making it simple to track the two. Soon they came to a steep rise and stopped at the top for a drink of water.

"Jesse's tracks are getting closer together, like he struggled to climb that last hill," O'Hallohan noted.

Leena was breathing hard but looked healthy and athletic. "You and I have gone all the way—I mean…come a long way. How far, do you think?"

O'Hallohan turned his back to her, smiling as he said, "Freud would probably say about five miles. But look at this. I think they decided to turn south here, probably so they wouldn't be seen by anyone climbing the hill across from here," he said, gesturing across the small valley.

The awkward moment passed.

"More likely he was too worn out to climb that hill," Leena said, worry evident in her voice. "I hope they're okay."

"You ready?"

"Always." She nodded and they set out again, the pace steady but fast. "Do you have rabbit genes in your family tree?" Leena yelled as she trotted to keep up with O'Hallohan's long loping strides.

She thought she heard, "Oh, yeah," drifting back over his broad shoulders.

It wasn't long before they crossed to the other side of the valley. O'Hallohan searched the ground for clues, and then started down the hill. He stopped, taking a long hard look.

"They went down the hill right here, and I bet when they got to that road they turned and headed toward the buildings over there," he said, pointing. "I bet they spent the night there."

Leena followed the direction of his finger and squinted in the bright morning light. "Let's go."

Soon they arrived at a large rock next to the road. O'Hallohan got down on one knee and touched a small depression in the dirt before he went to the road and began following the footsteps again, losing them often on the hard-packed dirt road. At last they arrived near the open-faced sheds at the end of the road. O'Hallohan studied the ground as Leena hurried past him and began calling Jesse's name.

"There's no one here," she said as she walked back. "Just a locked door and some empty barrels."

"Oh, someone was here all right." O'Hallohan held several small spent cartridges in his hand. "I picked these up over there by those black stains, which I'm sure are blood."

"Oh, dear God!" Leena cried.

"I don't know, look here," he said, holding up two larger casings. "These are from a 30-30 rifle. I kept seeing what looked like rifle butt impressions on the trail back there. Stay here. I mean, look around here and see if you can find anything else."

O'Hallohan began walking in ever larger circles until, satisfied, he returned a half hour later.

"The good news is, they didn't walk away into the desert. The bad news is, they either hitched a ride or were abducted. Either way, they're gone from here."

"Anything else?" Leena asked, frowning. "I found another blood stain and there are three different sets of tire tracks. I don't have a clue what that means."

"Show me," he said and followed her over to the prints and then up to the empty barrels, which he inspected. "Smells like gasoline. Wonder what's behind that locked door."

"Let's find out. Shoot the lock off."

"You know I'm a federal law enforcement agent. I can't just blow a lock off a door without a warrant."

"Well, I'm not. Watch out!" Leena reached into the front of her pants and pulled out the little .38 she had been packing.

"No kidding," O'Hallohan said, seeing the gun and moving to stand behind her.

"Sometimes a girl needs to be careful." Leena aimed and fired off a round. It shattered the lock.

O'Hallohan moved forward, opening the door. The stench hit him at once. He took a deep breath and went in. "Phew. Not much in there. Just a generator and pump, and of course a couple of dead bodies."

"Is it them?" Her voice trembled.

"Have you always been this susceptible? No dead bodies," O'Hallohan said, taking a deep breath and heading back in.

Leena peeked in and saw him going through some hoses and other equipment. "What's that horrible smell?"

"I'm not sure, but I remember reading about the making of meth, which uses smelly toxic chemicals. I bet this was a drug lab." He walked back out to the tire tracks. "But the pump, the generator, and this ladder were probably used to refuel an airplane here."

"Last night! Remember when I thought I saw an airplane's lights in the sky?"

"Oh, yeah. And we heard an airplane overhead. Does Jesse know how to fly?" O'Hallohan asked.

"I don't know. I know he was a parachutist."

"It's a lot easier getting out of one than getting it up."

"Oh, you have that problem then?" Leena asked with a grin. She saw his face redden. "Two dead bodies, huh?"

"Okay, we'll call it even for now. Let's get out of here."

They started up the road and after thirty minutes came to a gate with a No Trespassing sign written in both English and Spanish. After another two hundred yards, they came to the highway. Frank had the motor home parked in the entrance and was napping outside in a folding chair. They woke him and reported what they found.

He looked a little sheepish and said, "One part of getting old that's a bitch is it just sort of steals your memory. I plumb forgot to tell you I lent Jesse my old brush gun."

"Two separate pools of blood and two cartridges." O'Hallohan reached into his pocket and pulled out the spent bullets. "Thirty-thirty, I'll bet."

"Yep, open sights and only good for about two hundred yards, but up close she'll take your head off. Got many a deer with it."

"That's interesting. Why no scope?"

"Hell, that ain't hunting, more like killing. Shit! Maybe closer to target practice."

"I grew up on a farm and Dad used to say the same thing," O'Hallohan said.

"Hey, guys, could we get back to the issue at hand, here?" Leena moved toward the open door of the motor home. "By the way, how did you know we'd come out here."

"Now that it's light, I could see there weren't any other roads along this stretch for a long ways. In fact, I figured you'd be gone awhile so I went back to the main highway and refueled. Got some donuts back there on the table and coffee on the stove, if you're interested."

O'Hallohan sat down and began wolfing one donut after the other. Leena sat across from him and picked at one. She reached over and picked up Frank's cell phone and looked at the screen.

"You have a new voice mail, Frank. I wonder why you have service and I don't."

"Maybe it came in when I was getting fuel, back up the road there." He pushed the CALL button. "I got no service here, either. Guess we'll have to go back up the road."

"Speaking of driving, where are you going to go now?" Leena asked.

"I was headin' to Texas and can't see any reason to change my mind. I can drop you two in Vegas, if you want. It's on the way."

"What's in Texas?" she asked.

"You sure are a nosy broad." Frank smiled. "I own an old ranch there. Has an abandoned airport on it."

"If you don't mind, I would love to ride along…just to keep you company, you understand," Leena said as innocently as she could. "What about you, Agent O'Hallohan?"

"Wake me when it's my turn to drive," O'Hallohan said with a yawn.

"There's a queen-sized bed all the way to the back. Feel free to stretch out there," Frank said.

Leena turned to Frank. "Do you need some companionship to keep awake?"

"Nope, I'm fine. Go get some beauty rest. Feel free to shut the door; it'll be quieter."

Leena kissed him on the cheek. "Thanks."

Chapter 26

Veiled Deceiver

Like the previous morning, Lino was driving around the San Joaquin Valley seeking answers. Miguel called to tell him the guy they were supposed to kill had left the ranch with old Frank and Juella in Frank's motor home.

Lino had never figured out where Miguel acquired his intel. And until he did, there was no use thinking about it. Lino found the tire shop where Frank went to replace a bad tire. The kid working there said he saw a tall girl with big hooters and another guy with the motor home owner. That had to be the guy they were hunting.

He glanced out the windshield of the Mercedes toward the Sierras. If he was on the hoof, that's where he would go to hide. He pushed the gas pedal down and began driving toward the mountains.

His cell went off and he was surprised to see Miguel's number, breaking his long-standing security rule.

"Hey, what's up?"

"Where you at?" Miguel demanded.

"Uh, this phone okay to talk?" Lino thought he sounded pissed.

"Who knows? You close to an airport?"

"I'm almost into the Sierra foothills. I don't know."

"How far are you from Modesto?"

"Couple of hours, probably."

"Hang on." In spite of Miguel's hand over the phone, Lino could hear him asking how soon they could get to Modesto. "Okay, get to the Modesto airport and wait for me there. Might be awhile."

Lino put down the cell and found a wide place in the road to turn around. He arrived two and a half hours later at the midtown airport. Finding a secluded parking place, he locked the car and went into the terminal to a restaurant where he could hang out.

His cell rang again. It was Miguel, informing him they'd just landed and were in a blue and white Commander airplane at the general aviation terminal. Lino made his way there and saw a twin-engine, high-wing, low-slung airplane idling on the ramp with its rear door open. As he climbed the steps, he saw Armando, face bloody, hands tied together, and duct tape across his mouth. Armando also smelled of piss.

"Looks like you're having a bad day," Lino said, walking past him toward Miguel. He saw two guys he'd never seen before…and also didn't recognize the pilot, who closed the door and headed back to the front of the aircraft.

"What's going on? We taking Armando skydiving?" Lino asked as he sat across the aisle from Miguel.

Miguel didn't react to the joke. Instead he said, "You are not going to believe what happened. That bitch Juella stole one of my planes."

"Our…Juella? What?" Lino asked, wide-eyed. "She knows how to fly?"

"I don't know, probably the dude with her does." Seeing Lino's face, he continued. "The guy we're looking for, Christenson. She's with him."

Miguel told Lino the whole story and sat quietly as Lino digested it.

Lino tossed his head back and with a satisfied smile said, "I always wondered how you got the drugs north of the border. So the plane was kept in Mexico and then flew up to Mono Lake at night, returning before morning. Everything done in the darkness of night. That's good. Real good."

Miguel's hard look pierced Lino. He made a decision and said, "We have a vacant spot on the border we call the slot. We pay so the border guards don't watch it, once a week. They are provided a couple of cochinas. In and out while the border guards get their rocks off."

Lino thought hard about the set-up and asked, "Why are you taking Armando skydiving?"

"You know why. He was not a man."

"Yeah, sure. But I thought the reason we used him as a mule was because of his innocent baby face. Heck, we even put a child's car seat in the minivan to avoid suspicion. He was never brought on board for his gun."

"Yeah, but he forgot to unload the money before those two assholes made off in my plane."

"Uh oh! How much?" Lino asked.

"One point two mil. It don't matter. We know where it's at, since they set off the GPS."

"So that's where we're headed then?"

"We have the coordinates of the last signal. They have to be somewhere close to that, because they probably crashed nearby," Miguel said, staring over at Lino.

"Good. We'll get the money back. And if they're still alive, we'll take care of that problem at the same time."

"I like how you think." Miguel smiled wickedly and laid his head back.

"I think I'll go talk to Armando," Lino said as the airplane began its take off roll. "By the code, it's my job. I'm the one that recommended him."

"Okay, but don't kill him, yet. I might change my mind." Miguel subconsciously rubbed his crotch.

Lino questioned Armando, finding it interesting that the guy they were after took out both of their soldiers with one shot each, something he could relate to and appreciate. He replaced the duct tape and went back to his seat.

Lino got used to the whine of the Commander's turbo-props and after a few hours the pilot announced they were closing in on the last reported position of the GPS. Miguel went up to the vacant copilot seat as they began a pattern of descending left turns. He looked out and saw the mountainous terrain with its many clefts and hollows. There were a few stunted trees but a lot of pucker bushes and sage.

The terrain was also quite empty of a crashed plane. When they were a few hundred feet above the ground, the pilot started widening the circle outward. They flew for an hour or more before climbing again and straightening out. Miguel came back and spoke to the two men and sat back down across from Lino.

"Who are those two guys?" asked Lino. "I've never seen them before."

"Cubanos. Our new Venezuelan friends sent them and the plane to assist us."

Lino felt the plane slow, and the two Cubans went to the back of the airplane. The noise of rushing air filled the aircraft and before he could react, Lino saw them shove a struggling Armando out, immediately closing the door.

"It was my responsibility to take—"

"I decide who will die." Miguel watched Lino closely, a sadistic smile on his face. "This must be a good place to litter. Christenson must have thrown the briefcase out here, too. When it hit the ground it destroyed the homing device."

"How do you know they didn't just close the case back up?"

"Once opened, it's activated. The only way it can be stopped is by reversing the code. They only had five minutes. If they tried to disarm it, it was wired to explode. And we'd have seen the remains of the plane."

"What now? Come back on foot?"

"I don't think so. The pilot says we need to refuel. There's a small airport named Jornada not far from here. It's too small to handle fuel for this plane, so we'll fly to Santa Fe first for our fuel. Then we'll come back. They had to stop somewhere to refuel, and we'll find out where, find our plane, and then fucking kill them both."

Refueling the plane turned into an all-dayer. Miguel and Lino were up in the airport bar killing time when the pilot walked in and spoke quietly into Miguel ear. "Seems the airport's fueling system has experienced a break down. By the time it's fixed it will be dark."

"We might lose them in the night," Lino said

"Don't you think I fucking know that?" Miguel drummed his

fingers on the table. He took a deep drink of his beer. "It can't be helped; we'll get off early in the morning." He sat quietly for a few minutes and then said "Look, there's a guy I need to look up here in Santa Fe."

"The Indian art dealer?"

Miguel looked startled, "What do you know about the Indian?"

"Uh, everybody knows about him." Lino stumbled on. "They say he's a, uh money launderer."

"Strange. I never heard his name mentioned aloud before. Tell me more."

Lino hesitated and decided the truth might be best. "Word has it we buy expensive overpriced Indian art, mark it up a little, and resell it. Only it's really cheap fake art and we pretty much dump it and pay taxes on our small profit. We then have a butt load of legitimate money."

"Close, but no cigar. We don't pay for it; we trade drugs for it." Miguel glared at Lino. "Where did you say you heard about the Indian?"

"I don't honestly remember. You know, it's just talk you hear about."

"If it's such easy gossip, then the feds must of heard of it by now." Miguel spoke aloud almost like he was talking to himself. He pushed himself forcefully from the table. "I need to make some calls. You make sure we get refueled. I'll arrange a hotel for us and text you later for dinner."

The next morning Lino felt like he had a hangover. Something was amiss. He hadn't drunk much the night before, and he wondered if someone had slipped something into his drink. He took a long hot shower and when he came out of the bathroom, Miguel was sitting on his bed holding Lino's pistol.

"Shouldn't leave these things lying around. Someone could get hurt," Miguel said, laughing as he tossed it back on the bed.

"People are supposed to get hurt by them," Lino replied, warily eyeballing the gun.

Miguel abruptly changed the subject. "I was thinking they could have stopped anywhere for fuel after they dumped the briefcase."

Lino picked the pistol up, checked the magazine, and set it on the dresser. "Anything is possible, including that they crashed the plane."

"Nah, we would have heard about it on the news." Miguel scratched his scalp. "But I was thinking…why did they come this way? Why southeast? They could just as easily have gone north."

"Maybe they're just running," Lino replied. "You know how scared people don't always think about what they're doing."

"Not this guy. He's smart." Miguel pulled out a road atlas. "I bought this, this morning. If you trace a line from the ranch to our pick-up spot and then to the last GPS signal, it's pretty much a straight line," he said, opening the atlas and pointing.

Intrigued, Lino leaned closer. "That makes sense, in an airplane and all."

"Yeah, but if you extend the line, look where it goes."

"Texas."

"Not just anywhere in Texas, but close to the place old Frank took us as kids," Miguel said triumphantly.

"Yeah. It was out in the middle of nowhere and would make a good place to hide out. And it even had an old airport runway," Lino said, thinking aloud. "I don't think I can remember exactly where it was, though."

"Oh, I remember exactly where it was. That's where I pulled the top of Juella's bathing suit down. At least I had time to squeeze those big brown chichis before she punched me! That's another reason I'm gonna kill that bitch."

Chapter 27

Ancestral Commitment

The sun was much too bright to bear when he opened his eyes. Seeing the shiny aluminum top of the airplane's cabin, he sat up and uncovered himself. He didn't have a stitch of clothing on and realized it hadn't been a dream.

Then the recriminations began. The days were long gone when he treated sex lightly. It was the binding of two people…sometimes long before they were ready.

Juella certainly wasn't the kind of woman that if you woke up next to, you would chew your arm off to get away from. Quite the opposite. She had the kind of body men bought girlie magazines to get a peek at. She was great looking, courageous, passionate, and highly intelligent.

He put his head in his hands, feeling the scar. What was wrong with him? He got dressed, thinking how lucky he was. Lucky? And yet there was a persistent feeling that Juella was the wrong girl…

He got out of the airplane and walked around it, inspecting for any obvious problems and glad to distract himself from the previous line of thinking. He started walking toward the fuel pumps and saw an office, changing direction to go in. The old Indian man behind the desk looked up as he entered. The inevitable TV blared in the background.

"Morning," Jesse said.

"More like afternoon. You must be Clyde," the old man said.

"Huh?"

"You got that black Cessna 206 parked down at the end of the ramp."

"Yeah, but how did you—"

"Your wife Bonnie said you'd probably wander down here when you woke up."

"Bonnie? Uh, have you seen her?" Jesse asked, tilting his head to one side.

"Oh, yeah. She's sure is something. Talked me into loaning her my car and went into town to do some shopping." He slid his glasses back up his nose. "Bet you can't say no to her either."

"You got that right." Jesse walked over to a large map on the wall. "I'm going to need fuel."

"Yep, she took care of that, too. Gave me five hundred dollars as a deposit on my car. I told her you guys could use it for fuel."

"She's a handful sometimes. You got any current maps…uh… sectionals for sale? Mine's outdated," Jesse said, changing the subject.

"Sure. Over there in the glass case. Just reach in and get what you need." The old man gestured toward the far wall. "Your wife said you own a ranch in Texas. Whereabouts is it?"

Jesse saw the maps in front of him and said, "Oh, about an hour outside of San Antonio. Got our own dirt strip."

"Kind of figured that, with that airplane of yours. Cause she ain't no looker is she?"

Jesse laughed and picked up three different maps. "Hey, what can I say? I'm one for two."

"And speaking of your ladies, here comes the better looking of the two."

Juella pulled up in an old red Forerunner, and his heart fell as a flood of memories came bursting forth. How had he missed seeing it? Maps in hand, he walked outside as she was getting out of the car. She spotted him and walked up and put her arms around his neck. They kissed and it was her turn to be surprised when he held the kiss.

"We need to talk," he whispered. As she moved away he noticed she had on different clothes. And she had washed her hair. It smelled of apricots again, fresh and wholesome.

She recovered quickly and said, "Of course. I brought lunch. Here, Mr. Nogales, I brought you a sandwich and a Pepsi, too. Would you like to join us?" she asked.

"No, you two go ahead. I need to keep an eye on the store and the phone," he said, taking the offered food and drink.

Jesse and Juella walked out to the grassy area in front of the building and found a picnic table. She sat across from him and unwrapped a sandwich as he sipped a cold Diet Pepsi.

"When you drove up in that red Forerunner, I thought I was seeing a ghost. My deceased wife. She was also a nurse and had long hair like yours." She started to say something but he held up his hand to stop her. "She wasn't Hispanic or as tall as you...and there are many other differences. But I realized that the one thing you have in common—at least more than any other thing—is the look in your eyes when you look at me."

Juella's eyes brimmed with tears. "Give me your hands."

"What for?"

"To do what I promised myself last night."

He slowly placed his hands on the table and that was when he saw a new wedding ring on her finger. She placed his fingers on it.

"With this ring I thee wed," she said simply.

He sat there with a dumb smile on his face and eventually said, "What exactly does that mean?"

"Two things. I was serious when I told you last night about my cultural beliefs after you saved my life. I absolutely and totally belong to you and have surrendered. Now you have my life in your hands. It also means that I'm going to be having your babies. And after this morning, that might be sooner than later, since I'm not taking any type of birth control. And I have too much respect for human life to have an abortion...and I'm certainly not interested in being a single mother."

"But it was only once...okay, twice," he said, seeing her look.

"Yes, but it's right between my cycles. And do you think we're going to keep our hands off each other now?" She released his hands and reached into her new purse. "You might not love me now, but you will soon enough. Here, try one of these on."

She placed several gold rings in his hand.

"What am I supposed to do with these?"

"They're all different sizes. Find the right one, put it on your finger, and do the honorable thing."

"But...I don't love you."

"It takes years to fall in love. That doesn't stop millions of people who think they love each other when they say their vows. You can tell me you love me when you really do, and not before."

"We hardly know each other," he said, reluctantly trying on one ring after another.

"You didn't act like we didn't know each other a few hours ago, when you were making love to me. Hey, isn't making love, 'love making' in progress?" She watched him as he slipped a ring over his knuckle and flexed his fingers. Then she reached over and placed her fingers on the ring and looked into his far-away eyes. "It's not like I'm a dog or something."

She leaned forward in her new low-cut top, revealing just the right amount of cleavage.

He smiled. How did women just naturally know how to bait the hook? "Wasn't I supposed to have asked you to marry me or something?"

"Yes, I will and did. Now it's your turn. Won't you have me as your loving wife?" Juella asked so softly the words sounded as if they floated by on a gentle breeze.

Time seemed to stop as Jesse looked into Juella's smiling eyes. Deep inside he knew there were no accidents. All things happened for a reason, an unseen plan enfolding all about. He reached out and took her hands, placing them to his lips.

"Okay, how does this go? With this ring I thee wed." He smiled from the heart for the first time in what seemed to be decades. "Is this legal?"

"Yes."

"Don't we need a license and a witness?"

"I thought you were one of those anti-government guys. Why pay a marriage tax? Besides, God is our witness. You may now kiss the bride."

Juella came around the table and they kissed. Her lips parted, and he could tell that passion wouldn't be lacking in their marriage.

"What am I going to do with all these other rings?"

"Keep them. It's my dowry." She closed his hand. "I hear gold is a good investment."

"Gold, huh? Do you mind if I finish my uh…wedding feast? And then I think we better get out of here."

"Oh, I thought maybe we could stay in this cute little motel I found just up the street," Juella said, a pout mixed in with her smile.

"I don't think we have time for that. I was looking at the map inside and saw that we held a pretty straight course. If someone is chasing us…well, maybe we shouldn't be here when they arrive." He carefully studied her face and continued. "For a second there you forgot you were Bonnie, didn't you, wife?"

"Wife, I am." She looked up into his deep blue eyes. "I'll ask Mr. Nogales if I can drive the car down and unload our stuff."

She walked into the office and a short time later walked out to the car as he finished eating the remains of his wedding feast. She came over and handed him a new towel with the tag still on it and a ditty bag with soap, razor, and other personal gear.

"Mr. Nogales says there's a shower in the men's restroom." She leaned over for a quick kiss. "And quite frankly you smell like sex."

"I do?"

"Not really. You just smell of BO. Nice to have a wife with a great sense of humor, huh?"

After his shower Jesse walked back to the airplane and arrived just as Juella was transferring the money from the dirty pillowcase to a brand new backpack with the price tag still attached. He watched as she stashed the pistol on top of the money and then zipped it shut.

"Damn, did you buy the store out?"

"What can I say? I'm very organized. I've been to that airport in Texas, remember. And there is nothing even close, except a muddy old river. I wanted to make sure we have everything we needed for a while."

"That reminds me. What's the name of the town closest to the airport?" he asked, getting out a map.

"River Bar. It's right on the border of New Mexico, kind of by the Interstate. It's like an hour or two off the highway on a dusty road."

"Where?"

"Near Interstate 20. You know how it is when you're a kid… everything seems so far."

He pointed at the map. "Here's an abandoned paved airport. It's surrounded by an oil field, and there's a river nearby."

"That's got to be it. The oil wells are all dried up. Dad was always pissed about that."

"That's weird. It's almost the same course we've been heading," he said, drawing his finger across the map.

"You see? That's an omen, just like us. Made to be."

He never liked the word *omen* and quickly looked around the aircraft. "Where did you put the guns?"

"Pistol's under the seat, rifle's back here under the blankets. I stashed the other one in the storage with the money. And I bought myself a man's extra wide, extra large belt…seat belt. Am I efficient or what?"

"Sex, marriage, and pregnancy all in one day? I would say so." He folded his arms around her and held her close. "I'll taxi up to the gas pumps while you take the car back. Oh, and while you're there, don't forget to tinkle. You know how pregnant women are."

"You'll make a great father," she said over her shoulder as she walked away.

He got into the airplane, wondering if he would ever get the last word in. He taxied to the pumps, shut off the airplane, and checked the oil. Then he started to fill the tanks. It took much more gas than he thought it should hold.

"You must have long-range tanks," Mr. Nogales said, almost as if he was reading Jesse's mind. "How long did you say you've had this plane?"

"We just picked it up yesterday," Jesse answered, truthfully if not exactly accurately.

"You know, Mr. Clyde, if it wasn't for that wonderful woman

you have with you, I'd say this plane looks like a drug runner."

He stared into the old man's eyes and said, "We thought so, too."

"Course it ain't none of my business. But if the Texas ranch don't work out, we have plenty of hangar space here. And there's more than enough open land around here to get lost in, if'n you know what I'm talkin' about. Even way out here, we get to see people's faces on that damn time-wasting TV."

"Thank you for the kind offer," Jesse said, reaching out and taking his hand. "You never know."

"You take care of that fine woman, Mr. Christenson."

Jesse was still smiling when Juella came out and climbed up into the airplane. She looked over at him. "What were you two talking about?"

"Real estate. He offered us a place to live." He started the plane.

"We can live in Texas, can't we?" she asked over the din of the engine. "Oh, by the way, I bought a charger for your cell phone and recharged it. I called Dad just now and told him we were okay."

"You did what?" he yelled.

"Easy, stud. I'm not an idiot," she said crossly. "I got his voice mail. I just said we're fine and we are going to the place we agreed to go. Then I turned it back off. See?"

"Sorry, I…it'll take some time to get used to having a family. You're right. He was probably beginning to worry." Jesse tried to remember if they could trace a cell phone. Too late now.

They taxied to the end of the runway and this time did a complete preflight run-up before taking off. Jesse flipped some of the unmarked switches, and the radio came to life. He looked over at Juella and shrugged his shoulders.

"I was afraid to touch those last night. Didn't know what I might screw up." He checked for other traffic then picked up the mike and announced, "Jornada traffic, Cessna One-Bravo-Charlie, departing runway one eight westbound." He heard two clicks and started his take-off roll.

In spite of the thin air at the higher elevation, they climbed out easily. As they were flying across the numbers at the far end of the runway, they heard a report from another aircraft.

"Commander five-five-six reporting ten miles out on a long final approach for landing."

"Who is that talking?" Juella asked.

"It's another airplane approaching for landing. Doesn't have anything to do with us."

"Jornada traffic, Commander five-five-six cancel landing. We're going around, departing northbound."

After they made their turn east instead of west as he'd announced to the aviation world, Juella asked, "What was that you said on the radio?"

"Every aircraft has a call sign, usually the last the three of the registration. But it's probably not a good idea to tell the world this plane's call sign, seeing as how we stole the probably-stolen plane. So I made one up. One, because that's what we've become, Bravo for Bonnie, and Charlie for Clyde. That double click was probably from Mr. Nogales, meaning he understood, also."

"Oh, my. And on top of it all, I got a romantic." She reached over and put her hand on his leg as he busied himself with trimming and setting a course to follow.

They had been flying for an hour when Juella said, "The reason we have to run is because of the car. But why do they find it so dangerous? Do you think they'll ever leave us alone?"

"It's never the object they fear. It's the idea," he said as he did an accurate scan of the instrument panel and looked outside for other airplanes. "It goes something like this. Ideas mean change, change makes for new problems, problems cause instability, and instability most often reduces profits. The truth has zero agenda. It's just the truth. And truth is the most destructive thing on earth. It wipes out every lie it faces. As far as leaving us alone, probably not until they find something worse than me to fear."

"I decided after my husband died never to live in fear," Juella said, staring straight ahead. "I failed miserably."

"After my wife died, all I saw was darkness. Only someone who already has darkness in his soul can see the dark side for what it truly is. It was a long, lonely time before I realized it. The good news is, if you work on it you can allow the light to shine in and drive away the dark, replacing it with hope and optimism. It's an ongoing battle." He reached over and took her hand and brought it to his lips. "We'll be okay."

She smiled and looked down at the map spread across her lap and then looked outside for landmarks. Two hours later they crossed the interstate highway. Turning, they followed it until they found a dirt road and chased it into a small valley with a brown ribbon of a river running through it. Up ahead they could see a concrete runway. A dilapidated hangar was at the other end.

"That's it," Juella said, rising up in her seat.

Jesse started flying circuits around it, checking out the surrounding area. It was isolated, the chaparral tall and thick around it. He could see the abandoned oil wells scattered about. Roads had been cut to each of the well heads, and they looked like they'd been used quite recently. He made a low pass over the runway. With the exception of weeds growing in the cracks, it appeared to be in fair condition. He saw recent rubber tire marks, as if someone was using it to practice landings.

"I wonder why this runway was abandoned," he mused as he made the turn to set up the landing, figuring the wind was coming from the west.

"Dad said the government confiscated the land from the ranch. It was used in World War Two as a training base. After the war they gave it back."

He lined up with the runway and slowed the airplane. This time he flared a little early and bumped down hard on landing.

"Wow, is it supposed to feel like that?" Juella asked.

"I might be a little rusty. I haven't flown much in years."

"Now he tells me," she said. "But I do trust you, you know. And when the time comes, you can teach me to fly."

At the end of the runway, Jesse executed a one-eighty and taxied back to a patched up ramp that led to the old hangar.

He pulled up to the door and spun the aircraft around in case a hasty departure was needed. When he opened the door, the heat struck him.

"Whew, this might take some getting used to."

"It will cool off in a couple of hours when the sun goes down," Juella said, getting out and stretching, undaunted by the heat.

Jesse walked up to the large sliding hangar doors and saw a chain looped through the handles and secured with a relatively new padlock. He put his eye to the crack between the doors and looked into the darkened hangar. He could see daylight at the other end.

"Must be a door back there. I think I'll go around and check it out."

"Here take this, Clyde." Juella handed him a bottle of water and the pistol from under the seat. "I'll fix us something to eat."

Jesse had just disappeared around the corner of the hangar when Juella heard a loud bang. Her heart raced as she grabbed the rifle and ran after him, calling his name. By the time she rounded the corner, he was prodding a four foot rattlesnake with his shoe.

"Wow, that's a big one."

"I don't usually like to shoot them, but we might be staying awhile. Wonder where the rest of the family is," he said.

"You know, I like the outdoor type," she said, breathing heavily as she walked up and gave him a small kiss. "Don't get hurt, though. Remember, it's our honeymoon."

"Believe me, I haven't forgotten. Hey, do you know how to cook rattlesnake?"

"No." Rifle in hand, she turned and walked away.

He smiled as she walked away. He very much liked the way she moved, silken and shimmering. As she disappeared around the corner, he realized that when the time came he would die for her. Not if, but when.

Day Sixteen

Day Six of the Grand Pursuit

Chapter 28

Mendacious Revelations

Jesse woke late and smiled over at Juella as she stirred and opened her eyes. He had never felt so content in his entire life. Or had he? As something nudged his mind, he wondered briefly if his memory had totally returned. After a few seconds, he realized it didn't really matter. You could dream and plan all you wanted, but in an instant something unexpected could change things forever, and life would start all over again. It was only this moment and the imminent future that mattered.

"What are you thinking?" Juella asked sleepily. "Are you regretting marrying me yesterday?"

"Are you kidding? No way. I was thinking that if I could, I would bottle up how I feel right now and savor it for the rest of my life."

She scrunched up next to him. "We Mexican women know how to please our men."

"I don't know about all the other Mexican women but you are the most passionate—"

"Oh, stop it! You think too much with your head and not enough with your heart. Too many men hop from woman to woman looking for the perfect lover. But they don't realize that the more passion you put in, the more you get out."

"You sure have the passionate thing down. About the only thing I'm passionate about right now is a nice hot cup of java."

"I can change that, you know. Or wait! Do I sense a little bit of manipulation seeping out from you," she said, slapping his chest.

"Ouch."

"Oh, I'm sorry! Truly. In all the turmoil, I'd completely forgotten your wounds. How do you feel?"

"Are you kidding? After all this spousal abuse?" He reached up to stroke her face.

"I'm being serious. You still need to watch any sudden jarring of your head," she said, reaching below his waist.

He started laughing. "If only every day could begin this way."

"Oh, it can. I have many years to make up for." She climbed on top of him and kissed him deeply. "Someday we'll have a bed instead of this rocking airplane."

After a time, they got up and dressed. She fixed a cold breakfast, and he scouted for a way to heat the coffee pot.

Yesterday he'd found a rear door to the hangar but it was also locked. Today he circled the building further and found a place where the metal siding had been pried away. He pulled it back, creating a small opening, and then squeezed into the darkened hangar.

A large amount of equipment was stored in the middle of the floor. In the low light he couldn't make out most of it, but saw some pipes and pumps. It must have had something to do with the oil wells nearby. He made his way forward toward the large hangar door and looked out between the cracks at the parked airplane. He tried to slide the door further apart but the chain held it shut. When he jerked hard, a key fell off a board and onto the floor. He smiled as he realized that he'd spent many years in construction and knew they would hide a key nearby.

He went to the small door at the back of the hangar, let himself out, and circled back to the front of the building. Then he unlocked the padlock and removed the chain. Once he slid the hangar doors open, he entered the hangar and went back to inspect the equipment in the light.

Juella joined him, carrying a plastic bag with breakfast in it.

"I thought you told me the oil fields here were tapped out," he said.

"Dad told us years ago about a letter from the government saying the oil fields had dried up. They prohibited him from trying to get any more oil out and actually seized the wells, claiming some kind of environmental concern."

"But all these pipes and fittings are brand new. That doesn't make any sense." Jesse rubbed his chin and looked outside.

"Let's walk down to the river. You'll see some of the abandoned wells." Juella led the way back outside. "Maybe you can find some sticks and make us a fire for the coffee," she said. "Were you ever a Boy Scout?"

"A big one, a paratrooper. I can make a fire in a rainstorm." He picked up the coffee pot and reached into the plane to retrieve the big revolver and slip it into the hollow of his back under his shirt. "In case of snakes."

It was a half-mile hike to the river, and on the way they stopped at an old oil well. Jesse could tell there had been some recent work done, and he noticed a Department of Energy symbol emblazoned on the top of a one-way check valve he recognized. It was similar to the one used on the Take-Us car, only much larger. Something didn't look right but he couldn't put his finger on it.

"They must have recently sealed it up," he said. "It's strange how it still smells of oil after all these years."

"It sure does stink. Funny, I don't remember the smell. Of course, it was many years since I was here. Oh well, come on. I'm starved and I can't wait to see those fire-building skills."

Juella continued to lead Jesse down to the quiet brown river, where many tall cottonwood trees still survived. Off to one side they could see the remains of an old house, only the crumbling foundation and fireplace still standing.

Jesse had a fire going in no time, and the smell of coffee was in the air. After breakfast, they spent several hours at the river, at first just throwing rocks and soaking their feet, chatting happily like the lovers they had become.

"Do you know how to swim?" Juella asked.

"I grew up by a river, maybe not as wide or as strong a current as this one. It must be a hundred yards across from right here."

"Bet I can beat you across. You name the bet." She started

peeling off her clothes.

Jesse hesitated, watching the striptease going on in front of him. "We'll see about that after I smoke you."

When she was naked, he realized he hadn't appreciated how tall and athletic she was.

After he stripped down and joined her in the water, she said, "I'll give you a head start."

"You'll regret that," he said and took off for the other side.

Jesse was a good swimmer. But when he was about halfway across, he saw a streak go past him. Arriving at the other side, he found Juella holding onto a tree that had fallen into the water.

"What happened? Did you forget to take off the anchor tied around your ding-a-ling?" She laughed.

"You cheated. You didn't tell me you were a ringer."

"Swim team since I was twelve years old. You should have asked before you bet."

"What did I lose?"

Juella swam over to him and wrapped her arms around his neck. "I think you'll like what I have in mind. In fact, I'm sure I will."

He wrapped his arms about her as they kissed, holding their breath as they started sinking to the bottom.

They swam back to the other side and splashed around for a while before they climbed out and sun-dried themselves, both reluctant to get dressed again.

After so much sustained tension, Jesse was grateful for the respite. But it reminded him of the calm before a storm.

They were walking back toward the hangar, their feet crunching the hard pack, when Juella suddenly stopped and pointed to a cloud of dust in the distance.

"What is that?"

"It looks like a truck or something big. Whatever it is, it's going to beat us back to the hangar."

He touched the pistol under his shirt. His eyes darted back to the river, his head spinning, searching for a plan.

She caught his look.

"Let's not start our new lives by running." Juella reached out and grasped his hand. "Come on, let's go this way."

He looked into her face and let out the breath he didn't realize he was holding. Then he squeezed her hand and began walking next to her. The hangar blocked their view, but when they came around the corner they saw the large motor home they both knew so well.

"It's Dad!" Juella said, running toward the vehicle. The doors were already open. She heard a voice and saw Frank in the hangar at the same time she heard a woman's scream.

A woman ran past and threw her arms around Jesse, kissing him soundly. Shocked, Juella stopped and stared, not moving until Frank came up and gave her a hug.

"I knew you'd be safe in that guy's hands," Frank said.

Juella returned his hug and smiled inwardly. If he only knew where that guy's hands had been, she thought. She looked over Frank's shoulder at a tall red-haired man who was obviously checking her out.

"You figured out my message," she said to her father.

"I think I knew even before I checked my voice mail," Frank said.

Juella tried to read Jesse's face, as she and the man she called her father walked toward Jesse. The woman asked him something and turned to face Juella and Frank as they approached.

"Hi, I'm Leena. You must be Juella. I've heard so much about you. " Leena started to hold out her hand and instead gave Juella a hug. She only came up to Juella's chin. "Thank you for taking care of Jesse."

"Leena? I...I thought you were dead," Juella said, feeling herself blushing.

Leena let out a laugh. "I don't think so."

"But weren't you, I mean aren't you...I thought Jesse's wife was...you were...killed in an auto accident." She looked over at Jesse for help, but he was staring at the horizon, shading his eyes with his hand. She followed the direction of his gaze and saw plumes of dust.

O'Hallohan walked up next to Jesse, pulling out his MP5 machine pistol. "What do you think?"

"Looks like two cars." Jesse turned around and said, "Hey, Frank. The rifle's in the airplane."

"Don't know if I'll need it. Looks like more feds," Frank said, shading his eyes. Then he shrugged and went to retrieve the rifle. "What the hell, probably won't hurt."

"Oh shit, just what we need," Jesse said as he headed into the hangar and over to the pile of equipment. He put his foot on a pile of pipes and stared at the wall.

Frank joined him and put his arm around Jesse's shoulders. "Don't trust them. I don't give advice too often, but I don't trust them." Looking down, he said, "What are these pipes doing in my hangar?"

"Someone's been doing work on your oil wells," Jesse said. "Thanks for the advice. I'll do my best not to trust them."

Frank gave his shoulder a squeeze and walked out the back door of the hangar.

Juella and Leena walked over to stand next to Jesse, one on each side, with O'Hallohan taking position a step behind and off to Leena's side. They watched as two cars pulled up outside.

Car doors slammed as four men got out of what were obviously government cars. O'Hallohan moved a few steps to stand guard next to Leena.

"So I finally get to meet you in person, Mr. Christenson, and of all places here. You cost your country a lot of money and resources to track you down. Sorry, let me introduce myself. Agent Entersane, Energy Information Agency, Department of Energy." Entersane held up his credentials for Jesse to see. "This is my partner, and those two men are from another interested federal agency."

Jesse watched as Entersane and his partner stopped in front of him, while the other two took up positions on the other side of the hangar. He casually waved his arm at the other men.

"Four men and two cars. Couldn't cost that much," Jesse said.

"If you only knew how we found you. The EIA—"

"EIA, not CIA…what a coincidence," Jesse said, a hard edge to his voice. "What do you want?"

"Actually, it's what I can give you. New identity, a safe place to live, pension…and the funny part is that it would all be paid for by the big bad oil companies. All I need from you is—"

"I appreciate the offer but I think I'll just live my life the way I choose," Jesse said. "You know, Bill of Rights and all that."

"I'm afraid the information you have inside your head will not allow for peaceful coexistence. There are too many really nasty people out there who have sworn never to allow you to live out your life in peace. I'm sure you know there won't be any tranquility for you until the truth is sealed forever."

"Agent Entersane, that sounds very much like a threat," Leena said, having held her temper as long as possible. "And I will expose you a thousand different ways before I'm through."

The sound of an airplane landing interrupted her rant, prompting the agent next to Entersane to run toward the hangar door. Because of the dense vegetation, he could see only the top of a blue and white tail as it slowly made a U-turn at the far end of the runway.

"Ah yes, the reporter emerges," said Agent Entersane. "We have so many charges against you, Miss Delaney, that if you broadcast one word, we will haul you off to prison for so long—"

"Yeah, that will be great. But then you will have to give me my day in court," Leena interrupted.

"If I recall, your network did a story about the secret court we use to prosecute terrorists. Seems like just last week you were involved with…what was it, nineteen of them? All dead. For all we know, you're the twentieth, the one that got away."

"You can't blame—"

"Leena, let him show us his cards," Jesse said, placing a hand on her shoulder.

The three remaining agents watching Christenson turned to watch the noisy blue and white airplane. The DOE agent came back from the door and stood next to Entersane.

"He just turned around and took right off, probably just practicing his landings," the agent reported.

"Right. A safe landing, that's what I'm offering you all," Entersane said to the assembled group.

Frank walked into the hangar from the back door and said, "Ain't no such thing. All landings are nothing more than a controlled crash." He cocked the rifle and pointed at the smallish agent. "You listen to me, you lying feds. I got cancer and I'm gonna be dead soon, so I don't much give a shit. Just know that I'll shoot you down quicker than a Texas gusher."

Entersane shifted his weight and looked at the other agents with him.

"Tell me, Mr. Department of Energy," Frank went on, "I just came back from a little inspection, and I'd like to know what you're doing to my oil wells. Last I checked this was my property."

"It's Agent Entersane, and I really don't know what you're talking about."

"I'm just a farmer," Frank said. "But in California we have to irrigate our fields to grow anything, so I've learned a lot about pumps and valves and such. Why do you have a seal on a one-way check valve that's turned in the wrong direction, allowing oil to flow in but not out?"

"I have no idea what you mean," Agent Entersane replied.

"You were such a fountain of information just a minute ago. Tell you what I'm going to do." Frank took a knee and steadied the rifle on the pile of pipes, almost invisible in the darkness of the hangar. "I'm gonna shoot your right nut off at the count of three. One…two—"

"Wait!" Entersane blurted out, seeing the rifle barrel dip. "I'm a federal agent, you—"

"I think I was on two," Frank said.

"No! Okay." Entersane took a deep breath. "After Reagan was elected he decided, as a matter of national security, never to be held hostage by Middle Eastern oil interests again. He set up the Strategic Reserve and began storing oil."

"That's no secret. Everybody's heard of that," Leena interjected.

"No, you only heard what we wanted you to hear. We at the Energy Information Administration are the only ones who know the real truth of exactly how much oil we import and how much is consumed. We were out of storage capacity after the tank farms were full, as well as the old tanker ships leaking into the various bodies of water. We barely had enough crude stored to get us through a few months. So we started buying oil secretly. And when everyone thought we were unloading at the refinery—"

"I get it now," Frank said. "We used to pipe oil underground to the refineries from most of these oil fields. But once they were depleted, you started taking the oil from the ships and piping it backwards through the system…back into the ground for storage. That oil field right out there," he said, pointing, "pumped three hundred million barrels of oil out of the ground."

"Yes," Entersane said. "And now it's full again. And this is one of the smaller ones. We get million-barrel supertankers in everyday." He saw their stunned faces. "What did you expect? We've been doing it for over thirty years without a hitch, except for some of it bleeding out or being fracked."

"I knew there was something you weren't telling me," Leena said. "If the Take-Us car comes out you'll be stuck with all this oil. But far worse, you will lose your little fiefdom."

"It's a brilliant concept and a national security secret. We buy cheap, and the price continues to rise. It's like putting money in the bank," Entersane said, ignoring Leena. "Can you think of a better or safer place to put Arab oil than back into our own oil fields?"

"Why tell us all this now?" Jesse asked, stepping forward.

"Collection of data on energy is similar to the CIA's mission of collecting data on foreign threats. Whether you know it or not, there are many laws preventing you from sharing what I just told you. None of you will ever be allowed to disseminate what you just heard. And you, Miss Delaney, will never be allowed to publish."

Chapter 29

Unsealed Truths

"You! In the hangar! We have three AKs pointed at you." Miguel's shrill voice filled the shaded building. "Put your guns on the floor. All of you! Especially you, Mr. Secret Agent Man," he said to O'Hallohan, who already had his machine pistol leveled. "I'll shoot the women first…Good, that's good. Now back away from your weapons."

Miguel and his three gang members moved cautiously into the building.

"You two cover those feds," Miguel said to the two Cuban gang members and then stepped closer. "Oh, what's this?" He gestured at the silenced pistol in front of the skinny white agent. "I thought those were illegal. Gonna do a little back alley work?"

Miguel swept his AK back to his right. "You, too," he said, gesturing toward Christenson.

Jesse lifted his t-shirt and then put his hands in the air. "I'm not a fed," Christenson replied.

"Oh, right. You're the asshole gringo that stole my fucking airplane. In fact, you're the cause of all this." Miguel pointed the AK-47 at him.

"See here, young man," Entersane said, taking a step forward. "Stop this at once. I'm a federal agent."

"Lino, kill him," Miguel ordered, looking over to where Lino had separated himself from the group.

Lino had his Glock .40 caliber pistol out but not pointed in any particular direction. "But he's right, Miguel. It's better not to kill a fed."

"Kill him now, Lino!" Miguel screamed.

"No! Don't do it, Lino," Juella yelled.

Lino's eyes went to Juella. "Miguel, I'm telling you. It's a bad idea."

Miguel fired a burst directly into the little Energy Department agent, who crumpled to the ground without a sound. At the same time, Lino aimed at Miguel and pulled the trigger. No one but Lino heard the click, over the reverberations of Miguel's automatic rifle. Lino, with his lightning reactions, pulled back the slide and ejected the dud cartridge. He fired again.

This time everyone heard the click.

Miguel laughed insanely. "You should see your face, Lino."

Lino pulled the slide back again.

"They're all duds, Lino. I put them in while you showered yesterday. Right after I figured out it's F-B-I Special Agent Lino Santana." He said each word slowly with contempt. "I was hoping the leak wouldn't turn out to be you, but when I thought about it, you and Ronnie were always such good solid citizens, growing up," Miguel mocked.

"Fuck you, Miguel, you fucking pervert." Lino started toward him. "Oh, yes. I know all about your penchant for little boys."

Miguel took aim and fired once, hitting Lino in the leg and knocking him off his feet.

Juella screamed, "No!" She ran to Lino and put her hand over the wound, trying to staunch the blood.

"You're still a pervertido," Lino said though clenched teeth, looking up at Miguel.

"You couldn't help it, Miguel, after your dad molested you for all those years," Juella said, trying to sound calm.

"What do you know about it, you big-titty slut?" Miguel shouted.

"We all knew, but back then illegals couldn't go to the cops without everybody being hauled off. We wanted to help, but we were just kids. What could we do?" Juella asked. "We did tell Lino's mom, and she said she would help."

Miguel eyes were bugging out. "Hey, Lino, do you know how

many times you were standing on top of your mama when you were practicing your quick draw out in the walnut grove?"

"What do you mean?" Lino asked, pain evident on his face.

"Your mama, she talked to me." Miguel looked coldly at them. "But she knew too much about how my papa died. So I buried her. But not before...heh, heh." Miguel doubled over in laughter. "She was my first piece of ass."

"What?" Juella screamed. "Miguel, you're insane."

"I will fucking kill you!" Lino tried to rise to his feet, as Juella struggled to keep him down.

Miguel began to lower the AK to shoot again when Jesse shouted, "Hey, come on! I'm the one you came for. Shoot me."

Miguel looked over at Jesse. "Don't worry. I haven't forgotten about you. But you're business, and this is pleasure."

A desperate plan was forming in Jesse's mind and he kept talking. "Sure, I'm business. And you can kill me. But you still won't have the car."

"You fucking moron. I already have the car." Seeing the look on Jesse's face, Miguel said, "It's in a storage yard in the Bay area. Ask them." Miguel turned the barrel of the AK toward the tall black agent and took aim.

The agent glanced at his partner. "Yeah, we took it from the police impound lot, but then it was stolen from us," he said in a deep booming voice.

Leena's eyes hardened when she heard his voice. She studied his face.

"You see, Christenson? We control guns, drugs, money, and pussy." He pointed the AK back toward Lino and Juella. "There's nothing we can't find out or buy. Maybe I should sell you, Juella. You would make a really profitable cochina."

Christenson glanced backwards, nodded, and then edged over. "That's my wife you're talking about."

"Wife? You married that whore?" Miguel asked.

"Come on, asshole. Put down the gun and we'll settle this like real men." Jesse pulled off his t-shirt, walked directly in front of

O'Hallohan, and stopped. He felt the movement behind him and took a deep breath.

When Miguel began to move the AK toward him, Jesse dove to his right, tackling Leena and knocking her to the ground. He heard the distinct boom of the 30-30 while he was still in the air, followed by two loud gunshots from the .44 Magnum as he fell on top of Leena. He glanced up at O'Hallohan, who had the giant pistol still trained on the two downed Cubans as he ran forward to secure them.

Jesse's head began pounding from the sudden jarring as he stared into Leena's cold blue eyes. He seemed to remember them as not being so full of fire and yet…so distant.

"Did you really marry her?" Leena whispered so softly he barely heard.

"Well, kind of…yesterday." He rolled off Leena and held up his left hand to display the gold band. "No, that's not right. I did marry her."

Frank walked by and saw Jesse holding up his hand. "Saw those, first thing," he said as he reached down to help them up. "Figured you'd get around to telling me at the right time. Congratulations."

Jesse looked into the knowing eyes of the old man. "Thanks." Jesse glanced at Leena and then changed the subject. "That was a good shot you made, Frank."

"I couldn't save him." Frank looked over at Entersane and took a deep breath. "You two were standing in the way…That Miguel always was a crazy one. I can't believe he killed Ernesto's wife."

Jesse pinched his eyes shut, trying to relieve the pain. Before going over to Juella, he put his arms around Leena.

"I was very confused between the two of you. I couldn't remember. And I felt lost. But then Juella said she was going to be pregnant and wanted to have my babies. Somehow, that broke the locks on the dreams I had long ago buried. The truth took me back to my old life. But all of the tragedy—losing my first wife when she was pregnant, trying to survive when there was nothing left… It's like it was all erased, and God gave me another chance to live. Please forgive me, but I had to take it."

"I understand more about locks and former lives than you know." Leena straightened up and glanced over at O'Hallohan, who was speaking rapidly into his cell phone. "And I'll cry about it later, but right now I need to get a piece of my life back." She touched her finger to her lips and then to Jesse's lips, sighed deeply, and walked away.

Jesse went to Juella's side. She had the little Swiss Army knife out and was cutting Lino's jeans around the bullet entry point. Jesse bent over to listen to the conversation they were having.

"After Ronnie was killed, I wanted to avenge him. But I had already been accepted by the FBI," Lino was saying. "So I went to them. They staged a murder so I could go to jail undercover, to penetrate the Mexican Mafia. I could hardly believe it when Miguel's name came up and I had an instant in with the gang."

"But you've sacrificed so much of your future," Juella said, inspecting his wound. "The bullet must have missed the femoral artery. The bleeding has already stopped."

"Yeah, and the numbness is starting to wear off. I wish I could have come back sooner, but I had to stop Miguel. He had become a savage."

Jesse looked over at Miguel's lifeless body. Frank was kneeling beside it, head in his hands. Out of the corner of his eye, Jesse saw Leena reach under her shirt and pull out a small pistol.

The loud bang echoed through the hangar. Then it was deathly quiet as everyone stopped what they doing and stared at Leena.

"Which one of you raped me? Or did you take turns?" Leena asked in a deceptively calm voice.

"Look lady, you're crazy!" the skinny white USDA agent said.

"No. I heard your voices. And I will never forget them, especially yours, William. That is your name, isn't it?" Leena asked as she aimed the small gun at the black man's groin. "Just like someone said earlier: I'm going to blow your balls off at the count of three. One—"

"It wasn't me. He's the one that—"

"Shut the fuck up," the skinny man interrupted. "Can't you tell she's bluffing?"

Jesse and O'Hallohan reached Leena at the same time.

"Who are you guys?" O'Hallohan demanded.

"Federal agents, just like you," the skinny guy answered, with a smart-ass smirk on his face. His eyes traveled to Leena's cleavage.

O'Hallohan handed Jesse the Magnum and without missing a beat smashed the cocky man in the face. He went down hard and clicked out. "Federal agents don't rape women. Once again, who are you?"

"We're from the Department of Agriculture. And just for the record, I kept him from raping Miss Delaney," William said as Leena closely watched his face.

"What's the Department of Agriculture got to do with any of this?" O'Hallohan asked.

Frank walked up. "It's about corn and ethanol, ain't it?"

William nodded affirmatively.

"You two stole the Take-Us car—" O'Hallohan said.

"And the golf cart," Leena interrupted, her gun still pointed at William. "Over corn?"

"I'm afraid you have it right, Miss Delaney. It's about turf and money," William admitted. "We call it Wel-Ag, welfare for agriculture. In this economy we can't have thousands of farmers and millions of people unemployed. They may actually think they work for themselves, but we give them jobs growing corn and turning it into alcohol. It's a national security matter and a political decision to allow people to stay on their own farms, even if it does take more energy to make a gallon of ethanol than we get out of it."

"So the Take-us car would put an end to the make-work program," Leena said.

"Along with putting an end to rural America."

"So you didn't… I didn't get raped?" Leena slowly lowered the gun.

"No. I swear to you, ma'am. This clown is the one who knocked you out, and then he started removing your clothes, pretending to look for evidence. But when he unzipped his own pants, I stopped him and tried to get your clothes back on as best I could." William looked at the unconscious man at his feet. "I stopped him."

"Welfare for agriculture, oil back in the ground, a pretend war on drugs, common people losing their rights. How many more sealed truths are out there?" Jesse asked. "And all of this…this carnage, over something that was supposed to make life better."

Jesse reached up and squeezed his head. Juella put her hand on his shoulder. He turned and looked into her dark coffee-colored eyes and stroked her face. With shoulders slumping, he trudged toward the door of the hangar as if a ball and chain were being dragged across his soul. He stopped and blankly looked out into the arid nothingness beyond. After a few seconds, he nodded and went to the airplane.

"Hey, you can't go anywhere. We have a warrant," William yelled.

"Let him go. He's already paid the price," O'Hallohan said. "In full."

Juella walked over to Leena. "Honestly, I thought you were dead. He doesn't love me and he loves you so much. You should go with him."

Leena looked up. "No. You go. The story…my career," she said, her voice breaking and tears forming in her eyes. "You're going to have his babies."

They watched Jesse slowly climb into the airplane. The engine came to life and the hangar filled with the smell of hot exhaust.

Juella hugged Leena and slipped the little red knife with the flash drive into Leena's front pocket.

"If it's all over the internet, they'll leave us in peace," she whispered in Leena's ear as the airplane's engine revved. She turned and ran as the plane started to taxi, her long hair streaming back from the prop blast.

"Wait, Jesse! Wait for me."

Lino surveyed the remaining people in the hangar from his vantage point on the floor. Each of them had a different agenda, but he could tell by their body language they all wanted something good and right to come from this.

Juella's long legs carried her down the ramp toward an unknown future. Lino had known all along that having Juella was a pipe dream. Now he just wanted her to be happy. He was pleasantly surprised when the ugly black plane slowed and rolled to a stop.

Chapter 30

Grand Chase Terminates

From his work station in a quiet office at an Air Force base just outside Sacramento, the uniformed man closely inspected the face that appeared on the high-definition screen. The sky was clear, and from twenty-five thousand feet, the camera image from the Predator was sharp and well defined. He magnified and enhanced the face. The computer's facial recognition program quickly found a positive match, which popped up on the right side of the screen. He watched as the target climbed inside a black Cessna.

The drone pilot reached over and flipped up a red cover, arming the Hellfire missile. At the same time, he spoke into the microphone.

"We have a positive confirmation on subject one, Juliet, Charlie. Repeat J as in Juliet, C as in Charlie. Within range at five miles. Request permission to launch."

He knew that many others were looking at the same images he was seeing. He thought maybe he should wait until the airplane began to take off before launching. It would look more like an accident that way.

While scanning the different gauges and systems he was well aware that they were down to the last fifteen minutes of fuel before the drone would have to return to base for refueling. Someone better make a decision fast.

While he waited for a response, he calculated that from the current range the missile, traveling at Mach 1.3, would reach the target in less than twenty seconds.

He knew that only one man had the authority to order the launch. Hearing nothing in his headphones, he figured the Commander in Chief must have a tricky putt out on the golf course.

"I repeat, permission to launch."

About the Author

John R. Takacs was born and raised in Mishawaka, Indiana. As one of two boys among seven siblings, he had plenty of babysitters, fellow conspirators, and willing teachers growing up. But it was in the library that he developed his lifelong habit of reading. Following high school graduation, Takacs enlisted in the United States Army. He served with the famed 101st Airborne Division in Vietnam, where his helicopter was shot down by mortar fire. Takacs sustained serious injuries and was awarded the Purple Heart Medal. After an honorable discharge, he attended Indiana University.

Takacs landed a job as a high-rise ironworker, where he cultivated the need for an adrenaline high that his Army career had fostered. He also enjoyed tinkering, inventing a number of time-saving devices, and went on to own several small businesses.

After retiring and writing his first book, the award-winning *The Take-Us,* Takacs found he had become overweight and sedentary. He resolved to drop the extra weight and get back to the activities he enjoyed as a younger man. His nonfiction book, *Doing a 180 at 60*, details this journey, which started at the age of sixty. He enjoys racing motorcycles, skydiving, skiing, scuba diving, bicycling, and mountain climbing. As a leading proponent of active lifestyle, he hosts "Doing a 180 at 60" on KVGC Radio.

Takacs updated his first book, releasing it as *Hidden Truths* in 2017. The sequel, *Sealed Truths*, continues Christenson's quest to free America from dependence on OPEC and Big Oil. A third book in the series is planned.

Takacs, along with his wife Monika, resides in Pioneer, California.

Visit him at www. johnrtakacs.com.

Acknowledgements

While it has been said that writing is a solitary effort, which I totally agree with, that solitude ends with the beginning of the publishing process. Publishing a book is truly a team effort and it would not be possible without a quarterback to plan and guide through the process. Our quarterback is editor Betsy Beard, without whom this novel would not be nearly as good as it is.

Cover design by Sandra Miller Linhart, an award-winning author in her own right.

Red Engine Press and especially Joyce Faulkner, who picked me out of a crowd many years ago.

And it goes without saying that without a wonderful mate, my sweet wife Monika, and the members of my family, none of this would be possible. My heartfelt thanks go out to you all.